THE CASE OF THE BODY ON THE ORIENT EXPRESS

A DETECTION CLUB MYSTERY

KELLY OLIVER

Boldwood

First published in Great Britain in 2025 by Boldwood Books Ltd.

Cover Design by Alexandra Allden

Cover Images: Shutterstock and iStock

A CIP catalogue record for this book is available from the British Library.

Paperback ISBN 978-1-83617-556-8

Large Print ISBN 978-1-83617-555-1

Hardback ISBN 978-1-83617-554-4

Ebook ISBN 978-1-83617-557-5

Kindle ISBN 978-1-83617-558-2

Audio CD ISBN 978-1-83617-549-0

MP3 CD ISBN 978-1-83617-550-6

Digital audio download ISBN 978-1-83617-553-7

This book is printed on certified sustainable paper. Boldwood Books is dedicated to putting sustainability at the heart of our business. For more information please visit https://www.boldwoodbooks.com/about-us/sustainability/

Boldwood Books Ltd, 23 Bowerdean Street, London, SW6 3TN

www.boldwoodbooks.com

To Dorothy, and all the courageous women who have faced the hard decisions alone, made unacknowledged sacrifices, and kept their secrets.

1

ALL ABOARD

Crime writers were a special breed of animal. They circled one another like hounds scenting a fresh trail, each sniffing out plot holes and red herrings with the precision of bloodhounds.

From one end of a long table in their private dining room at Café Royal, Eliza Baker scribbled minutes in a worn notebook as members of the London Detection Club happily sipped claret and traded gory stories of murders and kidnappings gone wrong. Her bright eyes peering over the top of wire-rimmed spectacles, the club secretary Dorothy Sayers was recounting some gruesome detail about a body in a locked room. Looking dapper in his evening jacket and bow tie, Anthony Berkeley leaned back, grinning with amusement as he corrected her on the likely state of rigor mortis. When Agatha Christie chimed in, "Any murderer worth his salt can throw off an overly zealous detective by keeping the body warm through artificial means," everyone fell silent as if Her Royal Majesty the Queen had given a final proclamation ending all debate on the matter.

The ease with which they spoke of murder might have been

unnerving if Eliza hadn't known them so well. She'd been working as the secretary to the secretary for two years now, and she'd attended many of these dinners, where the writers relished the darkest corners of human depravity while drinking far too much wine. The fragrant scent of roast duck filled the air and reflections of the chandelier's soft glow danced in the wine glasses. Yet, while the writers tucked into their dinners with gusto, Eliza pushed a green bean around her plate. Despite her short-lived career at Scotland Yard, their talk of grisly murder put a damper on her appetite.

Of course, growing up on the streets and living through the war, she'd seen dead bodies. Far too many for her twenty-nine years. All the more reason not to talk about them over dinner. She closed her eyes and tried to shake the image of her poor mother, left penniless and destitute by a father she'd never met, and then dying of tuberculosis, leaving Eliza and her younger sister to fend for themselves. And then there was her partner at the Met. She'd watched him die, too. That tragedy at the docks had ended her career with Scotland Yard before it had really begun. Not to mention, it broke her heart.

"I second." Agatha's voice brought her out of her melancholy memories.

Drat. While Eliza was daydreaming, Dorothy had made a motion. Pencil at the ready, she tried to catch up to the conversation. From what she could gather, the writers were discussing sending a delegation to an International Writers' Convention in Constantinople to hawk their new collaboration, *The Floating Admiral*, a mystery novel they'd composed together in Exquisite Corpse fashion.

"All in favor, say aye." Gilbert Chesterton, the club president, tossed his cape over one shoulder with an air of solemnity befitting the House of Lords. A chorus of "Aye" rang out and pounding an imaginary gavel, Mr. Chesterton declared, "Motion passes. Dorothy will represent us in Istanbul."

"Excellent." Dorothy clapped her hands together. "I've already bought our tickets." She gestured toward Eliza. "Miss Baker and I will board the Orient Express the day after tomorrow."

Eliza's mouth fell open. Before she had time to question this plan, which involved dropping everything and running off to Constantinople/Istanbul with her boss, the writers were already onto another cold case. A recent double murder in a sleepy hamlet of Margate in Kent. Dorothy mused that the murder weapon must have been an aubergine or courgette given the area's local produce.

"Probably a murder-suicide," Anthony said. "A husband tired of eating black pudding while getting chewed out for taking the occasional nip." He chuckled. "Couldn't take it anymore." He dragged a finger across his throat. "And zip."

Leave it to a group of crime writers with minds sharper than razors to turn a perfectly civilized supper into a scene fit for a locked-room mystery.

"Or a wife who'd had enough of her husband sneaking around with his secretary," Agatha said with ice in her voice, no doubt the result of her recent divorce from her own cheating husband.

"Excuse me." A familiar figure appeared at the threshold. "I'm looking for Eliza."

A refrain of yips cut through the air.

A lump in her throat, Eliza got up from the table. "What are you doing here?" She stared at her sister. "What's happened?" It was unlike Jane to interrupt her at work. And even stranger that she'd bring Queenie. Pulling at the leash, the little beagle wagged toward her with Jane in tow.

"This arrived for you by special courier." Jane held out a blue-and-gold envelope.

"What is it?" Eliza bent down to give Queenie a pat.

"It's from the Orient Express line." Jane thrust the envelope at her. "I assume it's a railway ticket." One side of her lips twisted upward the way it did when she was annoyed. "When were you going to tell me you're leaving?"

"I'm not." Eliza glanced around at Dorothy, who was laughing and not paying the least bit of attention to Jane and Queenie. "At least, I wasn't... I mean, I didn't know." She took the envelope. It couldn't be. Surely, Dorothy hadn't bought her a ticket on the Orient Express. Not without asking her first. Not without approval from the Detection Club. Then again, knowing Dorothy, that was precisely what she'd done. She turned it over in her hands. Even the envelope was posh. Carefully, she opened it, making sure not to tear the shiny, gold edges. Geez. Sure enough. A railway ticket for the Orient Express. A second-class railway ticket, to be exact. "I guess I'm going to Constantinople the day after tomorrow," she whispered. "Dorothy bought the ticket without telling me." She shrugged. "Sorry, I didn't know until—"

"Well, I'm going away on an urgent assignment." Jane held out Queenie's leash. "So, you'll have to take your dog."

"On the Orient Express?" Eliza balked. "Her name may be Queenie, but I doubt they'll let her on board."

Jane's lips did that thing again. "True." She thought a moment. "Never mind." She wound the end of the leash around her palm. "I'll take her."

"Where are you going?" Eliza reached in her pocket and

produced a dog biscuit. The beagle's tail thumped against the floor and she crunched it into dust.

"Can't say." Jane tilted her head in that you-should-know-better-than-to-ask sort of way. And Eliza did know better. Her sister's work at MI5 was top secret. Only in extreme cases did Jane tell her anything about her urgent assignments. Like the time Jane asked her to spy on the members of the Detection Club because the War Office thought they were privy to classified information.

"Are you sure you can take Queenie... wherever it is you're going?"

Jane nodded. "She'll be good company."

Eliza knelt to the beagle's level. "Be a good girl for Auntie Jane." She gave Queenie's ears a scratch. "I'll be back soon." She looked up at her sister. "When will you be back?" She stood up and smoothed out her skirt.

"I can't say."

She couldn't say. Or, she wouldn't say. Probably classified. Hard to believe her sister had gone from picking pockets and using chess notations as their own private code to working for British Intelligence. Eliza had come a long way too. Thanks to Captain Hall and the French boarding school where she'd learned everything from forensic science to French and German.

Jane leaned closer. "Be careful," she said clutching Eliza's wrist as if she were sending her off to the gallows rather than a train journey. She looked into Eliza's eyes. "I mean it. Be careful."

Queenie, ever dramatic, let out a mournful whimper and flopped onto Eliza's boots as if to stage a last-minute rescue.

Eliza sighed. "You're both acting like I've got a one-way

ticket to doom." She pried Queenie off her shoe and arched a brow at Jane. "It's a train trip, not a murder plot."

"Just watch your back." Jane kissed her on the cheek. "Come on, Queenie. Let's go." She tugged on the leash and they disappeared into the hallway.

"I will," Eliza said into the echo of her sister's shadow.

Jane and Queenie. The only two creatures she loved in this world. More to the point, the only two creatures who loved her.

* * *

Two days later, Eliza found herself at Victoria Station. She threaded her way through the bustling crowd toward the platform. A whistle shrieked and a ghostly curl of steam floated through the iron archways. As she stepped onto the platform, Jane's warning echoed through her head. *Watch your back.* Through the hum of activity, raised voices drifted above the din of steam engines and clacking of giant, steel wheels. A curtain of steam rising from the locomotive obscured the faces of the well-heeled passengers pushing their way toward the first-class carriage.

Up ahead, she spotted Dorothy's distinctive porkpie hat tilted at a jaunty angle on her round head. Her boss was waiting with a mountain of luggage and no porter in sight. Eliza steeled herself for her employer's rough orders and marched toward the commanding woman who looked like an army general surveying a battlefield, her sharp eyes scanning the crowd as if expecting a wayward soldier to fall in line.

"There you are," Dorothy said. "I was beginning to think you'd abandoned ship." She smiled. "Thank goodness. I've had an awful time with my bags." She pointed. "Eliza to the rescue."

Eliza grabbed the handle on the largest case. "Good grief." The thing weighed a ton. "What have you got in here?"

"Books." Dorothy smiled. "Our latest Detective Club collaboration." She tugged on her gloves. "For the writers' convention in Constantinople."

"Good morning, ladies."

She turned to see Agatha approaching, a case in each hand.

"We'd best find our compartment and get settled in." Wearing a broad-brimmed hat, button-up cardigan, starched shirt, and men's tie complete with clip, Agatha Christie looked every bit the world explorer.

Maneuvering the leather valises through the jostling crowd, Eliza kept close to her employer. The coal smoke made her cough as she rushed to keep up with Dorothy. For a large woman, Dorothy L. Sayers was quick on her feet. The only things quicker than her feet were her wit and her temper.

Eliza had been working for the well-known mystery writer for two years now. And still she didn't understand why Dorothy took her secretary duties for the Detection Club so seriously. After all, it was just a silly supper club for crime writers with overactive imaginations, inventing trouble for their own amusement. Yet here they were making a special trip to Constantinople to sell the latest short-story collection put together by club members. Were they so short of cash they had to hawk their books by hand at a writers' convention?

Speaking of books, the case full of books weighed more than Eliza herself. Her right arm stretched to its limit trying to heft the monstrosity.

"Eliza, dear, are you alright with those bags?" Agatha gave her a sympathetic smile. Her fine features and soft eyes always gave the impression of congenial affability, even when she was put out or cross. Agatha Christie was a bigwig in the Detection

Club. As the bestselling author of the bunch, she carried a lot of weight, even more than a suitcase full of books. "Why don't we get help?" Agatha waved for a porter.

"And risk losing sight of our wares?" Dorothy was breathless. "Not a chance. We keep tabs on our precious cargo." And all she was carrying was her handbag and a Baedeker's guide to Constantinople.

So much for help.

Dorothy panted. "Those books are my babies." She'd edited the collection, a feat she'd compared to negotiating feuds between warring "clowders of cats." And she should know. She kept five cats living with her in her London flat. Five cats, along with one worthless husband. From what Eliza could tell, all Arthur did was drink and mope about the place. Sure, he'd been injured in the war. But so had a lot of men who weren't drinking themselves to death.

"My baby is back in Berkshire with Peter and Madge." Agatha sighed. "I hate leaving Rosalind and Peter." She slowed her pace until the three of them walked abreast.

"Rosalind is nine years old. Not a baby," Dorothy barked. "And she's with your sister. She'll be fine!" She huffed. "No offense to Peter, but he's a dog—"

"You don't know what it's like having a child," Agatha said, shifting the case in her hand.

Dorothy winced and quickened her pace again.

"I miss Queenie already." Her little beagle was in good hands with her sister. Slipping the strap of her own small handbag over her shoulder, Eliza clutched the heavy case with both hands.

"And at least Peter is loyal." Agatha sniffed. "An exemplary member of the Order of Faithful Dogs." She pursed her lips. "Which is more than I can say for Archie and the Order of

Faithless Rats." A cloud darkened her countenance. With a shake of her head, she quickened her pace. Eliza had heard about Agatha's unfaithful husband, Archie who, last Saturday, only one week after the divorce was final, married his mistress. Indeed, the mistress-cum-new-wife was why Dorothy had insisted Agatha come along on this trip. To take Agatha's mind off her faithless rat ex-husband.

"Yes, well, at least mine is a faithful rat," Dorothy said under her breath. "A boozy but faithful rat." She stopped and Eliza nearly ran into her. "But at least he's a good cook and he takes good care of the cats while I'm away. And Porky. Which suits me." Porky was the name of a porcupine Dorothy had rescued from the woods near her parents' house in the fens. Stabbing the air with a finger, she took off again. "Onward."

The sharp staccato of Agatha's heels hitting the platform tapped in counterpoint to the buzz of the crowd and hissing of the engines. Despite the heavy luggage, Eliza matched her pace. The symphony of sounds electrified the moist air and ignited a rush of adrenaline as Eliza anticipated boarding France's premier luxury railway.

By the time she reached the first-class carriage, her arm was throbbing. She sat the heavy case on the platform and took a deep breath.

"Don't let those books out of your sight." Dorothy peered over the top of her spectacles.

Eliza was used to Dorothy's commands. "You'd think you had bricks of gold in here." She grasped the handle and heaved the case onto the first stair and into the car.

"Let me help you, miss." Finally, a porter came to her rescue.

"Thank you," she said, glaring up at Dorothy.

The big woman shrugged and disappeared into the carriage.

"Good heavens." The porter laughed. "This is a load. A little thing like you carried this all the way from the station?" He winked. "Why so serious, Dolly? Come on, give us a smile."

Eliza got those kinds of comments all the time. Men acting amazed at her strength or her ju-jitsu moves or telling her to smile, or saying, "You're too pretty to be so serious." Yeah, if they'd grown up on the streets of London picking pockets and hustling chess to survive, and at twenty-nine years old were working a measly part-time job making peanuts, they wouldn't be smiling either.

She wished she hadn't thought of chess. Whenever she did, she thought of Theo. Theo Sharp. He'd run off to Paris before they'd even finished their first ever game. That was two years ago, just after she started working for the Detection Club—and spying on their members at Jane's bidding. He'd probably been afraid she'd beat him. Her head jerked involuntarily. Yeah, he was a sore loser. The pang in her chest betrayed her. It wasn't only about chess. She missed him. She exhaled a long breath. Tomorrow, after the boat train to Dover, the ferry to Calais, another train to Paris, a taxi transfer from Gare du Nord to Gare de l'Est Station, she could wave as they boarded the Orient Express.

Side-stepping through the train's narrow corridor, she followed behind Dorothy and Agatha as they made their way to their compartment. Dorothy was generous enough as employers go. But not enough to buy Eliza a first-class ticket. Still, Dorothy invited her to rest and take tea with them in their cabin. And she insisted Eliza call her and Agatha by their Christian names. As if that made them equals. Eliza and her meager luggage and forensics sample case, which she never left home without—a habit she picked up at the Met, could find her second-class accommodations later, after the train left the station.

A small but energetic steward gave them a tour of their cabin. He opened a mahogany door in the corner to reveal a small sink and brackets holding a water pitcher and glasses, along with a mirror, soap, and embroidered towels. Compact but elegant. Like the steward. Did the line intentionally hire small stewards to match the scale of everything in the cabin? He pointed to a wooden ladder attached to the wall across from the cushioned seat. "At nine o'clock, I set up the bunks and turn down the beds."

"I'll take the top bunk," Agatha said with excitement. You'd never know it from looking at her, but Agatha was quite athletic. Eliza had seen photographs of her in Hawaii with a surfboard. For her late thirties, Agatha was fit as a fiddle. And Dorothy was in better shape than she let on. Around London, she rode a motorcycle everywhere and swooped into Detection Club meetings wearing flowing capes over men's suits. She was nothing if not eccentric.

"I should hope so!" Dorothy laughed. "I'm not climbing that toothpick ladder."

"One last thing," the steward said. "Your robes are hanging here." He touched one of the plush, blue robes hanging from a hook on the wall. "And your slippers are there." He pointed to the floor where two sets of matching furry slippers waited like members of the Order of Faithful Dogs. He smiled. "I'll be nearby. Let me know if you need anything." He gave a little bow and backed out of the cabin to make room for the porter with their luggage.

"Why didn't the Detection Club sell baked goods or sponsor a car wash?" Eliza said, watching the porter struggle to slide the heavy suitcase under the seat. "It would have been easier on the back."

"A Detection Club bake sale!" Agatha grinned. "What a delightful idea." She smoothed her skirt and sat down on the upholstered bench. "We could sell Sinister Shortbread." She giggled. "And Poisonous Puddings... or Treacherous Trifle."

Leave it to a crime writer to come up with ideas for a deadly bake sale.

"Or Murderous Mincemeat." Dorothy took a seat next to Agatha. "Jealous Jammy Dodgers, and Scandalous Spotted Dick!" She chuckled as she laid her handbag on the seat next to her.

"Foolish Fool," Eliza chimed in, taking a seat across from them on a tiny jump seat.

Both women sat blinking at her. Maybe she should stick to what she knew: forensics, ju-jitsu, chess, and pickpocketing. Alright. Maybe not pickpocketing. After all, that was why she had a job as Dorothy's secretary. So she didn't have to pick pockets or hustle chess.

"Tiresome Tart?" Eliza raised an eyebrow.

"Stop!" Agatha waved her away.

Fine. Lesson learned. Don't compete with the wordsmiths. Again, she thought of Theo. Had he finished his second mystery novel? Was he busy writing a third? Or was he lolling about Parisian chess clubs picking up games and lithe French beauties? She bit her lip.

"Quit talking about puddings." Agatha put a hand on her wool-skirted tummy. "I'm already devilishly hungry. I only had time to gulp down a cup of cream and wolf a piece of marmalade toast before leaving home."

With a great belch of smoke and the loud squeal of metal on metal, the train lurched forward. Eliza grabbed onto the jump seat and pressed the toes of her boots against the floor to steady herself.

"Let's order tea." Dorothy adjusted her skirt. "And then you can tell me about your presentation for the conference," she said in Agatha's general direction. "Eliza, be a dear and find our cabin steward."

Clutching the woodwork as she went, Eliza swayed into the corridor to find the steward. When she returned, Dorothy and Agatha were in the middle of a tense discussion.

"What do you mean you're done writing?" Dorothy's voice went up an octave. "You're the crown jewel of British crime writing. You can't just quit. And everyone expects you to speak at the conference."

"My last book was a disaster." Agatha shook her head. "I only wrote it because I was strapped for cash." She closed her eyes. "It was painful. I had to dig it out of my soul like a splinter." She fiddled with the handle on her purse. "*The Blue Train*... It should be called *The Stinker Train*." She blew out a breath. "I won't have to quit writing. After my latest bomb, no one will buy another."

Were readers so fickle they would give up on a favorite writer after one bad book? Anyway, Eliza doubted the book was so bad. From what she'd seen, these writers were their own worst critics. Especially the women writers. The men, on the other hand, all seemed to think their own work was genius.

"I thought it was brilliant." Dorothy took her friend's hand. "Don't worry. You'll find your inspiration again. The last couple of years have been difficult. With your mother's death and then Archie." She patted Agatha's hand. "Give yourself time." Tilting her head, she gave Agatha a sympathetic smile. "Don't be so hard on yourself, dearest." She took a deep breath. "I do wish you'd reconsider and come to the conference." Her tone shifted from consoling to cajoling.

What was so wonderful about a writers' conference? All those windbag eggheads nattering on about make-believe crimes and fantasy romance.

"My heart is set." Agatha rearranged her handbag on her lap. "I had a ticket to the West Indies, but at a dinner party in London last week, Captain Howe made Baghdad sound so romantic." She smiled. "The next morning first thing, I went to Cook's and exchanged my ticket." Her face lit up. "So, here I am. On my way to the digs of Ur. At the invitation of my dear friend Katharine. Katharine Woolley."

The digs of Ur. Eliza was almost jealous. Doing something with your hands. Outside in the dirt. Not making up stories in a dark corner for a change. For a writer, Agatha was an adventurous sort. Archeology. Digging up the past. Eliza preferred the future to the past, especially when her own past was full of so much suffering and starvation.

"Of course, a bunch of boring old writers can't compete with mummies and ancient bones." For a moment, a wistful look passed over Dorothy's face. And just as quickly, it was gone. She tugged at the bottom of her jacket. "The living never can compete with the dead." She turned to Eliza. "Now, where's our tea?"

Just then, the cabin steward appeared with a tray. Thank goodness. Dorothy could be a bear, especially when she was hungry. The steward balanced the tray on one gloved palm and laid out the small table with the other. Quite a feat given the motion of the train.

"Darjeeling tea and raspberry macarons." The pastel-pink, cream-filled discs looked like stringless bandalores. He sat the plate of treats on the table and then laid out a silver teapot, teacups with matching, gold-rimmed saucers, and tiny, silver spoons. "Enjoy your tea, mesdames."

"Could I get a little pick-me-up in my tea?" Dorothy winked at the steward. "Brandy, perhaps."

"Of course, madame." The steward looked to Agatha. "Anyone else care for *un remontant*?"

Agatha glanced at her watch. "No, thank you."

Eliza shook her head. She wasn't on holiday, after all. She was working. Not that carrying luggage, taking notes, and arranging schedules took much brain power. Not like a challenging game of chess. A pang stabbed at her heart. Theo Sharp. Would she ever see him again?

"Very well." The steward gave a curt bow and then disappeared.

Dorothy resumed her attempt to persuade Agatha to speak at the Crime Writers' Conference. And Agatha held fast recounting the wonderful things she'd heard about the archeological digs of Mesopotamia from her friends Leonard and Katharine Woolley.

Not five minutes later, the steward reappeared with a carafe of brandy and a bottle of champagne.

"Champagne!" Agatha clapped her hands together. "How lovely."

Eliza wondered if the second-class passengers would be treated to champagne. A bed in second class was still better than sleeping on straw in the alcove of a church like she did as a child. She thought of Theo, who'd reported in his last letter that he and his roommate had taken up "tramping" to learn what it was like to live in poverty so they could write about it. Having grown up in poverty, she didn't see the allure.

"Compliments of a fellow traveler." The steward held out a folded card to Dorothy.

A bewildered look on her face, Dorothy took the note and opened it. The color drained from her face as she read it.

"What is it?" Agatha asked. "Bad news?"

"That remains to be seen." Dorothy's breath caught as she dropped the card onto the table. She turned to the steward. "I'll take my brandy neat if you please."

"You look as if you've seen a ghost," Eliza said as she plucked the note off the table.

"In a manner of speaking..." Dorothy gulped down the brandy and held out her glass for a refill, "I have."

Eliza stared down at the scrawling, black words:

Dearest Dottie,

Imagine my surprise when I learned we were on the same train en route to the Orient Express for the same convention in Istanbul, as the locals call Constantinople. Looking forward to catching up. It's been far too long.

All my love, Peachy.

She looked back at Dorothy, whose complexion had gone from pale to blotchy. "Who the devil is Peachy?" She passed the note back to Dorothy.

Rather than answer, Dorothy waved to the waiter and ordered another drink. "Make mine a whiskey."

* * *

The Hôtel des Bons Amis perched uneasily on a crooked street in the shadow of Montmartre, its peeling façade a weary testament to the years of whispered secrets and hurried goodbyes it had absorbed. Inside, the air hung thick with the acrid scent of stale cigarettes and spilled absinthe, clinging stubbornly to the faded wallpaper patterned with wilted fleurs-de-lis. Theo Sharp's room was no better: A dim, sagging space lit by a single flickering bulb that cast jittery shadows across the threadbare rug and the cracked mirror hanging lopsided on the wall. A warped table bore the scars of careless knives and scorched matchsticks, and the two narrow beds, their springs poking through lumpy mattresses, groaned under the weight of too many sleepless nights.

Theo applied a thick coating of Beauchamp's lotion to his cracked, red hands. He rewrapped the bottle in one of his union suits and hid it in the top drawer of his bureau, along with an envelope full of bank notes. The quest for writerly authenticity only went so far. His roommate, Eric Arthur Blair, an old friend from Eton, would break the bottle over his head if he found it. And he'd have a fit if he found out about the money. Eric believed in absolute faithfulness to the experience of poverty. Right down to the roaches and rats in their dirty little room in this dingy hotel in the bohemian, if not fashionable, part of Paris.

Theo shuddered to think what his mother would say if she could see him now. Sitting in front of their shared typewriter at a rickety table stacked with old newspapers in front of a greasy window. Almost two years ago, he'd hopped on a train to Paris in the romantic, if misguided, hope of becoming a real writer. Like Hemingway, Fitzgerald and Joyce. They'd found their inspiration in the dark basements of Parisian brasseries; why couldn't he? He still hadn't finished revising the novel he'd written before leaving London. Now, he wondered, why bother? After all, his first foray into detective fiction wasn't exactly a resounding success. Sure, he'd got it published, thanks to Dorothy and her pals at the Detection Club. His second attempt had been summarily returned by his editor, who called it "romantic drivel."

His elbows on the table, Theo held his hands up waiting for them to absorb the lotion before setting his damp fingers on the keys. His father had warned him not to go to Paris. It was a wonder the old man waited a whole year before cutting him off. Theo scoffed. And his mother... well, she couldn't bring herself to disown her only son. She regularly sent him care packages and money, which he kept hidden from Eric. In fact, the bottle of Beauchamp's had been in her last package, a little present she'd picked up on her trip to New York to attend his sister's wedding to a Rockefeller at the Rainbow Room. La-di-da. His parents must have loved hobnobbing with posh Americans.

His father may have a title, but the Yanks had money. Serious money. And more than anything else, his father worshiped money. Theo massaged a sore spot on his hand. An occupational hazard. He chuckled. His father should be happy. For years, he'd chided Theo for studying philosophy at Oxford, claiming he should do something useful with his life, as if being a member of the landed gentry and living the life of leisure was useful!

Well, Daddy dear, you should see me now. I have a job as a plongeur at a greasy spoon. Ha! I'm finally doing something useful: washing dishes.

A roach scurried across the table. Theo grabbed a newspaper from atop the pile and swatted at the vermin. "Gotcha!" As he dumped the carcass into the rubbish bin, he skimmed the headlines of *Le Figaro*:

Samedi 13 Octobre 1928

La rapprochement franco-allemande

Le perte sous-marin "Odine"

Un voleur de bijoux braque Chanel
L'affaire Harold T. Horan
Conférence internationale des écrivains

International Writers' Conference. In Istanbul. That must be the one Dorothy had invited him to. He'd had to decline because of the stupid dishwashing job. He wondered if Eliza was going along. Probably a good thing he couldn't go. Seeing her again would be too painful. It would rekindle the fire he'd come to Paris to extinguish.

With new resolve, he went back to the paper. To practice his French, he translated the rest of the news headlines aloud: "The French-German reconciliation. The Odine Submarine Loss. Jewel Thief robs Chanel. The Harold T. Horan Affair." His French was improving. No thanks to washing dishes.

When he wasn't washing dishes, he and Eric went tramping. Tramping was Eric's idea. Dressing up like hobos and frequenting the questionable parts of the city. All in the name of research. The upside: When he was dressed like a bum, the chess players in Tuileries Garden underestimated him, which meant he won a few extra francs. At least Eric didn't begrudge him making money from chess since he saw it as a sort of Robin Hood operation. Eric claimed to be writing an "award-winning exposé" on poverty in Paris called *A Scullion's Diary*. Theo would be happy to finish his second mystery novel. Although his first one had been such a flop, he wondered if his father was right about him wasting his life.

Then again, for Theo, writing wasn't about the money. Writing was hunger. The frenzied attempt to fill a void: the gaping abyss between experience and representation. In short: longing. He remembered someplace Hegel said, to be self-aware was to stare into an abyss called desire. Desire. Longing.

To reflect on one's life was always to want more from it. To yearn for something to fill the emptiness.

Poverty wasn't just an empty stomach. It was an empty soul. And Theo's soul was starving. His writing was a desperate attempt to stop the churning. To fill it. To plug it up with words. Words were his *bons amis* and more skittish than the roaches and the rats.

He wiped his fingers on his trousers and then started typing. As always, the first words he typed were:

For Eliza. Eliza, *mon amour*.

The more he tried to forget her, the more she bore a hole in his memory, a hole so deep that it threatened to consume his empty soul.

The door swung open with a bang. Eric stood smiling in the threshold. He was dressed as a bum, his short hair stuck up in all directions like a hedgehog, and a smudge of dirt ran down the side of his long face. But his eyes... his eyes shone as bright as beacons. "Theodore, old boy." He clapped his hands together. "Pack your bag!" He held up a box he'd been carrying under his arm. "I got us new jobs."

"Oh, no," Theo said without thinking. He didn't want to know where. If there was something worse than washing dishes, Eric would find it.

"Aren't you going to ask?" Eric's voice was full of excitement.

Theo pulled the sheet of paper from the typewriter and crumpled it into a ball. "I'm afraid to ask." He tossed it toward the bin before Eric could see it. *For Eliza. Eliza, mon amour*. How absurd. More like, *amour non partagé*: unrequited love.

"Guess!" Eric opened the lid to the box and pulled out a blue-and-gold uniform.

"Scrubbing toilets at the Ritz?" Theo rolled his eyes. "Shoveling coal at the Savoy?"

"Close!" Eric laughed. "Public Area Attendant on the Orient Express."

"Public Area Attendant?" Theo squinted at his friend. "What the—"

"Glorified toilet scrubber." Eric grinned. "Come on." He threw a uniform in Theo's direction. "Our training starts in an hour."

Merde! Theo smiled to himself. Progress. At least, now he was thinking in French.

2

AN OLD FLAME

That next afternoon, in the luxurious dining car aboard the famed Orient Express, the tension was palpable as Eliza accompanied Dorothy and Agatha to a table where they waited for the mysterious Peachy to join them for dinner. The train didn't officially depart Paris for another five hours, but the first-class passengers were allowed to board early and invited to take dinner in the dining room.

Like the rest of the train, the restaurant was gorgeously appointed with wood-paneled walls decorated with gold and pink inlaid flowers. Each table sported a white linen tablecloth, its own small candlestick lamp, and a single lily in a silver vase. And the chairs were high-backed, cushy, upholstered numbers that matched the drapes. Perfectly placed cucumbers and carrots sliced so thin, you could see through them glimmered like stained glass on Noritake china plates inlaid with blue-trimmed gold leaf. The only other time Eliza had seen such opulence was when, as a girl, she snuck into The Palm Court at the Ritz following a mark, a rich dandy who had entered the restaurant with a fat wallet in his pocket, which somehow got transferred to hers when she accidentally bumped into him.

Dorothy fiddled with her napkin and rearranged her silverware. She refused to talk about Peachy and flushed whenever Agatha or Eliza tried to pry information out of her. Dorothy's agitation was contagious. Eliza tried to shake it off by engaging Agatha in small talk. Although Agatha's idea of small talk was anything but small.

"What's so special about Ur?" Eliza took a sip of champagne. She could get used to this. Traveling with these ladies, she traveled in style.

"Ur, a port city on the Persian Gulf. The biblical home of Abraham." Agatha's eyes sparked with excitement. "As the Euphrates River shifted, the area became a desert. It's rich with ruins." Her hands were moving as she spoke. "My friend Katharine Woolley's husband, Leonard, is an archeologist and has a dig there." The more she spoke, the more animated she became. "Leonard is leading excavations for the British Museum."

Stealing artifacts for the British Museum, more like. Eliza kept her thoughts to herself and nodded along.

"Excuse me." A slender young man stood up from the next table. His narrow shoulders, long neck, bushy eyebrows, and chevron mustache gave him the bandit-like look of a Welsh polecat. A Welsh polecat wearing a black cassock and white clerical collar.

The mysterious Peachy, perhaps? Father Peachy?

"I couldn't help but overhear." He came over. "I don't mean to interrupt, but I'm going to Ur." He moved the cigarette he was holding to his side. "I'm Leonard Woolley's epigraphist on the Ur dig."

"Oh. My word." Agatha blushed. "What a small world."

"Not entirely." The priest smiled. "This is one of the only ways to get to Baghdad from London. And Lady Katharine asked me to look out for you."

"How kind." Agatha returned his smile.

A spark of recognition passed between the two of them. No doubt something spiritual that Eliza couldn't quite fathom. Dorothy was too distracted to pay much attention. Staring straight ahead as if in a daze, she sipped her gin cocktail in silence. Odd. Because usually, she was the most boisterous woman of Eliza's acquaintance.

"I'm Eliza Baker." Eliza held out her hand. "Secretary to the secretary of the Detection Club."

"Detection Club." The man sat his cigarette on the edge of the ashtray and gave her hand a pat. "How marvelous."

"This is Dorothy Sayers, secretary of the Detection Club." Eliza gestured toward her boss. "And you know Agatha Christie—"

Before she could finish her sentence, the man interrupted with a gasp.

"Not *the* Agatha Christie?" His eyes danced. "The mystery writer." The grin only made him look more feral. "I love your stories. No wonder Lady Katharine is so taken with you. She should have warned me I'd be in the company of greatness."

Agatha's blush deepened to a dusky rose. "And you are?"

"Oh, how silly of me." He patted his thinning hair. "I'm Father Richard. Father Richard Burrows. At your service." He nodded. "I would love to tell you about our dig." He glanced around the table, but his gaze landed on Agatha. "If you're interested."

"Very." Agatha's smile broadened. "Father, would you like to join us for dinner?"

Dorothy scowled and shook her head. Had she taken a

disliking to Father Richard already? Or was she so nervous about this Peachy person that she'd forgotten her manners?

"Or..." Agatha glanced at Dorothy. "Or... perhaps a drink later?" She stuttered on the words, perhaps worried the priest didn't drink.

"Perfect." Father Richard looked back at his own table where his companion was waiting. "I have plans for dinner already anyway."

Agatha followed his gaze. When she saw the woman sitting at his table, her smile faded. "Oh, I see." Obviously, she didn't approve of a priest dining with a pretty woman.

Father Richard gave a little laugh. "That's my secretary. Mrs. Daisy Boone." He emphasized the Mrs.

The tension visibly drained from Agatha's shoulders and she relaxed back into her chair. "Lovely." She smiled. "Lovely."

Eliza looked from one to the other and saw Agatha's fascination mirrored in his face. The spell of archeology must be worse than that of detection fiction.

Since Peachy was an hour late, Agatha suggested they start their dinner. Although Eliza was hungry too, she felt uncomfortable eating in public, especially in a posh setting like this one. She'd never had time to learn proper table etiquette. The burning questions of what fork to use with salad and which wine went with Victoria sponge had never ignited her imagination. She'd always felt lucky to have food on a plate.

When the waiter brought the first course, Eliza examined the plate. Perfectly fileted fish. The menu said it was *filets de sole meunière*. She took a bite and the tender, buttery filet melted in her mouth. How could simple fish with butter and herbs be so delicious? The second course was a moist chicken breast stuffed with a delicate ricotta and covered in a light cream sauce. Also, very nice. The *haricots verts* weren't just any green beans. They were garlicky and perfectly tender. The *rosbif à la gelée* was not as disgusting as it sounded. Still, she wasn't a fan of aspic or gelatin. After the beef came a romaine salad, followed by the best part of the meal: raspberry *coeur à la crème*, a light sponge, heart-shaped cake floating in raspberry puree. Eliza licked her spoon clean with each delightful bite. Pudding had always been her favorite part of the meal. And this was the most elaborate dinner she'd ever seen.

While Agatha and Eliza enjoyed the gourmet meal, Dorothy, usually a good eater, picked at her food. Was she still nervous about seeing Peachy? Or was she disappointed Peachy never showed up? And who the heck was this Peachy anyway?

"Looks like Peachy isn't coming," Eliza said between licks of her spoon. "So, can you please tell us who is this Peachy fellow? The suspense is killing me!"

Dorothy pursed her lips. "Hugo Fitzroy." She pushed a raspberry around on her plate. "We went to college together."

"Why Peachy?" Agatha asked. "His rosy cheeks?"

"The peach fuzz on his chin." Dorothy cracked a smile. "He was always trying to grow a beard. He never succeeded. His face remained soft as a baby's."

"Did you touch his face often?" Agatha raised an eyebrow.

"Don't be cheeky." Dorothy continued chasing the raspberry.

"Don't be so prudish." Agatha flashed a naughty smile. "We've both been married." She glanced over at Eliza. "And even if we hadn't, we're old enough." She cleared her throat. "At least some of us are."

At twenty-nine, Eliza was old enough—some would say, too old. But romance interested her about as much as the proper use of forks or appropriate wine pairings. From her limited experience, affairs of the heart ended up messier than the massacred cake splattered with red syrup on Dorothy's plate.

"Dottie!" a tenor voice squealed.

Eliza twisted around to face a chubby man wearing pants so tight, he looked like ten pounds of flour in a five-pound bag.

"Peachy?" Dorothy paled. "I thought you were joining us for dinner." She sounded hurt.

"My deepest apologies." He yawned. "Trying to get much-needed beauty sleep." He chuckled. "But I overslept." He moved around the table and leaned on the windowsill next to Dorothy. "But I'm here now." He pulled Dorothy into an embrace. "You haven't changed a bit."

She hugged him back and laughed. "I'd say years of pudding has softened us both."

"Indeed." He chuckled. "These days, I'm rather like a pond pudding." He patted his round stomach.

"We'd best not cut you then." Dorothy teased. She introduced him all around.

"You've done very well for yourself." He tapped a cigarette out of a gold case. "Want one?"

"Yes. Thank you," she said with a smile.

He snapped the case open and offered it to Dorothy. She plucked out a cigarette and once she had it between her lips, he held the flame of his engraved lighter under it and then lit his own.

"You've published how many novels now?" He tilted his head. "Three?"

"Four, actually." She grinned. "My latest just came out last week."

"Don't forget *Lord Peter Views the Body*," Agatha added. "Your book of short stories." She looked over at Mr. Fitzroy, AKA Peachy. "Dorothy also writes poetry, don't you know?"

Dorothy waved her hand in front of her face as if she were shooing a fly. "What have you been doing with yourself all these years, Peachy?" She shrugged. "I'm afraid you have me at a disadvantage. I should have kept up, but—"

"No. Not at all." He waved his hand. "I'm a writer myself. Investigative journalism, mostly." He took a drag off his cigarette. "Exposing corruption in the government or criminal activity among the peerage. That sort of thing."

"How fascinating." Agatha's eyes went wide. "So, you write about true crime."

"In a manner of speaking." He blew out a cloud of smoke. "Yes, you could say that."

"Your first book was on cold cases." Dorothy exhaled. "I remember it. Poisonings, wasn't it?"

"We've solved a few crimes ourselves, haven't we, Dorothy?" Agatha beamed.

"I suppose we have." Dorothy smiled. "We've even been consultants for Scotland Yard."

At the mention of Scotland Yard, Eliza nearly spit out her champagne. Sure, the Detection Club got together to discuss unsolved crimes and cold cases, but that didn't make them consultants for the Metropolitan Police. Eliza may not be an expert detective but after her forensic training and a month on the job at Scotland Yard, she was a heck of a lot more qualified to investigate than a bunch of novelists who sat around dreaming up fantasy crimes. Then again, her career at the Met ended in tragedy. At least this Peachy character wrote about real crimes instead of made-up ones.

Peachy leaned down and whispered, "Don't tell anyone, but I'm currently working on an exposé that will finally put me on the map."

"What kind of exposé?" Dorothy picked up her fork and started again on the raspberry.

"I can't tell you." He glanced around. "Otherwise, my subject might get skittish before I identify his handler."

"Oh, my." Agatha's eyes went wide. "Subjects and handlers. Sounds jolly exciting."

"Quite." Peachy smiled. He turned back to Dorothy. "I think you'll be pleased, Dottie dear."

"Me?" Dorothy looked up from her plate. "Why?"

"Let's just say I'm settling an old score."

"Goodness." Dorothy's icy-blue eyes were intense. "Sounds ominous."

"Indeed." He ground out his cigarette in the ashtray. "Bloody dangerous, too." He cleared his throat. "The train is going to be leaving Paris soon. I think I'll just eat in my cabin."

"Wouldn't you like to join us?" Dorothy sounded hurt.

"I really should get back to my cabin." He glanced at his watch. "Perhaps we can have drinks later, when the train is underway."

Dorothy nodded. "Alright."

"It really is good to see you again, Dottie." He put his hand on her shoulder and leaned down to kiss her cheek.

"You too, Peachy." Staring down at her plate, Dorothy stabbed the wayward berry.

Before he left, he whispered something into her ear, and the color drained from her face. Her mouth agape, she watched him make his way through the restaurant car and disappeared from sight.

"What was that all about?" Agatha said.

"Nothing, really." Dorothy bit her lip. "I hope he's wrong."

"About what?" Eliza said.

"Never mind." Dorothy stabbed the remains of her cake and

left her fork standing straight up in its center. For the next fifteen minutes, she buried her head in her Baedeker's guide to Constantinople and didn't say a word.

Agatha had just proposed a toast to "old friends" when the conductor made the announcement that the train would be departing soon. Amid the clinking of glasses, out the window, Eliza watched the hustle and bustle on the platform as the well-heeled Parisians waited to board the train. She thought of Theo, somewhere out there in the City of Lights.

"I say, look at that hat." Agatha pointed.

Eliza's gaze followed her finger. A striking woman wore a close-fitting, turquoise cloche with enormous, black feathers that stood two feet off her head. She stepped up onto the train. Behind her, a man with strong features like a hawk carried a metal case in one hand and helped her board with the other. Before boarding, as if searching for someone, he glanced up and down the platform. In a sea of gray hats, his disheveled, dark hair stuck out. And not just because he didn't have a hat, which was bad enough, and badly needed a haircut.

"He's not wearing a hat." Eliza gawked, hoping he couldn't see them through the dining car's tinted windows.

"Her hat quite makes up for his lack of one." Agatha laughed. "Oh, and her ruby brooch in the shape of a dog is just precious." She clapped her hands together.

"Only a man in a hurry, or with something to hide, leaves home without his hat," Dorothy said, lifting her gaze to the window. Her mouth fell open. "Good God!" The champagne flute slipped from her hand and crashed to the floor. "Peachy was right." As if cursing under her breath, she whispered, "Ivan Grigor."

* * *

Theo paced up and down the platform at Gare de l'Est waiting for the first-class passengers to board. The platform buzzed with a nervous, electric energy that seemed to hum in the very stones beneath his feet. The iron arches of the station loomed overhead, their shadows stretching like grasping fingers in the weak afternoon sunlight. A cacophony of shouts and steam punctuated the steady rumble of footsteps and the scrape of luggage wheels against the uneven tiles. Faces blurred into a restless sea of strangers: some animated with chatter, others tight with quiet resolve, each waiting for the train that would take them to Istanbul. He tightened his grip on his suitcase, his palms clammy despite the brisk October air. A faint whistle echoed in the distance, and his heart jumped, its rhythm quickening to match the frantic pace of porters darting between passengers with piles of precarious trunks. The faint smell of oil and coal mingled with the scent of wet wool and cigarette smoke. He tugged on the uniform collar, which was cutting into his neck. The cap precariously perched atop his head wobbled to and fro with only his ears to prevent it from sliding off.

"Calm down," Eric said, grabbing his sleeve. "Hold still, old man."

Theo stopped in his tracks and took a deep breath. It was one thing to dress like bums and tramp around the slums of Paris. It was quite another to board the Orient Express as a glorified custodian, cleaning toilets on the gleaming, blue jewel hurtling through the dark heart of Europe. What if he saw someone he knew? His uncle often took the train from London to Istanbul to buy rugs and enjoy warmer weather. Many of his parents' friends favored Greece in the winter and often traveled by luxury train. For that matter, his mother had been known to hop aboard the Orient Express for a shopping trip to Venice.

Theo pulled a toothpick from his pocket, stuck it in his mouth, and replaced pacing with chewing.

"Look, I was going to wait until we were aboard." Eric opened his knapsack and produced a glossy flyer. "But since you've got the jitters." He passed the flyer to Theo.

International Writers' Convention
7–10 October
Pera Palace Hotel, Istanbul

Theo glanced over at Eric. "We're going to the writers' convention?" His mood brightened. Then he remembered Dorothy's invitation. What if she was on this same train? More to the point, what if Eliza was with her? His palms started to sweat.

"How else could we afford to get there?" Eric grinned. "H. G. Wells is one of the speakers. A great political writer and a favorite with the women. Man after my own heart." He slapped Theo on the shoulder. "Let's get aboard before they leave without us."

Theo followed Eric to the back of the train where they boarded through the bar car. The train manager, Monsieur Fournier, met them for a brief refresher on the instructions they'd received the day before at the five-hour training session. He reminded them the only reason they'd got their jobs in such a rush was an outbreak of influenza among the staff—that and their ability to stand up straight and speak English, French, and Italian. Eric may have exaggerated their language abilities.

Monsieur Fournier had large ears and bloodshot eyes. The deep creases above his mouth looked like a second mustache. He wasn't exactly gruff, but he wasn't friendly either. He made it clear he expected military precision and the utmost courtesy to the passengers. "The slightest infraction and we won't hesitate to drop you off at the next station." He scribbled on his clipboard. "Now, go see to our guests. And remember, they are to be treated like royalty. *Comprenez-vous?*"

Theo nodded. "Yes, sir."

"Understood." Eric gave a brisk salute.

Monsieur Fournier scowled. "Don't mock me, Mr. Orwell."

"Never, sir." Eric kept a straight face. "Like you, I respect hard work."

After the manager was out of earshot, Theo turned to Eric. "Mr. Orwell?"

"Trying out a new pen name." He raised his eyebrows. "What do you think?"

"Eric Orwell." Theo shrugged. "Er-or, too many r's."

"How about George?" Eric tilted his head. "George Orwell. Has a ring to it." He grinned.

"What's wrong with your own name?" Theo didn't understand why authors had to change their names. Unless of course they had hideous names like Bracegirdle, or extra-long names that wouldn't fit on book covers like Wolfeschlegelsteinhausenbergerdorff, or women who needed to pass themselves off as men to sell books.

"Eric Blair." Eric waved him away. "Too commonplace and boring to be the name of a famous writer." He took off toward the passenger cars.

"Famous." Theo scoffed as he followed his friend. "That'll be the day." He didn't need to be famous. But he wouldn't mind making enough money to pay for food and shelter. His chapped hands would thank him.

"Excuse me."

Theo turned to face a lithe woman in a fox stole who was struggling with a monstrous suitcase.

"Might you help me with my luggage?" She dropped the case with a thud.

"Of course, madame." Theo used the French address as instructed. He grasped the handle and lifted. But the case was so heavy, he had to use both hands to get it off the floor. He resisted the temptation to ask what she was carrying, gold bars? Instead, he gritted his teeth and plastered a smile on his face. Yes, it would be nice to make a living writing. His soon to be aching back would join the chorus of thank-yous.

3

THE ENCOUNTER

Eliza spent the morning in the café car, drinking coffee and admiring the snowcapped Swiss Alps, which from the train window looked like the spine of a great prehistoric creature rising out of the green valley and into the blue sky. The bitter aroma of freshly brewed coffee mingled with the sharp scent of alpine air seeping through the seams of the train. Passengers murmured in hushed tones, their faces aflame in the glow of the rising sun, as the train hurtled through the mountains, its rhythmic sway lending an almost hypnotic cadence to the start of the day. Hypnosis verging on lethargy.

Fidgeting in her seat, she wished she could get out and explore, maybe go skiing or snowshoeing. Dorothy had given her a copy of her latest novel about the adventures of the aristocratic amateur sleuth Lord Peter Wimsey. But while Eliza had nothing against reading or mysteries, she couldn't abide sitting still. Unless, of course, she was playing chess. Reading was too passive for her tastes. She craved movement of the body and the mind. Most of all, she craved control. Stuck aboard this rattling tin can, she felt like a trapped animal.

Exploring the train cars seemed a poor substitute for the Alps. So, she resisted the temptation and resigned herself to another cup of coffee. Maybe Dorothy or Agatha would join her soon and provide an amusing distraction from the monotony: another mysterious stranger from their past or imaginative musings on a cold case.

Unfortunately, Dorothy was holed up in her cabin, insisting she had to work on her presentation for the conference. And Agatha was spending all her time with Father Richard discussing mummies and other buried treasure. Why not? After what her rotter husband did, she deserved some fun. Eliza laid her book on her lap and twisted around to peek at the pair. They were looking very cozy taking tea together at the end of the carriage; no doubt talking about dead people cheered Agatha to no end.

A young steward walked by and then stopped, turned, and stood next to her chair. "Why are you reading that rubbish?" He pointed to the book in her lap.

"What?" She sat blinking at him. Seriously? Was a waiter challenging her tastes in reading material? She resisted the urge to kick him.

"Lord Peter Wimsey." He bent down and read off the book cover.

She bristled. "It isn't rubbish." She may not enjoy reading, but that didn't mean Dorothy Sayers wasn't a good writer. At least she had strong women characters who disdained the conventions imposed in a world controlled by men. "The author is a brilliant writer." She omitted, *not to mention my employer*.

"Oh, apologies." The waiter's cheeks darkened. "It's just all that drivel about lords and ladies. How can you stand it?" He shook his head. "The Bellona Club." He leaned down to get a better look at the book's cover. "And Lord Whatshisname, entitled aristocrat."

"Have you even read it?" Eliza furrowed her brows.

"Well, no." He cleared his throat. "But I'll bet you—"

Another arrogant man judging another's work without knowing it at all. Talk about entitlement!

"If you fancy a bet, how about a game of chess?" She could use a few extra quid. And her idea of a wager was one she knew she could win.

"What?" He squinted at her as if she'd spoken Greek.

"Do you play chess?" She would love to beat this know-it-all, make some money, and teach him a lesson in the process. "It's a game of skill and foresight. Perhaps you've heard of it."

He grinned. "I'd love a game of chess. But I'm supposed to be working." He winked. "Maybe later when my shift ends."

"In the meantime, how about that cup of coffee I ordered?" She pointed at her empty cup.

"Righto." He smiled. "Coming right up."

A few minutes later, the bold young man returned with a steaming cup and a plate of biscuits. "I'm George, by the way. George Orwell." He glanced around and then whispered, "Actually, my real name is Eric, Eric Blair."

"Are you undercover?" she whispered back. If he was a spy, he wasn't a very good one, telling her his real name.

"In a manner of speaking." He leaned closer. "I'm a writer. I'm on my way to a big writers' convention in Istanbul." He beamed.

Good grief. Even the waiter was a writer. Was everyone on the bloody train a writer? Dorothy, Agatha, Dorothy's old friend Peachy, and now this George or Eric person.

"May I ask, what's your name?" He tilted his head and leered at her.

"Eliza." She wondered if she should have used an alias. Conversing with the steward was making her uncomfortable. Not because he was a steward but because he was taking liberties that made her uneasy.

"Eliza, let me tell you something..." Unfortunately, along with her coffee, he went on to deliver a lecture on democratic socialism. He was passionate, she'd give him that. But it was a relief when the train manager entered the carriage and the chatty steward trotted off in the other direction.

In an act of defiance, she waved the book above her head and then cracked the spine and started reading again.

By the time she thought to take a sip of her coffee, it was cold. She glanced at her watch. Golly. She'd been so engrossed by the book, she hadn't felt the time pass. She'd been reading for over an hour already. So far, it was the usual fight over inheritance and a dodgy will. And while Lord Wimsey was a toff and a bit silly, at least he was honorable and respectful toward women.

"May I?" The baritone voice caught her off guard.

She looked up into the hawklike face of the mysterious Ivan Grigor who'd boarded in Paris. His eyebrows looked like two awnings shielding his dark, sunken eyes, which only added to his inscrutability. His starched, white shirt, neatly knotted tie, and gold diamond tie pin with matching gold cufflinks suggested a man of means. And yet the frayed hem of his morning jacket and the slightly worn look of his trousers indicated otherwise.

"May I sit down?" There was a hint of a foreignness behind his posh, public-school accent.

She nodded.

"Thank you, miss..." The accent again. Was it Russian, or

perhaps Serbian? Too bad Dorothy didn't tell them anything about him.

"Eliza Baker." She laid the book on the table. "We haven't been properly introduced."

"Ivan Grigor, at your service." When he gave a little bow, his hair flopped forward. She wondered if it was a toupee. He slid into the seat across from her. "You're Dorothy Sayers's traveling companion, are you not?"

"Her secretary." Eliza stared into his face trying to get a read on him. A foreigner trying hard to eliminate any trace of his origins who happened to know she was traveling with Dorothy. "How do you know Dorothy?"

He chuckled. "Dorothy and I go way back." He raised his bushy brows. "Back to the days of our reckless youth, I'm afraid." When he folded his hands on the table, his ruby ring caught the sunlight from the window. "Where is the lovely Dorothy? Peachy told me she was here. But I haven't seen her yet."

"She's in her cabin." Eliza didn't know how much to tell him. Especially after Dorothy's reaction to seeing him board the train. "She's working."

"Working on her speech for the writers' convention, no doubt." He gave her a wistful smile. "She always was a clever one. And adorable, too."

"Indeed." She didn't trust Mr. Ivan Grigor. The way he talked about Dorothy. What gave him the right to claim such intimacy? She returned a forced smile, picked up her book, and then opened it to the place where she'd left off.

"Tell Dorothy I'd love to meet her for a meal or a cocktail and catch-up. Well." He slapped the table with his palm. "I'd best be going then."

She nodded but didn't look up from her book.

By the time she did look up, dusk was falling on a picturesque villa—she'd been so engrossed in the story, she'd missed lunch. Outside the window, terracotta roofs shimmering in the setting sun were reflected on a gem-green lake. They must be in Northern Italy. Glancing around for a waiter to ask, she glimpsed a steward darting out of the carriage. A shiver ran up her spine. His wavy, chestnut hair reminded her of Theo. She hugged herself. Two years ago, before he upped and left, she thought he'd fancied her. She must have been wrong. She never was good at reading people. That was her sister, Jane's department.

Her stomach grumbled. She glanced at her watch. Nearly teatime and she hadn't glimpsed Dorothy all day. She picked up her book and headed back to Dorothy's cabin to check on her. No doubt, she'd been working all day on her speech and hadn't taken a break to eat. When Dorothy was writing, she lived on sweet biscuits and strong coffee. Not exactly a well-balanced diet.

Eliza knocked on the cabin door.

No answer.

She knocked again. Had Dorothy gone out? If so, where to? Eliza hadn't seen her in the café car. Was she in the bar car? "Dorothy, are you in there?"

The door slid open. "Oh, it's only you." Dorothy poked her head out the door and glanced up and down the corridor. "Come in." She grabbed Eliza's sleeve and pulled her into the cabin. "Quickly."

"What's going on?" Eliza adjusted her jumper. "I thought you were writing."

"I am writing." She lit a cigarette.

"Did you finish your speech?"

"Not quite." She took a puff.

"But almost?"

"Not really." She blew out a cloud of smoke.

"How about you read it to me?" Eliza put her hands on her hips. What had Dorothy been doing all day if she wasn't writing her speech?

Dorothy paced the length of the cabin. All three strides of it. "Alright." She turned back and let out a loud exhale. "I'd like to thank the organizers for inviting me. It's an honor. And thank you ladies and gentlemen for being here this evening. Especially when you could be taking a sunset cruise on the Bosphorus." She waved her hand like a symphony conductor. Her hand trembled as she took another drag off her smoke. "That's it, I'm afraid." She dropped onto the bench seat.

"That's all you've written?" Eliza huffed. "What have you been doing in here all day?"

"Hiding." She picked at the hem of her blouse.

"From what?" Eliza sat down next to her.

"Regret, betrayal, heartbreak." Her cheeks turned blotchy and her lip started to tremble. "You name it."

"Peachy Fitzroy or Ivan Grigor or both?" Eliza went to the washbasin to fetch a glass of water. "Whatever happened, it's in the past." She handed the glass to Dorothy. "It can't hurt you anymore." She was dying to know what these men did to upset the usually unflappable Dorothy Sayers. "Perhaps it would help to talk about it." She gently touched her employer's hand.

Dorothy looked up at her with tears welling in her eyes.

Blimey. Whatever those rotten men did must have been bad, really bad.

"Ivan..." Dorothy's voice was jagged. "Ivan and I were close." She bit her lip. "A couple of years after college, I got a teaching job in London." She glanced over at Eliza. "That's where I met him." She sucked in a breath. "It was love at first sight. The trouble was, he didn't believe in marriage. Claimed it was a bourgeois institution designed to domesticate the passion out of men's souls." She scoffed. "Well, one thing led to another," she said, sniffling. "And as soon as I capitulated in the bedroom..." Using the backs of her hands, she wiped her eyes. "He upped and left." She closed her eyes. "A year later, he married a concert pianist from the old country." Cigarette ash dropped onto her skirt.

"You're going to catch fire," Eliza said, pointing at the ember.

Dorothy jumped up and brushed it off.

"The old country." Eliza sighed. "Let me guess: Russia."

Dorothy nodded.

"So, he did believe in marriage after all," Eliza said softly. "The scoundrel."

"When I heard about the wedding, I went to bed for a week." She stared down at her shoes. "What I did next was shameful." Her eyes flicked up to meet Eliza's. "So much so, I can't speak of it."

She obviously hadn't killed him. So, what was so shameful she couldn't speak of it?

Of course, Eliza was dying to find out. But she knew Dorothy well enough not to press her. "Why don't we go get some dinner?" Eliza stood up. "Some food and wine will lift your spirits."

"What if he's there?" Dorothy looked terrified.

"I'll protect you." Eliza sliced the air with her hand. "I'm an expert at ju-jitsu." It was true. During her short-lived stint in the Metropolitan Police, she'd learned martial arts. She'd also learned her own lessons in regret, betrayal, and heartbreak. "Come on. It will do you good."

Eliza led Dorothy through the corridor to the dining car.

The light outside the windows had turned a violet blue. Illuminated with candle sconces, the restaurant car was bathed in a soft peach color. Each table was set to perfection with silver, gold-rimmed china, and a tiny vase of fresh lilies. The hum of voices blended with the clickity-clack of the train to create a soothing symphony of sound.

"See?" she said. "Isn't this better than hiding in your cabin?"

From across the car, Agatha waved and beckoned from a table where she was no doubt plotting to uncover hideous mummies or jars of pickled internal organs.

Holding her arms askew for balance, Eliza picked up her pace as she made her way toward the table. Agatha was all smiles. In fact, Eliza had never seen her looking so happy.

"I hope we're not late," Eliza said, taking a seat across from her.

Agatha clutched something in her palm. "Not at all." She held out her hand and opened her palm. "Look, isn't it dear?" Her voice was as bubbly as the free-flowing champagne. "Father Richard gave it to me." She quickly added, "On behalf of my dear friend Katharine Woolley, or so he claims." She blushed. "I think he just didn't want to admit he bought it for me himself. Maybe he thought it would give me the wrong idea." She giggled.

"Really, Agatha." Dorothy huffed. "He's a priest, for heaven's sake."

In the palm of her hand, Agatha held a large, ruby-studded gold brooch in the shape of a schnauzer. "At breakfast, I mentioned missing Peter, my dog, and at lunch, Father Richard gave me this." She beamed. "Isn't it sweet?"

Eliza and Dorothy exchanged a telling glance. With their shared interest in archeology, Agatha and Father Richard's friendship was moving faster than the express train. Did Father

Richard carry a supply of adorable gold pins to present to lady travelers? He hardly had time between breakfast and lunch to make a purchase, especially since the train hadn't stopped since Simplon when they exchanged dining cars.

"It's darling," Dorothy said, admiring the jewelry. "But isn't it a little soon to be exchanging gifts?"

"Oh, don't worry, Dorothy dear." Agatha giggled. "I didn't give him one." She took a quick sip of her red wine. "Anyway, he says he got it for me on behalf of my dear friend Katharine. And I always send her an advanced copy of my latest novel."

"Speak of the devil," Eliza said under her breath.

Father Richard was all smiles as he approached the table.

"Please join us." Agatha beamed.

"Don't mind if I do." Father Richard slid in beside her.

"Good evening, ladies." The deep voice came from over Eliza's shoulder. "Good evening, Father Richard."

Eliza turned to see Ivan Grigor dressed in an evening coat and bow tie with his hair slicked back. The shine on his black shoes couldn't conceal their wear and again he had the look of an aristocrat who'd fallen on hard times. But how did he know Father Richard?

"I would join you, but my lovely wife Lena is waiting for me." He smiled back at an attractive woman with short, dark hair, lovely, sad eyes, and a stunning, scarlet, silk scarf. "But Dorothy, I wonder if we might meet for a drink after dinner." He put his hand on Dorothy's shoulder, revealing a stunning cufflink that sported a yellow gold scarab on turquoise enamel encircled by a band of delicate pearl.

The effect was palpable even to Eliza, who felt Dorothy shudder.

Dorothy cleared her throat. "I'm afraid—"

"Oh no you don't." He held up his hand. "I won't take no for an answer." Under his charming tone was a lingering threat. "We have so much to catch up on." His eyes brightened. "What has it been? Almost five years ago now since you last wrote to me?" He grinned. "And what a letter it was. You remember. Don't you, Dorothy dearest?"

"Ten o'clock in the bar." Dorothy turned the color of the claret. "One drink. That's all."

"Wonderful!" Ivan gave a little bow. "Until then." He turned on his heels and returned to his lovely wife.

"What in the world was that all about?" Agatha asked.

"A new friend," Father Richard said, dabbing at his mustache with his napkin.

Agatha turned to Father Richard. "You know him?" Her tone was accusatory.

"No," Father Richard said softly. "I only just met him this afternoon. In fact." He lowered his voice even more. "He sold the brooch to me."

"Oh. I see." Agatha turned back to her friend. "Dorothy, who is this Ivan Grigor to you?"

"A chapter of my life I was hoping to forget." Dorothy stood up, dropped her napkin on her plate, and marched out of the dining car.

* * *

Theo had seen her. She was on the train. Eliza Baker. His tormenter and the object of all his desires. He rolled over on his upper bunk to face the wall, as if closing in on himself could shield him from the pain of seeing her again. As the train rolled along, it seemed to whisper her name. Eliza. Over and over again. He covered his eyes with his arm.

She'd looked the same as the last time he'd seen her. Flaxen hair, steely eyes, rosebud lips. He scoffed. Clichés. All clichés. He never could do her justice. Seeing her again now, he realized why. At least in part.

It wasn't just the limitation of words, their inadequacy to reach into the chest of life and tear out its beating heart, nor that experience always outstripped the representation of it. No. It was something else. Something beyond Eliza's physical beauty. Something inside her. Her determination and resolve. Her grit. More than that, it was the way she moved through the world. With force. Force and grace. How could he put into words the power of Eliza? Or her power over him? Every time he took up his pen, he tried. And every time, he failed. Like the queen, she was the most powerful piece on the board. And like the queen, she could swoop across the squares between them and snatch his heart if he wasn't careful.

Whoosh. The door to the cabin opened.

"What are you doing in bed, old boy?" Eric's voice was chipper. Too chipper. "I met the most gorgeous girl in the café car." He plopped down on the lower bunk. "The sweetest little piece." He chuckled. "I'd love to sink my teeth into her."

"Aren't you forgetting your station?" Theo rolled over and peered over the edge of the bunk. "We're lowly staff, remember. No fraternizing with the upper classes." He surveyed their second-class cabin, which was a narrow, airless box, its walls closing in with the faint scent of damp wool and stale tobacco. The overhead luggage rack sagged ominously, and the single dim light flickered as the train jolted, casting jittery shadows that seemed to press closer with every mile. Not like the opulence of first class. An opulence bought at the expense of creativity and imagination—at least that's what Eric would say.

"She's different. Defiant and dangerous. Practically daring

me to take her." He lay back on the bunk and put his hands behind his head. "How I'd love to run my hands over her—"

"How about we keep our fantasies to ourselves, old boy." Theo really didn't want to hear about Eric's erotic daydreams. It was bad enough keeping his own in check.

"She was reading a stupid mystery book." Eric snorted. "Genre fiction. Up your alley, I suppose."

"And what's wrong with genre fiction?" Theo hung his head further over the edge and stared down at his friend. "Genre fiction can do anything your political literary writing can, only it will keep the reader turning pages and interested instead of putting them to sleep."

"A good book should educate and not entertain." Eric stabbed the air with a finger. "The theater is for entertaining. Serious literature must expose the unseen power dynamics at work in social hierarchies."

"You mean like the power dynamics of taking young women and sinking your teeth into them?" Theo rolled his eyes. Sure, he believed in exposing the oppression of the lower classes. But he also believed in women's rights. Women were people and not property to be taken.

"Women are different." Eric sighed. "They're here to tempt us. To fulfill us. To mother our children. They aren't cut out for politics or the dog-eat-dog world of powerful men."

"What's with all the eating metaphors?" Theo's stomach growled.

"Take my little piece in the café car, for example." Eric propped himself up on his pillow. "She is enamored of a lord, the romantic protagonist of her silly mystery novel." He laughed. "What she doesn't know is hard work is what makes a man manly. She's probably a virgin who deserves a good—"

"Alright." Theo hopped off the bunk. "Enough with what

women deserve." He ran his hand through his hair. "What they deserve is to be treated with respect as the equals to men."

Eric laughed. "Talk about fiction, my friend."

"Fiction can be aspirational. Even hopeful." Theo went to the window and stared out into the darkness. "It doesn't have to be all maggots and filth."

"If life is maggots and filth, then fiction should describe what is and not some utopian ideal." Eric sat up. "People need to know what they're up against. They need to be warned."

"The truth goes beyond descriptions of squalor, my friend." Theo turned back to Eric. "I agree. Fiction should be truthful. The truth about an experience, a life, a perspective. Not the truth—there is no one truth. Your dogmatism about the way things are is as bad as the totalitarianism you claim to expose." He exhaled. "Especially when it comes to women."

"I suppose you believe in love between equals and all that hogwash." Eric scoffed. "Like the delicious Eliza from the café car, you've read too many idiotic romance novels."

"Did you say Eliza?" Theo balled up his fists. "Stay away from her."

"Or what?" Eric guffawed. "You'll challenge me to a duel at dawn?" He laughed. "You'll never escape the mores of the upper class, old boy."

"And by pretending to be poor, you'll never know what it's like to actually be poor. You and I can dip in and out of poverty. But we'll never know what it's like to have no escape." Theo yanked the door open. Speaking of escape, he had to get out of there before he did something stupid, like punch Eric in the face.

4

THE FLAKY BROOCH

The next morning, Eliza went to the dining car at eight o'clock sharp to meet Dorothy and Agatha for breakfast. Even at this early hour, almost every seat was taken. Although judging from their pale complexions, the dark circles under their eyes, and the way they were leaning on their tables, some of the diners could be suffering from hangovers, the result of a late night in the bar car. A few shielded their eyes from the glow of the pale morning light hitting the polished wood and brass fittings, making them gleam like the belt buckle of a waking giant. The soft clink of china and the quiet murmur of early risers mingled with the faint aroma of coffee and fresh bread, promising a hopeful if precarious start to the morning.

Agatha waved from across the room. She was alone at a table for four.

"Where's Dorothy?" Eliza plunked down across from her.

"She refused to get out of bed." Agatha chuckled. "Such a lazybones."

"That's odd." Eliza poured herself a glass of water from the jug on the table. "She never misses a meal. And she never, ever sleeps in."

"She'll be along soon, I'm sure." Agatha ran her hand across the dog brooch pinned onto the lapel of her jacket. "Such a glorious morning." When she smiled, she looked ten years younger than her nearly forty years. Wistfully, she turned to gaze out the window.

It was true. The sunrise over the vineyards transformed the landscape into a fantasy of lush, emerald valleys and rows of flame-tipped grape vines.

The waiter offered them coffee. Agatha asked for tea instead. Eliza gladly took a cup of hot coffee with plenty of cream and lots of sugar.

Breakfast was a feast of smoked salmon, eggs with truffles, and toast points with caviar, along with fresh berries and crème fraîche. Agatha was particularly fond of the crème fraîche, asking for an extra dish of the light, airy goodness.

"Dorothy doesn't know what she's missing," Agatha said, taking another heaping spoonful of cream and popping it into her mouth. She was eating it straight, not bothering with the berries.

"Maybe I should go check on her." Eliza fidgeted. Dorothy was already thirty minutes late, which was unlike her in the extreme; according to her, unless you were ten minutes early, you were late.

"Let her be." Agatha petted her doggie brooch again. "She'll be along when she's ready." A tiny flake of gold floated in the air and drifted down onto the table linen.

A waiter whisked by. Eliza did a double take. "Doesn't that waiter look like Theo? Theo Sharp?" Her cheeks warmed.

Agatha twisted around for a look. "Why, you're right." She

turned back. "But it couldn't be. He's a waiter." She smiled. "People tell me I look like someone they know all the time. I have one of those faces." She played with her pin. Another tiny flake fluttered to the table.

"I think your dog is shedding." Eliza pointed to the tablecloth where the second flake had landed.

"What?" Agatha blanched.

"Your brooch." Eliza nodded toward the pin.

Agatha removed the brooch from her lapel and examined it. She picked at it with a fingernail. Another gold flake came off. She glanced over at Eliza. "Good heavens. It's fake." She picked up her knife and tapped one of the rubies. It fell out onto the table. She pressed the back of her spoon against it. "Paste." The ruby chipped under the spoon.

"Do you think Father Richard knows it's fake?" Eliza asked.

Agatha blinked.

"Speak of the devil." Eliza motioned with her eyes.

Mr. Grigor glanced around and then tucked a bottle of champagne under his coat. He scurried out of the carriage, but not before grabbing a fancy pastry off the tray on his way out.

"What's he up to?" Agatha squinted.

"No good." Eliza stood up.

"You're not going to follow him, are you?" Agatha's gaze intensified. "What if he's dangerous?"

"Why would he be dangerous?" Eliza huffed. "No, I'm going to fetch Dorothy. She can't hide in your cabin the whole trip." She dropped her napkin on the table. "And she can tell us about her friend Ivan Grigor and why he's selling fake jewelry."

"I'm surprised Father Richard would buy a paste ruby." Agatha's face fell. "He's an archeologist. He knows the real thing when he sees it." She glanced up at Eliza. "You don't think he knew it was fake and bought it on the cheap?" Pursing her lips, she wrapped the brooch in a handkerchief and tucked it inside her purse. "Perhaps that's all I'm worth. Paste rubies."

"Don't be silly." Eliza put her hand on Agatha's shoulder. "I'm sure there is a reasonable explanation. And I'm going to find it." She gave Agatha a sympathetic smile. "I'll be back. Hopefully, with Dorothy in tow."

"Thank you, dear." Agatha went for another consoling spoonful of crème fraîche. "I'm to meet Father Richard in five minutes. So I may not be here when you get back."

Eliza nodded, took one last sip of her coffee, and then took off toward Dorothy's cabin. As she traversed the corridor, she wondered if Dorothy could shed light on why her old pal Ivan might sell paste jewelry. Was Dorothy really having a lie-in? Perhaps she was so engrossed in writing her speech, she'd lost track of time.

Eliza knocked on the cabin door. "It's me, Eliza."

"Come in." Dorothy's voice sounded strange. Muffled, like she was in a well.

Eliza pulled the door open. "Why weren't you..." She stopped short when she saw Dorothy lying on the lower bunk, her eyes red and puffy and a letter in her hand. "What's wrong? Have you been crying?" If it was unlike Dorothy to be late, it was unheard of for her to cry. She was more likely to growl and bark than cry.

"I'm fine." She tucked the letter into an envelope and slipped it into the pocket of her dressing gown.

Eliza tilted her head and squinted at her. "Bad news?"

"It's nothing." She sat up and patted at her hair. She really didn't look well. Her face was blotching. The bags under her eyes looked like two purple plums. And her hair was a messy bird's nest. There was obviously something wrong.

"Are you ill?" Eliza sat across from her on the jump seat. "Is it your husband, Arthur? Have you had news from home? One of the cats?"

"Arthur is fine." Dorothy shook her head. "The cats are fine." She tightened the belt on her gown. "I'm fine." She slipped her feet into the slippers provided by the line. "Everything is fine."

"You don't look fine." Eliza narrowed her brows. "And you missed breakfast." She leaned closer. "You need to eat. You'll feel better after some strong coffee and French pastries." She stood up. "Come on. Get dressed. We're going to get you some food." Given Dorothy's distressed state, the interrogation about Ivan Grigor and the brooch could wait.

"Can't you find the cabin steward and order me something to eat in here?" Dorothy stared down at her feet.

"You really need to get out." Eliza went to the window and opened it. "For one thing, it's terribly stuffy in here." A blast of cold air tore in through the window. She considered closing it again, but decided Dorothy needed a bracing breeze to get her moving. "You can't hide out in here for the whole trip." She went to the cupboard and retrieved Dorothy's shoes and skirt set. "Get dressed. We're going to the dining car."

"Please—" Dorothy whimpered.

Eliza held up her hand. "It will do you good." When she opened the door, the cross-breeze made her shiver. "I'll wait for you outside in the corridor." She stepped into the hallway and then turned back. "Don't take long. My coffee is getting cold."

Hugging herself, Eliza paced back and forth in front of the door to Dorothy's cabin. Raised voices from the corridor made her stop and listen. Agatha and Father Richard were having a tense discussion. Perhaps Agatha had presented him with her flaky brooch with its fake jewels. She stood stock and listened.

"My reputation is at stake," Father Richard said. "Next time I see that man, I'll throttle him."

She couldn't make out what Agatha was saying, but her tones were consoling.

"I'm going to demand my money back!" Maybe Father Richard wasn't as soft-spoken and easy-going as he appeared to be. "I swear to you, I examined it carefully." Thud. Did Father Richard drop something? "How could I have fallen for a fake?" Another thud. Had he kicked the wall? "How humiliating."

"Now, now." Agatha's voice was calm. "Don't fret. I love it just the same. It was very thoughtful of you... I mean of Katharine."

When the pair came into view, Eliza dashed back down the hall. She knocked on Dorothy's door again. What was taking her so long?

"It's me." Eliza knocked again.

"Come in." Dorothy's voice was weak.

Eliza slid the door open and entered the cabin. "You're still in bed!" She couldn't believe it. Dorothy must be ill. That was the only explanation.

"I'm really not feeling up to facing the dining room... and my ghosts." Dorothy sat on the edge of her bunk, wringing her hands.

"You can't sit here stewing all day." Eliza stood, arms folded across her chest. "I'm not leaving until you get up, put on your clothes, and leave this room."

By the time Eliza coaxed Dorothy out of her cabin, it was almost dinner time. They went to the bar car for predinner cocktails. The bar was packed with women wearing evening gowns, long strings of pearls, and feathered tiaras. The men wore long evening jackets sporting silk pocket squares and bow ties. Given her morning and afternoon were spent cajoling Dorothy, Eliza hadn't had time to change for dinner. In her brown, tweed skirt and jacket, she was as drab as a pheasant among peacocks. Which seemed somehow fitting for a secretary to a secretary of a writers' supper club.

At the far end of the car, a pretty woman was playing the piano. Wait. She did a double take. It was Mrs. Grigor, Ivan's lovely wife.

"Do we really have to listen to this?" Dorothy waved her hand in front of her face as if she smelled rotten fish.

"I think she's rather good." Eliza didn't know much about music, but the halting, melancholy tune appealed to her.

"That is Ivan's wife," Dorothy hissed. "The circus performer turned concert pianist." She shook her head. "And to top it off, she's gorgeous. Figures." She marched up to the bar.

Eliza followed close on her heels.

"I'll have a Gin Rickey." Dorothy leaned against the bar. "Make it extra strong."

"And what would you like, mademoiselle?" the bartender asked Eliza.

"A glass of water, please." She needed her wits about her to keep an eye on Dorothy.

"Oh no you don't." Dorothy smirked. "Make that two Gin Rickeys."

"Why don't you ladies have a seat and I'll bring you your cocktails." The bartender's smile was a mile wide.

Finding a seat was easier said than done. Weaving through the boisterous crowd, Eliza spotted an unoccupied bench on the other side of the bar. She beckoned to Dorothy. They squeezed onto the bench. They didn't have a table, but they did have an excellent view of the pianist.

Swaying to the music, her hands floating over the keys, Lena Grigor looked like a melancholy angel as she played her strange tune. From her crescent brows and pouty lips to her high forehead, long nose, and large, dark eyes, her features were an uncanny mix of fine and striking. As she played, she kept glancing over at a fellow sitting alone sipping a cocktail.

When Eliza followed the pianist's gaze, the man looked right at her. In self-defense, Eliza closed her eyes and lost herself in the otherworldly sounds.

"Two Gin Rickeys, as ordered."

She opened her eyes to see Dorothy's old friend Peachy holding out two glasses.

Dimples sprouted at the sides of his mouth when he smiled. "May I join you?"

"Standing room only, I'm afraid," Dorothy said. "Unless you plan on sitting on my lap."

Peachy laughed. "I haven't had such a nice invitation in a long while." He glanced back at the bar. "I'll be right back. Going to grab my martini." When he returned, he stood near Dorothy, sipping his cocktail. "Tell me what you're working on these days, Dottie, dear."

Dorothy's face brightened. "A woman is accused of poisoning her faithless husband." She gave him a knowing look. "And my chivalrous sleuth Lord Peter Wimsey comes to her rescue."

"Nothing quite like a damsel in distress." Peachy grinned.

"Oh, don't worry." Dorothy pursed her lips. "My Harriet Vane gives as good as she gets. Believe me, Wimsey has met his match."

"So, it's a love story, then." Peachy raised his glass. "You always were a hopeless romantic."

"Very funny." Dorothy waved him away. "Enough about

me." She lowered her voice. "Tell us about your top-secret exposé."

"If I told you, it wouldn't be a secret, would it?" Peachy drained his glass and sat it on the tray of a passing waiter.

Eliza held her glass in mid-air. It was him. The waiter. It was Theo Sharp. What in heaven's name was he doing on the Orient Express? And why was he wearing that uniform? When did he start working for the railroad? Last she'd heard, he'd run off to Paris to find himself among the bright young things of the Lost Generation or some such. She watched Theo carrying drinks to other passengers. Had he seen her?

"If you promise not to tell a soul," Peachy said in a whisper. "It's about Ivan Grigor." He grinned.

Dorothy gasped. The color drained from her face. "What about him?"

"Let's just say, I never forgave him for the way he treated you." Peachy adjusted his tie. "And my exposé is my way of repaying him for his cruelty."

"You're doing it for me?" Dorothy raised her voice. "Why?"

"I know what happened after he left you... the suffering you endured... it was heartless." He tapped out a cigarette from a gold case. "Want one?" He held out the case.

Dorothy plucked up a cigarette.

He held the case out to Eliza.

"No thank you." She shook her head, but her eyes still followed Theo across the carriage.

"I have my own reasons, too." Peachy pulled a gold lighter from his pocket and lit both cigarettes. He took a puff and blew out a cloud of smoke. "This book is going to make me famous." He tilted his head. "Maybe not as famous as you, dear Dottie. But it will put me on the literary map." He glanced around and then grabbed an ashtray.

"What's so special about Ivan?" Dorothy asked, the cigarette trembling between her fingers.

"Let's just say the French authorities have a special interest in our old friend." He winked. "I'm going to get another drink. Would you like one?"

Dorothy sat blinking at him.

"Will you excuse me?" Eliza said finally. "I see someone I know."

As Eliza snaked through the crowd toward Theo, the haunting strains of Lena's music followed her—and so did the eyes of a mysterious man wearing a monocle and smoking from a long cigarette holder watching from the corner. Who was he? Turning back to take stock of him, she bumped into Eric Blair, who was waiting tables. "Sorry," she said without looking up.

"You can touch me any time." Eric's whispered breath was too close for comfort.

Without another word, she hurried past him and found Theo hunched in a corner, scribbling on a notepad.

* * *

Filling in for one of the sick waiters, Theo was serving cocktails to patrons when he noticed something odd about the music. Yes, he'd seen her. Eliza Baker sitting with Dorothy. But he'd kept his head down and made a beeline for the furthest corner. To distract himself from her, he concentrated on the music. The pianist was changing tempos and keys in a highly unconventional way, even for non-Western music. At first, he thought it was random, some idiosyncrasy of the pianist's moods or fancy. But as he was delivering a Sidecar to a gentleman from Bulgaria, he noticed a pattern, a pattern as complicated and risky as the Rousseau response to the Italian game in chess: At first, it seems daft but it is actually very sneaky. Like the Rousseau opening, the rhythms and cadence of this song seemed unmoored. Yet, at some points, the tune sounded more like Morse code than a melody.

As the pianist played, he wrote down every key change and tempo change. Over and over, she played the same sequence of notes. Then the tempo changed and she played them over again and again. Odd. As she played, the pianist repeatedly glanced over at a well-dressed man sitting alone at the bar. Did those notes mean something to him? Something more than the music? As music, it was plain bizarre. But what if it was more than music? Did the sequence of letters corresponding to the notes mean something?

"What the hell are you doing here?" The strong, familiar voice startled him.

He looked up from his notepad and was face to face with the woman who occupied all his dreams, both night and day. The woman he'd tried to no avail to replace with various Parisian girls. But none of them could compare to her. Eliza. Eliza. ELIZA. That was the sequence of letters stamped on his heart. "Eliza," he stammered. "I didn't expect to see you—"

"You didn't expect to see me ever again." Her eyes hardened. "You left without finishing our game... without saying goodbye." She flushed and looked away.

"I'm sorry. I... I..." He didn't know what to say.

She gave her head a little jerk and then put on a forced smile. "You were afraid I'd beat you." She crossed her arms over her chest. "That's why you ran away. Either that..."

"I was afraid," he said. It was true. He had been afraid. Not that she'd beat him at chess. Players rarely did. And even if she had, he didn't care. No, the game wasn't what scared him. It was the way she played, the intensity of her focus, her concentration, her passion—and those chameleon eyes changing with the light from green to blue to gray. Being so close to her, close enough to feel the heat emanating from her body, made him shiver. That's why he ran away. He was falling. Falling for her. He'd had to run before he hit the ground and his heart shattered into a million pieces.

5

THE BANQUET

Later that evening, Eliza dined with Dorothy, Agatha, and Father Richard, all of whom were sullen and unusually quiet. They seemed to take turns glaring over at Ivan Grigor and his wife, Lena, who were seated at the table across from them, holding hands and cooing at each other and sharing their food like newlyweds.

Once again, the dining car was a symphony of opulence and precision that reminded Eliza of how far she'd come. Polished mahogany paneling reflected the warm glow of ornate sconces, while brass fittings gleamed like knife blades. Crisp, white linens draped the tables, each adorned with delicate, crystal stemware and silver cutlery that caught the gentle sway of the train without actually toppling over. The air carried the mingling aromas of roasted chicken and spiced wine, underscored by the faint, metallic tang of coal smoke from the engine far ahead. Passengers murmured in a dozen languages, their voices blending with the occasional trill of laughter and the wheels clattering against the tracks. It was a space at once intimate and theatrical, where every glance and whispered word seemed to hold the promise of intrigue—except, perhaps, for the glares coming from her own table, which held the promise of homicide.

The chef had prepared a special fixed banquet menu. First, they were served a glass of 1847 Oloroso that Theo described as "a dark and brooding sherry," which seemed appropriate given the mood of the table. Next came a cup of cold bouillon, "a very strong, good soup set to a clear jelly." The first gelatinous spoonful was enough to put Eliza off. The others, particularly Agatha, appeared to enjoy it—although there was much whispered speculation as to why Theo Sharp was serving aboard the Orient Express. The fish course was a lovely turbot in a light Hollandaise sauce, followed by *poulet en casserole*, which they enjoyed with a bottle of Corton. Across the aisle, as Ivan and Lena Grigor ate off one plate and fed each other spoonfuls, Eliza wondered if they weren't putting on a show for Dorothy's sake. Regardless, it rather turned her stomach to watch the lovebirds going at it, especially since whenever he finished with a course, Ivan Grigor ground out his cigarette butt in whatever was left on the plate. Disgusting.

The final course was a sweet omelet stuffed with jam prepared tableside by none other than Theo himself. Only once did the flame threaten the hem of his jacket. He may have grimaced while flipping the omelet, but he succeeded like a pro. Impressive. If he didn't make it as a writer, and was forced to give up hustling chess, he had a talent for flipping food.

"Mr. Sharp is a regular renaissance man," Agatha said. "Cooking, waiting table, and writing."

"Peculiar behavior if you ask me," Dorothy said. "Why can't he mooch off relatives or rich benefactors, or marry a duchess like respectable writers do?"

Although Eliza refused to countenance the idea of Theo

marrying a duchess, all through dinner, she couldn't take her eyes off him as he hustled busing tables, refilling champagne glasses, and flipping omelets. Despite her dower colleagues, by the end of the meal, she was in high spirits.

Father Richard must have felt the effects of spirits, too. And not the holy sort. He drained his wine glass for the sixth time, threw his napkin on the table, and marched over to confront Ivan Grigor. His face went red as he accused Mr. Grigor of tricking him and selling him a fake. Sputtering and sweating, Mr. Grigor adamantly denied it. After a few minutes of the two men spitting at each other like snakes, Lena Grigor intervened. "Ivan, please." She reached across the small table and put her hand on his sleeve. "Let's simply return the Father's money and he can return the brooch." She smiled. "We don't want to make a scene and ruin this lovely banquet."

Pouting, Ivan nodded in agreement. "Very well."

"Come to our cabin tonight after my performance," Lena said, her smile broadening, "And we'll set everything right." She glanced across at her husband. "Won't we, dear?"

He mopped his brow with a handkerchief. "Of course, darling."

After the last course, the diners gradually left the restaurant car and retired to the bar car. Eliza trailed along with her group and they took a table together near the piano, where Lena once again performed a haunting melody. She swayed to the music as if possessed. Her husband had taken their bottle of wine from the dining room and sat at the bar watching her. Unfortunately, Mr. Grigor looked like he'd had quite enough alcohol already. His face was blotchy and beads of sweat sparkled on his forehead. He leaned on the bar for support as he sipped his wine. And the unnerving man with the long cigarette holder and monocle sitting alone was there again, in his regular corner giving Eliza the creeps. Was he watching Lena or her? And why?

"Excuse me." Dorothy rose from the table and went to the bar. She sat next to Mr. Grigor.

"What's she up to?" Eliza asked, twisting to get a better look. "I thought she hated him."

"I don't blame her." Father Richard balled up his fist. "The man is a scoundrel."

"Yes," Agatha said thoughtfully. "Women often fall in love with scoundrels."

Like two conspirators, Dorothy and Ivan were engaged in an intense conversation. At one point, Ivan threw his head back in laughter. Obviously, Dorothy didn't think it was funny. She had a sour look on her face like she'd bit into a lemon. Ivan leaned close and whispered into her ear. Dorothy's look turned from sour to murderous. She flinched when Ivan wobbled into her and nearly knocked her off her stool. The man was soused.

Eliza wondered if she should intervene.

The color drained from Ivan's face and he doubled over, panting. Was he going to be sick? He bolted upright and grabbed Dorothy by the neck.

Eliza jumped up from the table and sprinted to the bar. If necessary, she was ready to give him a Flying Guillotine around the neck or a Cartwheel Kick to the torso. She may not have made the cut at Scotland Yard but her training sometimes came in handy. She pulled him off Dorothy and propped him up against the bar. The man didn't resist. Instead, he was as limp as a noodle. As soon as she let go of him, he collapsed at her feet. Obviously, the man couldn't hold his liquor. His body spasmed once and then went rigid. Alarms started going off in her head.

Lena quit playing and suddenly, the bar car was as quiet as

a grave. Everyone was staring at Ivan lying motionless on the floor. "What's wrong with him?" Lena's shriek pierced the air. "Ivan." She dashed over and knelt next to him. "Ivan, dearest." She brushed the hair away from his face. "Wake up."

"He's just had too much wine." Eliza knelt too. At least she hoped it was merely too much alcohol. She put her hand on his forehead. His skin was cold and clammy. She had a sinking feeling in her stomach. Her training kicked in and she felt his neck for a pulse. Her mouth fell open and she glanced over at Lena, who was patting her husband's face. "Mrs. Grigor..."

Lena ignored her and continued caressing her husband's face. "Ivan, darling. Wake up."

"Mrs. Grigor." She stared over at Lena, wondering how to tell her.

"Wake up, dear." Lena let out a frustrated laugh. "You're making a scene."

"Mrs. Grigor." Eliza reached out and touched the other woman's sleeve.

Except for a tremble in her lip, Lena went as still as a statue.

"Mrs. Grigor... Lena. I'm sorry." Eliza took her hand. "I'm afraid your husband is dead."

Lena blanched. She fell to her hands and knees over her husband's body and started wailing. The rest of the passengers gawked and gasped.

"I'll get a doctor," a bartender said as he stepped out from behind the bar.

"Too late for that, I'm afraid." Eliza grimaced. She lifted Ivan's wrist and tried again to find a pulse. She shook her head.

"I'll find the manager, Monsieur Fournier." The bartender zipped out of the carriage.

While trying to calm Mrs. Grigor, not to mention getting her out of the way, Eliza did her best to examine the body.

Foam had formed on Ivan's blue lips. The pupils in his eerily staring eyes were dilated. His jaw was clenched and all his muscles were rigid. These symptoms were not caused by drinking. The combination of foaming at the mouth, dilated pupils, and muscle rigidity could suggest a neurotoxin.

She glanced around until her gaze met Theo's. He was standing at the end of the bar holding an empty serving tray to his chest. She gave him a signal with her eyes. He sat the tray on the bar and weaved his way through the crowd until he reached her side. She stood up, took him by the sleeve, and whispered, "He may have been murdered."

"Murdered?" Theo did a double take. "Why do you think so?"

She pointed to the dead man's mouth. "Foam, dilation, rigidity are all possible signs of poisoning." She leaned closer and whispered in Theo's ear. "A neurotoxin, to be precise." His hair smelled of cedarwood and lime and brought back memories. Memories inappropriate to a murder scene. "What did Ivan eat or drink this evening?" She was betting on a quick-acting agent. Although it was possible the poison had been administered earlier in the day or even days ago.

"As far as I know, he ate the same as everyone else." Theo ran his hand through his hair. "The menu tonight was fixed, so he couldn't have eaten anything else. And the aperitifs and wines were paired with the food." He looked back toward the bar. "Unless he ordered a cocktail before dinner, he consumed exactly what everyone else did. In fact, he and Mrs. Grigor shared a plate."

Eliza turned back to Lena Grigor. "Are you feeling alright?"

"Of course not!" She put her hand to her mouth. "My husband's dead."

"Right." Eliza grimaced. "Sorry. I meant, did the meal have an adverse effect on you?"

"Why would it?" Lena gave her a puzzled look.

"Food poisoning or something disagreeable—" Theo's voice broke off. Either he didn't accept her theory of toxin or he was sparing Mrs. Grigor.

"*Mon Dieu.*" Monsieur Fournier blustered into the car. He gasped as he stared down at the body. "Is he...?"

"Dead," Eliza said.

"Stand back!" Monsieur Fournier motioned to the passengers to move. "*S'il vous plaît.*" He softened his tone. He turned to a porter and whispered. The porter trotted off. Presumably to find a doctor or railway security or ring the police. What country has legal jurisdiction on a train that passes through so many? The last stop, not long ago, was in Belgrade. They must still be in Serbia. What was the next scheduled stop? Sofia? They wouldn't be there for hours. Not until morning.

"Mrs. Grigor," Theo said. "Allow us to take you back to your cabin." He nodded to Eliza and she nodded back.

As they escorted Lena from the bar car back to her cabin, Eliza grilled her about the meal. Was anything out of the ordinary? Did Ivan have any health problems or a bad heart? Was she absolutely sure she ate everything he had at the meal?

Cheeks red and blotchy, the grieving widow assured her the dinner was wonderful, and no, Ivan was in perfect health, and yes, she'd eaten and drank everything her husband had.

By the time they reached Lena's cabin, the poor woman was sobbing. Eliza put her arm around her shoulders. "There, there." She looked over at Theo, whose lips twitched in sympathy.

"And you're sure you feel alright?" Eliza said softly. "Physically, I mean. No ill effects from the meal?"

"I do feel rather dizzy." The flush on Lena's cheeks deepened.

Theo offered her his handkerchief. Lena took it and dabbed at her face. "Perhaps I ought to lay down," she said weakly. "I am feeling poorly."

Eliza gave Theo a knowing look. "Stay with her while I go fetch a doctor."

Theo nodded.

Eliza returned to the bar car where Monsieur Fournier and another railway official stood guard while a man with a medical bag bent over the body. Around them, a crowd had gathered. Where was Dorothy? In the commotion, all eyes were on Ivan. But Dorothy had been next to him at the bar. They'd been arguing. Eliza's stomach soured. Could Dorothy have poisoned Ivan Grigor? She had a past with the man. An unhappy one. Had she taken this opportunity to exact revenge for past wrongs? Dorothy had committed murder in fiction. But would she have the gall to do it in real life?

"Everyone needs to leave the bar." Monsieur Fournier shooed everyone away. "Go to your cabins and stay there, *s'il vous plaît*." He waved both arms in the air. "We will bring breakfast to your cabins in the morning. In the meantime, please stay put in your own cabin." He stopped Eliza from coming any closer. "Mademoiselle, you must go."

"I'm looking for a doctor." She glanced down at the man tending to the corpse. "For Mrs. Grigor. I'm afraid she may have been sickened by the meal, too."

"You aren't suggesting it was our cuisine that caused Mr. Grigor's death, are you?" The manager scoffed. "Our chef is one of the finest on the Continent. We have the best reputation. It's preposterous that the meal in any way had anything to do with Mr. Grigor's demise."

The doctor stood up. "Heart attack, I expect."

"See!" The manager's expression was gleeful. "What did I tell you?"

"Doctor, I wonder if you might check on Mrs. Grigor." She didn't mention poisoning or the food again. "She has had quite a shock and she's not feeling at all well."

"Certainly." The doctor gathered up his medical bag. "Lead the way."

Eliza glanced down at the body and then quickly surveyed the room. She wished she could take a closer examination, check Ivan's pockets, and look for clues. But that would not be possible with the manager standing guard. She'd resigned herself that she'd got all the evidence she was going to get and led the doctor back to Lena's cabin.

Theo was waiting outside, pacing the hallway. His countenance brightened when he saw Eliza approach with the doctor. "She insisted I wait out here."

"Mrs. Grigor." The doctor gently rapped on the door. "It's Doctor Feldman."

"Come in." Lena's voice was barely audible over the noise of the train.

The doctor turned back to Eliza. "I'll take it from here."

"Thank you, doctor." She only hoped he got to her in time. "Please check for toxins."

"Toxins?" The doctor furrowed his brows. "Whatever for?"

"I suspect someone tampered with Mr. Grigor's meal." Eliza bit her lip.

"Good heavens!" The doctor blinked. "You can't be serious."

"Deadly serious." She met his gaze. "You'd best act quickly."

"And who are you to tell me what to do?" He stood blinking at her.

"I used to work for Scotland Yard." She let out an audible

breath. "I know something about poisons and I'm worried she may have consumed whatever killed her husband."

"Good Lord. Leave it to me." The doctor opened the cabin door and disappeared inside.

Eliza turned to Theo. "Can you get me into the kitchen?" She had an idea. If she couldn't examine the body or the crime scene, she could examine the food. Or what was left of it.

"Probably." He put his hands in his pockets. "Why?"

"Come on." She tugged on his sleeve. "Before they do the dishes." There might still be traces of whatever toxin the killer used. But how would she know which dishes were Ivan's? She'd figure that out in the kitchen. If the poison was in the food, how did the murderer isolate it to Ivan's plate?

As they made their way through the corridor, her mind was racing. Who had access to his food? The chef? The waiter? Other diners? His wife? How could the chef ensure the food went to Ivan and no one else? No. It had to be someone further along the food-delivery system. Either that or someone close to Ivan's table. Surely not the waiter, since that was Theo. Other diners, perhaps? Or his wife, Lena herself? She was close enough. But if she ate everything he did, then she would have poisoned herself. And if the toxin was quick acting and deadly, as Eliza suspected, Lena would be dead, or dying, too. Not to mention, the poor woman was genuinely distraught.

Whatever the case, it was worth a look in the kitchen, and certainly better than sitting in her second-class cabin twiddling her thumbs.

* * *

As Theo led her through the corridors on the way to the kitchen, he marveled at how Eliza acted without hesitating. She didn't mince words or beat about the bush. She was no shrinking wallflower. No, hers was a commanding presence. And he admired her for it.

Before he'd left London, he'd taken every chance he could to see her. Back then, he'd memorized every freckle on her face, the slight angle of that one eye tooth, the way her right brow was slightly higher than the left, and the frayed wool suit she favored. Those details were the same. And yet, there was something profoundly different about her. A neat chignon had replaced her long curls, and maybe she'd added a touch of rouge and lipstick. But that wasn't it either. It was something deeper. Invisible. The way she carried herself. More confident than defensive. Calmer. More self-assured. He held the kitchen door open for her. Nicer.

The kitchen was a battlefield of gleaming steel and scattered remnants, with smudged plates and empty pots stacked high like trophies of a hard-won victory. The air was thick with the fading aromas of roasted meats and spices, mingling with the metallic tang of soap as weary chefs scrubbed away the evidence of the evening's indulgence. As they stepped inside, they were met by a chorus of clanging of pots and pans. Due to the staff shortage, most of the dishes were stacked by the sinks still waiting to be washed. The chef was busy overseeing preparations for breakfast, which undoubtedly had just become more complicated since Monsieur Fournier ordered everyone to stay in their cabins where breakfast would be delivered.

Eliza zeroed in on the unwashed dishes from the fish course. "The poison would be best administered in a sauce or liquid."

Theo followed her to the sink.

"Passengers aren't allowed in the kitchen." The chef brandished his breadknife.

"She's with me," Theo said. "She's investigating—"

"Shhhh..." Eliza put her finger to her lips. "Don't tip our hand," she whispered.

Theo squinted at her. The chef would never allow her to stay if they didn't tell him why. "I work here and she—"

"As long as you're here." The chef stabbed his knife in the direction of the dirty dishes. "How about attacking that pile? Everyone in my kitchen pulls his, or her, weight."

Lucky the kitchen was short-staffed. Otherwise, the chef would have expelled Eliza *tout de suite*.

"Gladly, sir." Eliza examined the stack.

What exactly was she looking for? To him, all the plates looked the same. Slimy and grotesque.

"Here," Theo said, taking a plate off the top of the stack. "Let me do it." He turned on the tap. "I'm a pro." He lifted the first plate off the stack and ran it under the water.

Eliza examined each plate he removed.

"You could at least pretend to help," Theo said, picking up another dish. "Why don't you dry as I wash?"

She shook her head. "I'm busy." She leaned closer to what was left of the stack.

"Doing what?" Theo scrubbed at a bowl, put it aside, and then grabbed the next plate.

"Wait." Eliza bent closer and stared at the plate in Theo's hand. "Look." She glanced up at him, her bright eyes dancing. "A cigarette butt."

He shrugged. "So?"

"Ivan Grigor had the disgusting habit of using his dinner plate as an ashtray." She glanced around as if looking for something. "Get me a clean dish, preferably a small bowl." Her voice was full of excitement. "This must be Ivan's. Who else on the

Orient Express would grind a cigarette butt into their gourmet meal?"

He went to the cupboard and fetched a bowl.

"And a spoon."

He obliged.

She used the spoon to scoop congealed Hollandaise sauce from around the cigarette butt into the bowl. "The trouble is, if he was poisoned, the toxin could have been in any course from the soup to the pudding."

"What are you going to do with that?"

"Test it for toxins, of course." She smiled.

"Let me guess." He'd forgotten how lovely she was when she smiled. "You just happen to have a laboratory back in your cabin."

"No." Carrying the bowl of leftover sauce, she opened one cupboard and then another.

"What are you looking for?" Theo followed close on her heels.

"Black tea," she said, continuing to open cupboards.

"I'd be happy to make you a cup of tea." Theo went to the tea cupboard, removed a large tin, and waved it at her.

"Are you two going to wash those dishes or not?" the chef barked. "If not, get out of my kitchen now."

"Make it a pot, extra strong," Eliza said. "Bring it to my cabin as soon as possible." She pointed to another dish in the stack. "And bring a sample of that one, too."

Sure enough, a bit of omelet with a cigarette butt sticking out of it.

"And I'll need a control sample." She glanced around. "Bring a small dish of uncontaminated Hollandaise."

"Yes, ma'am."

"The dishes," the chef shouted.

"As soon as possible," she stage-whispered and then bolted to the exit and was gone.

"The dishes!" The chef ran the back of his sleeve over his forehead.

"I'm making a pot of tea for a passenger." Theo held up the tea tin.

"No tea until you've finished washing the dishes. All of them."

Theo stood holding the tea tin, blinking at him. "But—"

"But nothing." The chef picked up his knife and sawed a baguette in two. "My kitchen. My rules."

He blew out a loud breath, set the defiled bit of omelet aside, and set to washing the dishes. He hoped the last two years also had made Eliza more patient. As he scrubbed, tiny soap bubbles took flight and floated up from the sink. Some must have reached his face, which would account for the stinging in his eyes—but not for the clenching in his chest.

6

RAILWAY FORENSICS

Eliza had waited long enough. She left the sample in her washbasin, gave her roommate strict instructions not to touch it, and then went to find Theo. On her way through the dining car, she overheard the waitstaff discussing Ivan's collapse. The head waiter said he'd heard it was definitely a massive heart attack. When one of his underlings suggested food poisoning, he was sent back to the kitchen to tidy up.

How often did seemingly healthy men in their late forties keel over from heart attacks? And if it was food poisoning, why wasn't anyone else affected? Everyone had eaten the same dinner. And Lena had even eaten the exact same meal from the same plate. They'd even shared the wine: the bottle Ivan carried with him to the bar.

Monsieur Fournier and the doctor may think Ivan died of natural causes, but Eliza suspected foul play. The question was, who would want to kill Ivan Grigor and why? Had he found out about Peachy's exposé and threatened him and Peachy silenced him for good? Or, had Dorothy got her revenge after all these years for treating her cruelly? And then there was Lena. The spouse was always a suspect.

First things first. She must prove Ivan's food was poisoned. Not by spoiled fish or chicken, but by the intentional addition of a neurotoxin. She made her way through the dining car, which was an abandoned battlefield of indulgence, its elegant linens now speckled with coffee stains and crumbs. Crystal glasses sat half-filled with flat champagne, and the air hung heavy with the mingled scents of overripe fruit, cigarette smoke, and faintly sour perfume. Moonlight streamed mercilessly through the windows, illuminating tired faces and bloodshot eyes behind the clink of glasses and adrenaline-fueled murmurs of catastrophes and accidental deaths. Obviously, like her, these passengers were ignoring Monsieur Fournier's pleas to go back to their cabins.

In between the dining car and the kitchen, she found Eric Blair smoking a cigarette. "What do you think of the dead bloke?" he asked as she approached.

"Think of him?" She really didn't have time for another lecture on socialism and the evils of class hierarchy. "I hardly knew him." She continued on her way.

"I think his friend bumped him off."

She whirled around.

Eric blew out a cloud of smoke. "People talk after they've had a few whiskeys."

"What friend?" She stood face to face with him. Well, not quite. He was a good head taller.

"Speaking of..." He grinned. "If you want me to talk, you'll have to buy me a few whiskeys." He dropped his cigarette and ground it out. "How about it? A nightcap. Just you and me?" He put his hand on her shoulder.

She flinched.

"I have a bottle back in my cabin." He tilted his head. "What do you say?"

"Why don't you just tell me what you heard." Eliza took a step back.

"I'll tell you." He moved closer. "If you have a drink with me. Just one teeny weeny drink."

If some friend of Ivan's had told Eric something, she wanted to know. Her Scotland Yard instincts told her she needed to know. Her womanly instincts told her to stay away from this cad. "Alright." Her head jerked involuntarily. "Just one drink and you'll tell me what you heard."

"Deal." He held out his hand.

Reluctantly, she took it. His hand was dry and cool and he didn't bother shaking hands. He just held onto hers.

She pulled her hand free. "Let's get this over with, shall we?"

She followed him back through the bar car to his cabin, hoping she wouldn't regret this. Her senses on high alert, she was ready to give him a swift kick to the head if necessary. He'd better have some useful information or she just might kick him anyway.

Eric opened the door to his cabin and gestured for her to enter. As she stepped across the threshold, a lingering scent of cedarwood and lime filled her nostrils. She couldn't help but think of Theo. Why hadn't he come to her room with the tea? He'd probably been waylaid by Monsieur Fournier or that grumpy chef. What if he came looking for her? She'd better get this drink over with as soon as possible, so she could check back at her cabin, and then find Theo. The sooner she got out of Eric's, the better she'd feel.

Eric put his hand on the small of her back and maneuvered

her into the room. "Sit." He pointed to the bench. "Please." His tone softened.

Cautiously, she sat down. She ran through all the ju-jitsu moves she could do from a seated position. Knee cut, Yoko Sumi Gaeshi Sweep, Sit-up Escape. Eric was tall and wiry, but he didn't look too strong. She could take him if she had to.

He poured out two big glasses of whiskey. No ice. No soda. No water. Straight whiskey. "I'm here; now tell me about this friend of Ivan's." She held the glass in both hands.

"You promised to have a drink with me first." He nodded toward her glass.

She took a sip.

He did the same, eyeing her from over the lip of the glass.

She took another. It burned in her throat. She could feel it grazing her esophagus and dropping like hot lava into her stomach.

"Tell me about yourself." He leaned back against the seat cushion. "No, let me guess." He narrowed his eyes. "You're from London." He cocked his head. "Thames Estuary with remnants of the East End." He smiled. "I have an ear for dialects. All good writers do."

"Of course." He wasn't wrong. She'd grown up in Devil's Acre not far from the docks in the morning shadow of Westminster Abbey, where, as a girl, she'd learned to pick pockets and hustle chess to survive and fed her little sister after her mother died. She nodded. "How about Ivan's friend? Where was he from?"

"Uh-uh. Not until you finish your whiskey." His eyes lit up. "What the heck. This could be fun." He squinted up at the ceiling for a few seconds. "I'd say Ivan's friend is from the West Country." He pursed his lips. "I'd say Dorset. Maybe Somerset." He took a drink. "Now, Ivan Grigor, his accent is—was—interesting. That ever-so-slight Russian inflection filtered through just-a-bit-too-proper Oxford education." He looked at her. "Not unlike your employer, who uses her education as a shield to hide her East Midlands origins." He raised his eyebrows. "How am I doing so far?"

"Impressive." Cajoling him was her best bet. She took another sip. "So, Ivan's friend is English. That narrows it down some." Although not much. "Half the passengers on the train are English." Obviously, he wanted her to play along. "What other hints can you give me?"

"Hmmm..." He stretched his arm across the top of the bench so it rested behind her shoulders. "He's also a writer going to the International Writers' Convention in Istanbul." He grinned. "Like half the passengers on this train."

"He." She smirked. "A man. That narrows it down even more. An Englishman and a writer." She thought for a minute. Who had she met on this train who fit that bill? Eric Blair. Sitting next to her. She furrowed her brows. He wasn't that tricky, was he? To refer to himself in the third person? With writers, you never knew. Then there was Father Richard. He was English, a priest, and an archeologist. "Dorothy's friend Peachy!"

"Who the heck is Peachy?" He got a funny look on his face.

Drat. What was Peachy's real name? She thought for a minute. "Mr. Fitzroy!"

"Very good." He gave an exaggerated applause. "You deserve a reward." He leaned in and kissed her on the cheek.

"But you don't." She pushed him away. "Not until you tell me what Mr. Fitzroy said about Ivan."

"Alright. Alright." He exhaled loudly. "After a few too many drinks, Hugo Fitzroy told me he was writing an exposé on Grigor, one that could land the Russian in jail."

She already knew he was writing an exposé. She gritted her teeth. Would he hurry up and spill the beans already? She wanted to get away from him as soon as possible. "Go on," she said encouragingly.

"Aren't you going to give me a little incentive?" He raised his eyebrows. "Something to keep me going?"

She tightened her lips. She'd like to give him a sharp knife-hand to the jaw. Instead, she smiled sweetly and reached out and caressed his face. "Please, Eric. What else did he say?"

"Well." Eric blushed. "Fitzroy was worried that Grigor found out what he was writing." He leaned close and whispered in her ear. "And apparently, Ivan Grigor has some rather nasty associates. Men you don't want to mess with, if you know what I mean." He brushed his lips against her hair.

The smell of whiskey on his breath mixed with stale onions turned her stomach. She put her hand in the middle of his chest and gently pushed him away. She needed to hear the rest before she gave him a shove. "Tell me about these associates of Mr. Grigor's."

"Russian thugs, apparently." He waved his hand dismissively. "What does it matter?" He shrugged. "All bad men are the same." He grazed her neck with his hand. "Or do you believe Tolstoy? All good men are alike and only the bad ones are interesting?"

She didn't know much about Tolstoy, but she knew from her experience with the London Metropolitan Police, a boring, good man was preferable to an interesting, bad one. And right now, she wished Eric Blair wasn't trying so hard to be interesting.

"I kept my end of the bargain," Eric said, moving his hand to her knee. "Now you keep yours."

As she recalled, the deal was one drink in exchange for

information. But given his wandering hand, she was pretty sure he wasn't asking her to finish her drink. She grabbed his hand and was about to fling it off her knee when the door opened.

"What the hell?" It was Theo. "No wonder I couldn't find you." He shook his head, turned on his heels, and left.

"Theo, wait!" she called after him. Theo's entrance distracted Eric just long enough for Eliza to wrestle free of his grasp. For good measure, she delivered a quick palm strike to his nose.

He grunted and covered his face with his hands. "Why you little—"

She was long gone before he finished his insult. She sprinted up the corridor. "Theo, wait." Surely, he couldn't think she'd consented to Eric's bad behavior. Didn't Theo know her better than that? "Theo, stop!"

He disappeared into the next car. She ran after him. She caught up to him in the bar car. "Dammit, Theo, stop already." She grabbed onto his sleeve. "Come on. Calm down."

He stood glaring at her.

"It wasn't what it looked like," she said. What did it look like? A handsy, arrogant arse thinking he was entitled to grab. That's what.

"I left the tea in your cabin as instructed." His tone was formal. "I should get back to work." He yanked his arm away.

"Don't be a nitwit." Geez.

"I'm sorry you think I'm a nitwit." He reached into his pocket. "Now I really should be going."

"Wait." She moved around him to block his path. "Don't you want to know what I'm going to do with the tea?"

"Drink it, I suppose." He looked down at her with sad eyes.

She had a sudden urge to kiss him. "No." She bit her lip. Why was her heart racing? Why did she want more than anything to explain? To make it up to him. To tell him it wasn't Eric she wanted to kiss. It was him. Oh right. He'd left London without even saying goodbye. After telling her she was cruel, no less. She stepped out of his way. "The tea is for an experiment." Not to mention, the last time she got close to someone, he'd died. At the docks. On that terrible night that ended her career at the Met. And she could never let that happen again.

"What kind of experiment?" His tone was softer now.

She resisted the urge to reach out and brush a stray lock of hair from his forehead. "A forensic test." Plus, her urges were hardly appropriate for such an old friend. Theo was more like an older brother. Right? She'd met Theo when she was thirteen, after Captain Hall caught her picking his pockets and sent her to boarding school instead of arresting her. Theo had been the captain's son's friend and roommate at Eton, but he'd barely noticed her. They lost touch until she ran into him at Gambit Chess Club two years ago: a month before he ran off to Paris.

"Sounds fascinating." He smirked.

She couldn't tell if he was serious or making fun of her. "I thought you'd be interested." She glanced up at him and couldn't help but return his smile, even if his was fake.

***

What was Eliza doing with Eric and why was he drooling over her? Theo's heart was racing. What had he just witnessed? Did Eliza fancy Eric? She'd just met him, for God's sake. He balled up his fist. Eric's "sweetest little piece." Disgusting. Of course, she'd go for Eric. He was tall and charming and a brilliant writer. Everything Theo wasn't. But he was also a cad. Back in Paris, he'd brought home a new girl every week. And the way he talked about them. Theo tightened his lips. The way he'd talked about Eliza. It turned Theo's stomach.

The train lurched and Theo bumped into Eliza. "Sorry." He regained his balance.

The narrow corridors were a challenge to traverse, especially carrying a tray of drinks or food. Yesterday, the swaying had made him drop a load of dirty dishes that clanked up and down the first-class corridor. He'd be lucky not to be sacked before Istanbul. Monsieur Fournier had made it pretty clear that if they hadn't been short-staffed, Theo would have been fired the first day.

"So, explain to me why you need the tea?" Theo touched the wall to steady himself.

"You'll see." She opened the door to her cabin.

As he followed her inside, the scent of jasmine caressed his nostrils. The memories that came with it hit him like a freight train. Eliza sleeping in his arms, before he ran away to Paris. "Your tea." He pointed to the teapot, which was sitting on the small table. "It's probably cold by now. And very strong, too."

"Good." She fetched a bowl from her washbasin. He recognized it as the one she'd taken from the kitchen. The one containing Hollandaise sauce from Ivan Grigor's plate. "Hand me the tea."

He grabbed the pot. Standing behind her, he peered over her shoulder at her experiment. The warmth of her penetrated his soul and ignited his brain. Fear of what else proximity could inflame, he took a step back and watched from a safer distance. "I brought the omelet you asked for." He glanced back at the little dish on the table with the cigarette butt in the center, standing at attention. "And the fresh sauce."

"Obviously, this test is rudimentary," Eliza said, scooping a smidge of sauce into a water glass. Using the handle of her toothbrush, she mixed the tiny bit of sauce with water. "Our test subject." She poured a splash of tea into the glass. "Strong tea contains high levels of tannic acid." She rotated the handle around in the glass. "And when tannic acid comes in contact with the proteins in various neurotoxins, it creates a reaction."

"Don't tell me." Theo was impressed. "Your police training."

"My forensics training, to be exact." She swirled the mixture. "Now..." she said, her voice full of concentration. "We watch for a distinct precipitate reaction."

"What kind of reaction?" Theo stared at the glass. White clouds formed in the brownish water. "Blimey!"

"Exactly." Eliza held up the glass. "The toxin proteins interacting with the tannins." She smiled over at him. "Now, let's test the control sample." She pointed at the table. "Hand me the uncontaminated sauce."

He gave her the small bowl of Hollandaise sauce he'd scraped out of the cooking pot. She repeated the same steps as before. Once she'd mixed everything together in a glass, she held it up and swirled. Nothing but light-brown water. No clouds. "See." She beamed. "No reaction. No toxins." She poured the control water into the basin. "Proof, however rudimentary, that Ivan Grigor was poisoned."

He wanted to wrap her in a tight embrace. She was so devilishly clever. He'd never met anyone like her. "By whom?" He held his hands behind his back to resist the temptation. "Who would want to kill Ivan Grigor?"

"Peachy Fitzroy, for one." She rinsed out the glasses. "We'd better save the contaminated sauce for the police."

"The fellow writing the exposé?" Theo cocked his head. "Dorothy's friend. I know his early work on true crimes."

"Does everyone know about his so-called exposé?" She snorted. "I thought it was top secret."

"He was nattering on about it last night in the bar." Theo squinted. "Wait a minute." His mouth fell open. "Oh my God." He looked over at Eliza. "You'll never believe this. His first book included a chapter on unsolved poisoning cases."

"Well then." Eliza stabbed the air with a finger. "I'd say we may have identified our killer." When she smiled, a sweet dimple formed at the side of her mouth.

His hands still clasped firmly behind his back, he dug his fingernails into his palm.

7

PEACHY'S MANUSCRIPT

Later that night, defying Monsieur Fournier's orders to stay in her cabin, Eliza tagged along with Theo as he tidied the public spaces on the train. They ended up back at the bar car, which was now a hushed and hazy retreat. Its earlier lively energy had faded into the eerie creak of the train and the ghostly clink of abandoned glasses. The dim glow of low lamps reflected off empty bottles and half-melted ice, while a faint haze of smoke lingered, the last gasps of a dying night.

The manager had made it clear the staff were to continue doing their jobs. But she was surprised they hadn't closed off the bar car. There could be important evidence there. Then again, the medic had concluded Mr. Grigor died of natural causes, a heart attack or a stroke, although he couldn't be sure which without an autopsy. Since they were only another day out from Constantinople, Mr. Grigor's body was being stored in the refrigerated car where blocks of ice kept perishables cold. The local police would meet the train when it arrived at its final destination.

No one else suspected foul play. She wondered what

Agatha and Dorothy, whose imaginations usually ran wild, thought of the situation. Especially Dorothy, who'd been the last one to talk to Ivan and had a pretty good motive to want him dead. She may have a motive, but did she have the means? Surely, she wouldn't travel with a spare vial of poison just in case she ran into an old lover who'd spurned her.

"So far, we know this much." She watched Theo emptying ashtrays in the bar car. "Ivan Grigor was poisoned. The toxin was in the fish course." Every time he took a step, she did too. "Whoever put it there had to have the opportunity."

"And a motive," Theo added.

"And a motive," she repeated. "According to your charming roommate, Dorothy's old friend Peachy had a motive." She pointed to a butt he'd dropped. "If Ivan found out about Peachy's exposé, Ivan may have threatened him. And Peachy might have decided to get to him first."

"And Peachy knows poisons." Theo wiped off a bar table. "He's written about several real-life poisonings."

"Alright, he had the means and a motive." She leaned against the bar. "Did he have the opportunity?"

"The dining room was so busy and everyone was moving around and chatting up everyone else," Theo said, wiping another table. "Peachy might have been able to mix a drop of poison into Ivan's meal without being detected."

"But in that case, why wasn't Lena affected?" Eliza said. "She ate from the same plate."

"True." Theo scowled. "And she seems fine. The doctor says her symptoms were from shock." Theo shook out his dishrag. "Not poison."

"But he can't know for sure, can he?" Eliza cocked her head. "You really think Peachy could have contaminated Ivan's plate without anyone noticing? He'd have to be a magician to pull off a stunt like that," she said, blowing at her fringe. "Anyway, unless he planned to kill Ivan even before he boarded the train, why would he bring poison along to the writers' convention?" She pursed her lips. "We need to get into his compartment and conduct a search."

Theo stopped swabbing the table. "You can't go snooping around other people's cabins." His eyes went wide. "You're not with the Met anymore. And even if you were, we're..." He glanced out the window. "In Bulgaria."

"Maybe I can't." She raised her eyebrows. "But you can."

"Me!" He laughed. "I'm not the former copper. Just a lowly custodian."

"Precisely." She repressed a smile. "And I strongly suspect Peachy's cabin needs a good cleaning" She tilted her head. "What do you say?"

"I say, you're going to get me fired." He shook out his rag.

"So what?" She shrugged. "You aren't seriously considering a career cleaning up other people's mess."

"Why not?" He bristled. "Someone's got to do it."

"Great." She took his arm. "Why doesn't someone start with Peachy's cabin?"

He didn't resist as she led him across the bar car toward the passengers' quarters. "Look for any incriminating evidence." She tugged at his sleeve.

"Like what? A vial of poison?" He scoffed.

"Exactly." Halfway down the corridor, she realized she had no idea where Peachy's cabin was. "I should be following you, not the other way around."

"Finally." Theo smiled. "You recognize my value."

"Don't get carried away." She pressed herself up against the wall to let him pass. "Although your current occupation does have its advantages for sleuthing."

His body brushed up against hers as he squeezed past. She shuddered. Why did he have to smell so darn good?

When they reached Peachy's cabin, she stood back while Theo knocked. "Housekeeping." He knocked again. No answer. Using a key from the chain attached to his belt, he opened the compartment. She took a step forward but he stopped her. "It's best if you wait here."

"I want to conduct the search." She furrowed her brows. "I am the professional."

"Former professional." He held his arm across the threshold. "You'll have to trust me on this."

She'd learned on the streets of London not to trust anyone. A lesson she'd taken to heart. Queenie and her sister Jane were the only creatures in the world she trusted. And lately even Jane was testing her. "But—"

Theo held up his hand. "I know trust isn't part of your game plan." He softened his tone. "Believe me, I've done enough research on murder to search a suspect's room."

"Fictional murder." She stood arms akimbo.

"True-crime murder," he corrected.

"Books about murderers aren't the same as tracking real murderers." She winced, remembering the terrible night at the docks that ended her short-lived career with the Met. If she hadn't lost her footing and slipped on the dock, her partner wouldn't have turned back to help. His fatal flaw was helping her. "All the deductive reasoning in the world won't replace good empirical forensics."

"What I just witnessed with the tea and sauce was as much speculation and interpretation as experimentation." He smirked. "Now let me get on with it before Peachy comes back and finds me snooping around his room." He stepped inside and closed the door in her face, but not before she'd got a good look inside.

The first-class cabin was a cluttered den of creativity with scattered papers and crumpled drafts dotting the plush carpet, along with an overturned ashtray and the faint smell of burnt tobacco. A leather-bound notebook lay open on the small, mahogany table, its pages covered in a sprawl of ink-smudges. A fountain pen rested precariously on the edge of a teacup, and the gentle sway of the train made the hanging lamp cast ominous shadows across the velvet upholstery. Of course, there were no vials of poison sitting out in the open. Once the door clicked shut, she'd have to trust Theo to find it.

Trust. Not her favorite word. She paced the corridor. Back and forth. Up and down.

Waiting for Theo was like waiting for a slow opponent to make a move in a game of chess. The difference being she never played chess without a timer. And when she had her druthers, she opted for speed chess. Theo would probably say it was because she trusted her instincts more than her foresight. It wasn't her instincts that craved a challenge. It was her intellect. And not the abstract, philosophical kind Theo preferred. But practical intelligence and applied analytical skills. With an emphasis on skill. Even the most talented chess players needed to practice. Why? Because like detective work, chess was a skill. Not an art.

"Miss Baker." The voice startled her. "Eliza. What are you doing?"

Drat. It was Peachy. His disheveled clothes rivaled his messy hair for most frowsy. His complexion wasn't brilliant either. "Spying on me?" His lower lip trembled.

"No." Her heart raced. She had to warn Theo. "Of course not." She raised her voice. "Why—"

"My manuscript is missing." He looked like he might cry. "Someone took it." His face reddened. "Was it you?" He slammed his hand into his palm. "I'm in a world of trouble."

"Of course I didn't." She backed up against his cabin door. "Calm down." She clasped her hands together as if in prayer. "Please. Calm down and tell me what happened." Had Ivan stolen Peachy's manuscript before he died? Is that why Peachy poisoned him? And now he was blaming her to cover his tracks?

"Ahhhhhhhh." He put both hands to his face and exhaled a nearly silent scream. "I've been working on that book for the last ten years. How could this happen?"

"When was the last time you saw your manuscript?" She considered trying to tap the door to the cabin with her foot to warn Theo. Could she do it nonchalantly? Just an accidental kick of the foot? "Where did you keep it? Did you have it locked up?" She intentionally backed up until she bumped the door. Hopefully, Theo wouldn't open it. "You know what?" She put her hand on Peachy's sleeve. "How about a brandy? To settle your nerves."

He stared at her with wide eyes.

"Then you can tell me exactly what happened. All the details." She took a step away from the door.

"The train manager told us to stay in our cabins." He turned his face to the wall and leaned his head against it.

"Apparently, neither of us is following orders." She tilted her head, trying to make eye contact.

"What am I going to do now?" He pounded the wall with his fist.

"Don't despair." She had to get him away from his cabin before Theo came waltzing out. "Your manuscript must be someplace on this train."

"Unless the thief threw it out the window or burned it." His voice broke. "My life's work. My baby." He sniffled.

"Steady on." She watched him writhing in his own wretchedness. "Come on." She gave him a sympathetic smile. "We'll get your manuscript back."

The door to his cabin slid open and Theo emerged holding up a small vial. "Look what—" He stopped himself and quickly put his hand behind his back. "Mr. Fitzroy. Your cabin is ready, sir." He raked his hand through his hair. "I've turned down your bed for the night and tidied up."

"Mr. Fitzroy's manuscript is missing." Eliza caught Theo's gaze. "Seems someone took it." She raised her eyebrows. "He's beside himself." She gestured toward the distraught man.

"Why would someone steal your manuscript?" Theo sounded incredulous.

"Mr. Fitzroy is writing an exposé, not some made-up whodunnit." She couldn't resist.

"Not just any exposé!" Peachy balled up his fists. "For the last decade, I've been following Ivan Grigor, rooting out his secrets." He stared into the distance. "His secrets are worth stealing, even killing, to protect."

Was Peachy confessing to killing Ivan? Eliza bit her lip. "Tell us more about these deadly secrets. Could they be a motive for murder?"

"The manager told me Ivan died of a heart attack." Peachy glanced back and forth from Eliza to Theo. "You don't think he was..." His voice trailed off. "Good God." His eyes went wide again. "The Obsidian Cartel. If they found out I was about to expose one of their central operatives..." His shoulders slumped.

"Obsidian Cartel?" She squinted at him. "What's that?"

"Only the largest organized crime outfit in Eurasia." He put a hand to each side of his face. "And the most dangerous." He pressed on his cheeks. "I think I'll take that brandy after all."

Blimey. If Ivan was involved with organized crime, there could be any number of people who wanted him dead. Out of the corner of her eye, Eliza noticed Theo wiggling a small, brown bottle behind his back. She took a step closer to him to block Peachy's line of sight. Theo must have found the vial in Peachy's cabin. Could the bottle contain the poison used to kill Ivan? Were Peachy's emotional outbursts genuinely the result of losing his manuscript? Or was he a murderer? An emotionally unstable killer? For all she knew, Peachy had disposed of the manuscript himself to implicate someone else in the murder of Ivan. Or, to hide the evidence.

"I have a bottle of whiskey in my cabin," Theo said. "If you don't mind slumming it in second class."

"After today, I'd gladly drink out of a hog's trough." Peachy's thin lips turned up in a weak smile. "Not that your room is a hog's trough."

"At the end of the game, sir"—Theo tapped his cap—"the king and the pawn return to the same box."

She thought of Ivan Grigor. Was death indeed the great leveler? she wondered.

Theo held out his arm. "After you, sir."

* * *

After a whiskey in his cabin, Theo had to get back to work. Peachy was shaking so badly, he could hardly speak. And Eliza. Well, she acted like it was an interrogation instead of a consolatory drink. The night's events put Theo on edge. And the whiskey didn't help.

Around midnight, Theo finished cleaning all the public

spaces on the train. He put away his broom, dustpan, and unused rags in the cupboard in the kitchen car. Exhausted, he couldn't wait to get back to his cabin and fall into the arms of Morpheus. Although given his dreams lately, it wouldn't be Morpheus's but Eliza's long arms tempting him onward. And whether awake or asleep, against his better judgment, he would follow her to the ends of the earth and back. His jacket unbuttoned and his cap under his arm, he trudged through the dark bar car. Where was she now? Asleep in her bunk? Or performing another makeshift and miraculous experiment. He smiled to himself. Eliza Baker, alchemist of his heart.

A shuffling sound made him stop. Slowly, he turned in its direction. In the dark, the glow of a cigarette pulsated like the bloodshot eye of Cyclopes. A soft sigh bled into whispers from the piano, keys caressed so gently, you could hear them lightly clicking before being coaxed to give up their secrets.

"Mrs. Grigor?" He stared in the direction of the piano. "Is that you?"

"Tell me." Her voice was small but steady. "What's your opinion on sacrifice?"

"Sacrifice?" He thought of chess. The best player was willing to sacrifice his queen to save his king. To lose something now in order to win everything later. "Necessary sacrifice, yes. Sacrifice for its own sake, no. I'm not one to be a martyr." Following the glowing ember, he made his way to the piano. "How about you?"

"I believe in committing to a cause and sticking with it." With one finger, she played a version of the same haunting melody from last night. "Don't you?"

"I do." Although he wasn't sure what his cause was yet. Except breaking out of his father's stifling grip, and writing. He was committed to writing. Then again, he needed to write to survive. So maybe it didn't count. Can you commit to something you need to live? "What's that tune you're playing?"

"Something I wrote." She touched the sheet of music in front of her. "Do you like it?"

"It's unique." He stepped behind the piano to get a look at her composition. In the dark, it was impossible to read.

"I'm still working on it." She picked up a pencil and made a mark on one of the pages.

"I've never heard anything like it." He wished he could study the score. The key changes and alternating times were so unpredictable.

"Are you a musician? Mister..." She looked up at him with sad eyes piercing the darkness like two dying stars.

"Sharp. Theodore Sharp." He started to extend his hand but thought better of it. He was just the hired help, after all. "Can I bring you something? A cup of tea or a nightcap?" He fiddled with the band on his cap.

"No, thank you." She stood. "I should go to bed." She put out her cigarette in an ashtray on the piano and then gathered up her sheet music.

"I'm sorry about your husband." He winced. What do you say to someone who has just lost their beloved? Words had to be inadequate to the depths of her grief. And yet, so many great writers tried to give words to sorrow—and longing and love. The stuff that made life worth living was impossible to translate into words. All the more reason to keep trying.

"I am too." She sighed. "Good night, Mr. Sharp."

"Good night, Mrs. Grigor." He watched her float out of the carriage, a ghostly apparition in a long, flowing gown.

Sitting at the piano, he tried to recreate her melody. Hardly a composer or anything close, he had studied piano when he was young. Of course, his father didn't approve. Music was for girls. Hunting was for boys. Theo played the one piece he remembered. Chopin's Prelude in E Minor. He always did prefer the minor keys. Tears welled in his eyes. He'd forgotten how unbearably sad it was. His hands fell to his lap.

What would he do if he lost Eliza? His beloved. He closed his eyes. A chortle escaped his lips. He'd never had her. How could he lose her? She wasn't his to lose. He swallowed hard. Too bad he hadn't become a composer. Perhaps it was easier to translate love and sorrow into music than into language.

As he scooted off the piano bench, his foot kicked a piece of paper and sent it scuttling. He bent and picked it up. A sheet from Lena Grigor's composition. He glanced at the exit. Should he take it to her?

No. Not yet.

He flew to the light switch and flipped it on. Studying the notes on the page, he meandered back to the piano and attempted to play Lena's haunting tune. One note at a time.

8

THE FRENCH INSPECTOR

The train slowed to a stop. Eliza stopped too. Standing in the corridor outside Theo's cabin, she looked out the window. In the darkness, she saw a dimly lit station. A sign read NIŠ. Was this a scheduled stop? She watched as a man boarded the train. He was wearing the belted navy uniform and tall disc hat of a French train inspector. Eliza put her hand to the glass and pressed her face closer. No one else got on or off the train. Perhaps they'd made a special stop to let the inspector on board. Was he here to investigate Ivan's death? Did someone finally believe Mr. Grigor didn't die of natural causes? It was about time.

She pushed away from the window and continued her search for Theo. He wasn't in his cabin. Where the heck was he? Even though the train had stopped, there was a great squealing commotion outside. Another midnight train, perhaps? By the time she reached the bar car, the train was moving again.

"There you are." Eliza marched over to the piano. "I've been looking all over." She furrowed her brows. "I didn't know you could play."

His wistful smile matched the melancholy song he was playing. "I guess there's a lot you don't know about me." He continued playing, swaying more dramatically as he went. "Did you do the test on the vial I found in Peachy's cabin?"

"Of course." She sat the bottle on the piano. "But it was empty. So I could only test for residuals."

"And?" he said, continuing to play the sad song.

"Nothing." She shrugged. "No reaction. If it did contain poison, it's been cleaned." Her lips twitched. "Then again, my tea test wasn't exactly state-of-the-art." She picked up the bottle and shook it. "We need to get this to a proper laboratory for testing."

The sound of whistling signaled someone was approaching.

"*Excusez-moi.*" The French train inspector appeared in the carriage. "I thought all passengers were confined to quarters." His tone was crustier than a day-old baguette. "Is this the carriage where the Englishman fell dead?" His beady eyes and beaked nose gave him the look of a carrion bird.

"It is." Eliza met the inspector near the bar. "He was right about here." She pointed at the spot where Ivan had collapsed.

"You are a witness?" The inspector's accent was as thick as his bushy eyebrows. "Both of you?"

"Yes," Theo said, still tinkering on the piano. "One minute, he was alive and the next, he was dead."

"Isn't that always the way." The inspector surveyed the bar. "Was the Englishman exhibiting signs of illness? What was he drinking?"

"Come to think of it," Eliza said, "he was sweating a lot after dinner." She remembered he kept mopping his brow with his handkerchief. Another sign he was poisoned.

"I was working." Theo tinkled away. "I served the dinner and wine for the table: Mr. Grigor and his wife, Lena."

The inspector's eyes narrowed. "His wife."

"Yes."

"Are you investigating the mur… er… death?" Eliza asked.

"Preliminary investigation." He waved his hand. "A formality. Nothing more." He leveled his gaze. "If you know something, speak up." His dark eyes shot accusing darts at Eliza.

"I believe Mr. Grigor was poisoned." She looked straight into his eyes. She wasn't about to let his piercing stare unnerve her.

"Poisoned, you say?" His mustache twitched. "And what makes you think that?"

She recounted his symptoms and her experiment with the Hollandaise sauce.

"Impressive work." He gave her a pleased smile. "And do you also know who poisoned the Englishman?" His tone was smug.

She debated on whether to tell him their suspicions about Peachy.

"I'm waiting." He cocked his head.

She was beginning to dislike him.

"Our prime suspect is Hugo Fitzroy," Theo said, glancing up over a sheet of music. The song he was playing had gone from sad to mad as his fingers hit the keys. "He is writing a book to expose the criminal activities of Mr. Grigor."

Eliza shot Theo a look. The inspector's interest in the dead man felt simultaneously disingenuous and prurient.

"What about criminal activities?" The inspector's sharp tone cut through the night.

"About his involvement with a criminal organization called the Obsidian Cartel." Theo leaned in and squinted at the sheet music. The melody became erratic and dissonant.

"What's that you're playing?" The inspector crossed over to the piano.

"One of Lena Grigor's compositions." Theo kept playing.

"Where did you get that?" The inspector's face reddened. He looked like he was going to grab Theo by the collar and toss him off the train.

"Mr. Sharp!" A bellowing voice made them all turn to the doorway where Monsieur Fournier came racing toward them. "The staff are not allowed to play the piano." He strode over and ripped the music off the piano. "Furthermore"—he glanced at Eliza—"the staff shall not fraternize with the guests." He hissed his disapproval. "*Excusez-moi.*" He turned to the inspector. It was as if only now he'd seen him. "I didn't know we had an inspector aboard."

"I just came aboard in Niš," the inspector said. "I'd best get on with it." He tipped his hat and made for the exit.

"I'm so sorry." Theo's apology seemed genuine. "It won't happen again."

"It better not." Monsieur Fournier tugged at the bottom of his jacket. "Now hadn't you, both of you, better get back to your cabins?"

"Of course." Theo stood up. "Sir, I wonder." He cleared his throat. "Might I have the music?"

The manager stood blinking at him.

"The sheet music, sir." Theo pointed at the piece of paper in the manager's hand.

Monsieur Fournier looked down at the page and then back up to Theo. "No, you may not."

"It belongs to Mrs. Grigor." Theo held out his hand. "I'd like to return it to her, if I may."

"No, you may not." The manager huffed.

In two long strides, Eliza was at his side. She plucked the paper from the manager's hand. "I'll do it." She flashed a smile. "Lena is a friend of mine."

"Very well." The manager scowled. "Now, please. Both of you, go to bed." He exhaled a long breath. "If only I could do the same."

Once they were in the corridor, and out of earshot of the manager, Eliza handed the sheet music to Theo. "What's this all about?"

"I don't know." Theo pulled a toothpick from his pocket and clamped down on it. "There's something odd about this music." He tightened his lips around the pick. "Look at this," he said, holding out the sheet. It had black notes with letters written above them. "Notice anything strange?"

She read over his shoulder. "B-A-G-B-A-G-D-A-D-D-A-D-C-A-C-A-F-E-F-E." She glanced up at him. "What does it mean?"

He shook his head. "Damned if I know." He tapped his cap onto his head. "But it's the refrain she played over and over again."

"Why don't we go ask her?" She shrugged.

"It's after midnight." Theo scowled. "And she's grieving."

"All the more reason to go." She tapped her foot.

"What about your investigation?" Theo gently folded the sheet music and tucked it into his jacket pocket.

"Since you told that French train inspector everything we know"—she smirked—"our job is done. We sit back and watch him arrest Hugo 'Peachy' Fitzroy."

Theo gave her a suspicious look. "You aren't convinced he did it, are you?" he said, chewing on the toothpick.

She shrugged. What did it matter since a train inspector hardly had the authority to arrest anyone, even a murderer. They would have to wait until their arrival in Constantinople when no doubt the local police and British authorities would have something to say about Ivan Grigor's death. "We need to get into Lena's cabin."

"I clean up other people's messes, remember." He led the way to the first-class carriage, throwing his toothpick in a trash bin on the way.

Lena's cabin was in the same car as Dorothy and Agatha's. She waited while he knocked.

"Housekeeping," he said somewhat sheepishly.

Eliza stepped in front of him and knocked louder. "Mrs. Grigor?" She knocked again.

"Maybe she's sleeping." Theo removed his cap and tucked it under his arm.

"After what happened to her husband, I doubt anyone is sleeping." Eliza knocked again. "Lena, are you in there?"

"If she is, she's not answering." Theo sighed. "Let's forget it and go to bed. I'm completely knackered." He did look tired.

"Do you have the passkey?" She pointed to the keys jangling from his belt.

His brows furrowed in concern. "You want me to open the door to a passenger's room at..." He glanced at his watch. "Nearly one in the morning."

"That's exactly what I want." She put her hand on his sleeve. "Look, if she's out then it's the perfect time to search the dead man's cabin."

"I don't know." His lips twitched.

"Please." She looked up at him and softened her gaze. "I'll owe you."

He thought for a second. "Alright." He let out a big breath. "The last time someone died right in front of us, you made it into a competition, remember?"

"Yes, and I won." She smiled. "My prize was playing you in chess. But we didn't finish our game because you ran off to Paris, remember?"

"I didn't run off to Paris." He inserted a key into the lock. "I had an opportunity and I took it."

The door creaked open.

She squinted against the darkness. Now was not the time to argue about him running away. The chess game was another story. "As long as you give me the opportunity to beat you at chess," she said, moving closer.

"I doubt you'll ever get the opportunity to beat me." With a broad grin, he stepped over the threshold.

"It will be fun to try." She put her hand on the small of his back and gave a little shove. "Let's do what we came for before Lena gets back from her nocturnal activities."

"We came to return her sheet music." Theo lit a match. She couldn't help but notice that his face looked lovely in the soft light. "Not to snoop around her room."

"Luckily, since she's not here, we can do both." Eliza shut the door and flipped on the light.

They both stood, speechless, gawking around the room.

Clothes and papers were strewn everywhere. The cabin was chaos. The room was ransacked. Eliza glanced around. An open suitcase lying on the floor haphazardly spilled men's clothes.

"Speaking of cleaning up other people's messes." Theo scratched his head. "What the heck happened here?"

"I'd say Lena rifled through her husband's luggage looking for something." She picked up a stray sock and dropped it into the open case.

"Unless Ivan's killer came looking for something." The color drained from his face. "And found Lena and..." He didn't finish the sentence. "I saw her an hour ago. I hope she's alright."

"The sooner we search the place, the sooner we can go find her." Eliza looked up from rummaging through the pockets of Ivan's evening coat. "Of course, you're welcome to go look for her on your own."

"Good idea." He clapped his cap back onto his head. "I'll leave you to do the breaking and entering."

"Hey, there was no breaking involved." She snorted. "You opened the door."

"Yeah." He squeezed his eyes shut. "And now I regret it."

"Why?" She moved to the pockets of Ivan's trousers. "No one will ever know."

"We'll know."

She shrugged.

He shook his head. "I'll know." He opened the door, stepped into the hall, and without even a tiny glance back, shut it again, hard.

Geez. What's wrong with him? A teensy, green-eyed monster of a thought rapped on the entrance to her brain. Did he fancy Lena Grigor? Is that why he went running off again? *Come on, Eliza, old girl. Get a grip.* Anyway, what did she care?

She slammed the nightstand drawer shut with a wee bit too much force. Muttering to herself, she continued going through pockets and looking in cubbyholes. She yanked on the cupboard door. Ivan's jackets and trousers hung askew on their hangers. Someone had already done exactly what she was doing now. She stood there staring down at Ivan's shoes. Nice shoes. Expensive leather, probably Italian. She peeked her head inside the small cupboard. Where were Lena's shoes? Where were Lena's clothes? She went back to the suitcase, picked it up off the floor, and sat it on the bench seat. If this was Ivan's suitcase, where was Lena's? Did the husband and wife share one case? Surely, they didn't share clothes! And surely, Lena hadn't worn the same white gown for the entire trip. No, she'd also worn a bright linen dress to breakfast one morning.

Eliza ran her hand across the silky lining of the case. Underneath the cloth, the suitcase bottom was uneven. She knelt next to the bed and examined the edges of the liner. In one corner, a tiny tab stuck out from the bottom of the suitcase. "What have we here?" She pulled on the tab.

Aha. With a click, the liner snapped out to reveal a hidden compartment under a false bottom. Carefully, she lifted the false bottom. A black, velvet bag with yellow drawstrings lay in the secret section. She lifted it free and weighed it in her palm. Slowly, she loosened the strings, opened the bag, and dumped the contents into the empty suitcase.

Like a slice of holiday fruitcake, assorted gemstones sparkled up at her. Red rubies, green emeralds, blue sapphires, set in gold or silver bracelets and necklaces. And one ruby-red schnauzer exactly like the one Father Richard—supposedly on behalf of his benefactor, Katharine Woolley—had given to Agatha. She picked up the brooch and examined it. Odd. It was *an exact replica* of Agatha's. She took a closer look. No. This one wasn't shedding and it wasn't chipped. Its gold plating was intact. She scratched its surface. It seemed real. No flaking. No shedding.

So why did Ivan have a second doggie pin? And why was it hidden in the lining of his suitcase?

* * *

The train's corridors late at night were silent and dim except for the soft hum of the wheels on the tracks. Flickering sconces cast long, wavering shadows on the polished wood walls, and the faint scent of smoke and spilled wine lingered in the still air as if the evening's secrets had seeped into the very fabric of the train.

Theo passed through one carriage after the other, looking for Lena. If she wasn't in her cabin at one in the morning, where would she be? He checked the bar car. Empty. The new restaurant car. Deserted. The new kitchen car. No. Anyway, why would she be in there?

As he surveyed the new kitchen car, he wondered how the chef kept track of everything, changing dining cars and kitchens every time they crossed a border.

He went from one end of the train to the other. No sign of Lena.

As he walked the length of each carriage, he thought about Eliza. What was it about her that he found irresistible? He must be attracted to danger. Why else did he have such a crushing obsession with the foot-fighting, heart-stomping, law-breaking Miss Baker? She never listened to him. She was abrupt and rude. She had a blatant disregard for authority. Wait. Is that a strike against her? He'd caught her holding hands with his roommate. All in all, she was infuriating. And the most fascinating woman he'd ever met.

Argh. He grunted. Obviously, Paris wasn't far enough to get away from her crushing presence in his psyche. There was nowhere on earth far enough away from Eliza Baker to make him forget about her.

Sure. He could live without her. He would have to. But he

couldn't forget her. Not ever. The king may move only one square at a time. But no matter how long it took and where he ended up, he would follow his queen.

As for Lena, he was beginning to wonder if she was still on the train. If she was, she was well hidden. Perhaps in the arms of a secret lover. Hugo "Peachy" Fitzroy perhaps?

What better motive for murder than forbidden passion? He sighed. Or unrequited love.

9

THE LETTER

Early the next morning, Eliza went to Dorothy and Agatha's cabin. When she arrived, the two women were deep in conversation. Holding her fist in mid-air, she hesitated. Instead of knocking, she listened at the door.

"I had no idea," Agatha said. "Poor dear. Why didn't you tell me?"

"I couldn't." Dorothy's voice was hoarse. "My parents would have disowned me. I would have been fired from my job. And I'd never have been allowed in polite society again." She sounded like she'd been crying. "Not to mention, it would have ruined my literary career."

What in the world had Dorothy done? Was this the shame she'd spoken of earlier? Eliza turned the handle and, without knocking first, opened the door. "I hope I'm not interrupting."

Both women went as silent as a cemetery. Dorothy's eyes were puffy and bloodshot. She looked at Eliza and then quickly gathered up a letter from the table, stuffed it in an envelope, and tucked it under her pillow. That blasted letter again. This time, Eliza was going to get to the bottom of it.

"What's that?" Eliza tilted her head.

"What's what?" Dorothy played dumb.

"The letter you hid under your pillow." She pointed.

Dorothy flushed.

"Are you in some kind of trouble?" Eliza looked from Dorothy to Agatha. "Does this have anything to do with Ivan Grigor?"

Silence.

"Tell me," Eliza said softly. "Maybe I can help." She wiggled her fingers. "Please. I can keep a secret. And I can kick the stuffing out of anyone stupid enough to threaten you." She gave her boss a sympathetic smile.

Wordlessly, Dorothy reached under her pillow, retrieved the envelope, and held it out. Still in her dressing gown, she sat on the bottom bunk staring down at her bare feet.

"You mustn't tell anyone," Agatha said. "Otherwise, Dorothy will be ruined."

What could be so bad it would ruin her? "Alright." Eliza took the envelope. She turned it over. Scrawled on the front in thick, black letters was:

Dorothy Sayers, Confidential

Slowly, as if handling a poisonous snake, she slid the letter out of the envelope. She glanced over at Dorothy, who gave her a sad nod. As she read the letter, she let out a little gasp. What in the world! "Blackmail?"

Dorothy nodded again.

She reread the letter:

Dorothy dearest,

I hate to put you on the spot, but you see, I'm in a bit of financial trouble. As you know, I have a weakness for cards. I'm wondering how much my silence about John Anthony is worth to you. Shall we say 1000 pounds sterling?

To be crystal clear, if you don't pay me 1000 pounds when we reach Istanbul, I will go to the newspapers and tell them about John Anthony. Do we have a deal?

"Who is this from?" Eliza held out the letter. "And who is John Anthony?"

Dorothy's lip quivered. "Do you swear to secrecy?"

Eliza nodded.

"You won't tell another living soul?" Dorothy's tone was desperate.

Eliza shook her head.

"Promise?"

"I swear." She put her hand over her heart.

Dorothy let out a long exhale. "It's from Ivan Grigor."

"He was blackmailing you?" Eliza's mouth fell open. Oh dear. Blackmail was an excellent motive for murder. *No.* She pushed the thought from her mind.

"Terrible thing." Agatha fanned herself with the morning paper. "And now he's dead."

"And John Anthony?" Eliza was almost afraid to ask. Did it have something to do with whatever "shameful" thing Dorothy claimed she did after Ivan left her? "Was he your... lover?"

Dorothy hung her head. "John Anthony is my son."

A knock on the door startled them. They looked at each other. Dorothy quickly hid the letter again. Agatha folded the newspaper and laid it on the table. As Eliza smoothed her skirt, a headline about a robbery in Paris caught her eye.

Another knock. No time to read the paper. She answered the door.

"Breakfast, mademoiselle." The waiter stood outside next to a cart laden with trays. The staff had prepared trays of fruit, croissants, marmalade, coffee, and juice. Unlike earlier in their journey, everyone would eat the same thing no matter want they wanted or who they were. It appeared the first-class and second-class passengers were getting the exact same trays down to the silver bud vase containing a single, white rose. Maybe death was the great equalizer after all.

"Please." Eliza gestured for him to put their tray on the table.

Like a dormouse, he scurried in and left the tray. Even the waiter could feel the tension in the room: tension so thick, you could butter your croissant with it.

After a morose breakfast with the two melancholy writers, it took Eliza nearly an hour to persuade Dorothy to get out of bed and get dressed. Hiding under the covers wasn't going to solve anything. While Dorothy dressed, Eliza tracked down the cabin steward and ordered another pot of strong coffee and more pastries. Nothing like a big dose of caffeine and sugar to jump-start the brain.

Eliza poured another cup of coffee for each of them. Given Dorothy's precarious state, she was reluctant to question her. But a man had been killed. And Dorothy had a strong motive to kill him. "Ivan Grigor is dead. He can no longer hurt you." Brushing crumbs off her skirt, and taking another fortifying drink of coffee, she got down to business. "Who else knows about your son?"

"Only his father." Dorothy bit her lip. "And Peachy."

"Could Peachy be involved..." Eliza lowered her voice. "In this blackmail threat?"

Dorothy shrugged.

"How bad could it be if people found out about John

Anthony?" Agatha sipped her coffee. "You're a married woman and a successful writer."

Dorothy scoffed. "You really haven't a clue." She grabbed another croissant from the plate. "First off, my family would disown me. Second, my readers would abandon me. Third, well... I can't face it." She slumped back into the bench. "I'm so ashamed."

"Ashamed of your son?" Eliza asked.

"Of course not!" Dorothy straightened her spine. "John Anthony is a perfect little angel."

"Where is he?" Eliza resisted asking, *Where do you keep him hidden?*

"My cousin Ivy runs a foster home. He's with her and has been since he was born." A hint of a smile curved at the corner of her lips. "He's a cute little fellow. A perfect little gentleman... not like his father."

"You know, about the father, I was wondering—" Agatha said nonchalantly, as if she were about to ask after the weather.

"Don't." Dorothy held up her hand. "His father is a man I met at my boarding house. I was so distraught over Ivan... I threw myself at Bill." Her lips twitched. "Neither of them wanted to marry me when they found out I was pregnant."

"So, Ivan knew about Bill and the baby?" Eliza nibbled on a croissant.

"I didn't know who else to turn to." She closed her eyes. "And I still loved Ivan." She sighed. "Now he's dead and I don't know who else he has told."

"Hopefully, no one." Agatha patted her friend's hand. "Don't worry, dear. It will be alright."

"It's not fair," Eliza said. "Men can go around fathering babies all they want and not suffer the consequences."

"Tell me about it." Dorothy puffed.

"Talk about double standards." Eliza stomped the heel of her boot. "It makes me furious."

"Think how the world would change if men could have babies," Agatha mused and then giggled.

"If only..." Dorothy let out a chortle. "Then maybe they'd learn their lesson."

A cloud of dark thoughts stormed into Eliza's mind. Dorothy was talking with Ivan at the bar when he collapsed. Did Dorothy decide to teach Ivan a lesson? Eliza narrowed her eyes and assessed her employer. Was Dorothy capable of murder?

The Detection Club members maintained anyone was capable of murder under the right circumstances. If the winds of guilty motives weren't already blowing in Peachy's direction, they could easily be gusting in Dorothy's.

* * *

With all passengers having breakfast in their cabins, it was a busy morning. Theo hustled back and forth to the kitchen refilling his cart and delivering trays. Eliza had kept him up half the night. When she wasn't giving him commands and cajoling him into breaking and entering, she was haunting his dreams. Yawning, he pushed a newly filled cart up the corridor. He was so tired, he was practically tripping over his own feet. And he still hadn't located Lena. His back was beginning to hurt. Maybe he should make up with his father and slip into the life of a gentleman. It wouldn't be all bad. He could play chess whenever he wanted. In fact, he could spend all this time at the chessboard. He thought of one of his father's favorite sayings, an adage attributed to the American chess prodigy, Paul Morphy: "The ability to play chess is the sign of a gentleman. The ability to play chess well is the sign of a wasted life." He chuckled. A wasted life didn't sound so bad right about now.

He knocked on the next door and delivered yet another tray of fruit, croissants, coffee, and juice. As he rolled the cart up to Peachy's door, he stopped and wondered if he might find the newly widowed Lena Grigor in the loving arms of Hugo Fitzroy. He knocked on the door. "Breakfast service."

No answer.

He knocked again. "This is the steward with your breakfast."

Nothing.

He put his ear to the door and listened. If Peachy was in there, he was very quiet. Were the lovers holding their hands over their mouths, waiting for him to leave? He knocked once more. "Mr. Fitzroy?"

A grunting sound came from the other side of the door. He put his ear to the door again.

"Mr. Fitzroy. Is everything alright?"

The next sound emanating from inside was downright eerie. Like the air being let out of a balloon.

"Mr. Fitzroy? Peachy? Is that you?"

Silence.

"Alright." Theo clicked his tongue. "I'm coming in." He used his passkey to open the door. As he stepped inside, a strange smell hit his nostrils. A metallic, rusty smell. He flipped on the lights. "Mr. Fitzroy?"

Theo stumbled backwards. His hand flew to his mouth and he gasped into his palm.

Mr. Hugo "Peachy" Fitzroy was sprawled on the floor in a pool of his own blood. The stain on the carpet bloomed around his head like a deadly halo. His eyes were wide and his lips moved, his mouth sputtering blood.

"Oh God!" Theo dropped to his knees. "What happened?"

Peachy gripped Theo's arm. "My manuscript." He gasped. "Key." He got a startled look in his eyes and then his hand dropped to the floor. All life ebbed from his body and his dead eyes stared up at the ceiling.

Tears in his eyes, Theo looked away. He got up and staggered back out into the hallway. "Help!" He ran back toward the kitchen. "Help!" He tripped on the threshold and stumbled into the kitchen. "Peachy." He panted. "Mr. Fitzroy." He put his hands on his knees and bent over.

"What's wrong with you?" the chef asked. "Hungover, I suppose."

His hands still on his knees, breathless, Theo somehow managed to get the words out. "Hugo Fitzroy has been shot." Then everything went black as he collapsed in a heap.

10

THE KEY

Later that morning, Eliza watched from the corridor as Monsieur Fournier cordoned off Peachy's cabin. Like Ivan's, it had been ransacked. Obviously, the murderer was looking for something. Something they didn't find in Ivan's luggage. Did they find what they were looking for in Peachy's? An unpleasant thought niggled at her. The blackmail letter. It gave Dorothy a strong motive to kill Ivan. And if Peachy knew about the baby, or was in on the blackmail, she had a motive to kill him, too. Eliza winced. How well did she really know Dorothy? The mystery writer dreamed up lots of complicated murder plots. Had she performed one, or two, in real life? Crime writers' imaginations were full of homicide. Were their hearts also full of murder?

If only she could get into Peachy's room to investigate. No doubt the killer left clues. They always did. Locard's Principle of Exchange was the first lesson she'd learned in forensics. The perpetrator of a crime will introduce material to the scene and leave with material from the scene: hairs, fibers, paint, pollen.

"Everyone back to their cabins," the manager said, waving

away the few passengers who had gathered in the hallway. "And stay there until we arrive in Constantinople. We will make sure you get *quelque chose* for meals." His voice was loud but shaky. "In the meantime, if you need anything, ring for your steward. But lock your doors, *s'il vous plaît.*"

Eliza hung back, hoping to get a better look inside the dead man's room.

"Mademoiselle." The manager stood face to face with Eliza. "*S'il vous plaît*. Return to your cabin immediately." He sighed. "The police have asked me to secure the train until we reach Constantinople." He softened his tone. "You may be in danger. Please go back to your cabin and lock yourself in."

She took one last look over his shoulder. Peachy's dead body sprawled on the floor. The bloodstained carpet. His clothing and papers strewn around the room. What was the killer hoping to find? Another blackmail letter, perhaps?

"Go!" the manager barked.

She started and then turned on her heels and headed back to the second-class carriage. But she didn't stop at her own cabin. She continued on to Theo's. If the Orient Express was delivering lunches and had stewards on call to attend to passengers, then Theo wouldn't be confined to quarters. He'd be free to move about the train and enter passengers' rooms. Clearly, when it came to investigating murder, cleaning up other people's messes had its advantages.

She knocked on Theo's door.

Eric answered. "Why Eliza, how nice to see you again." His big ears, beady eyes, and pointy nose reminded her of a pine martin. His toothy smile reminded her of a wolf.

"Is Theo here?" She tried to get a look inside but Eric blocked her view.

"The old boy has had a bit of a shock, I'm afraid." Eric

chuckled. “Right upstanding Englishmen dropping like flies.” His voice dripped with sarcasm. “Theo’s a sensitive soul.”

“Yes. One of his best qualities.” She stood on tiptoes to try to get a look over his shoulder. “Theo, are you home?”

A muffled “No” came from inside.

Eric laughed. “See, I told you.” He leveled his gaze. “We could always go to your cabin. I’ll bring a bottle along and we can make our own party.”

“No, thanks.”

“Suit yourself.” He shrugged. “In that case, I’ll get back to writing.” He glanced back at a typewriter on the table. “I’m writing a short story to read in Istanbul.” He raised his eyebrows. “Want to hear what I’ve written so far? It’s called *A Day in the Life of a Tramp*.” He cocked his head. “Did you know spikes won’t allow tramps to spend two consecutive nights?”

“Spikes?”

“The workhouse shelters.” He huffed. “Tramps walk over twenty kilometers a day just getting from one spike to another.”

She thought of her childhood spent wandering the streets of London. Almost daily, she made the rounds from St. Katharine Dock to Westminster, picking pockets, begging for handouts, and hustling chess in St. James’s Park.

“You see, I’m making political writing into an art.” He leaned against the door frame, one long arm across the doorway.

“Yes, very impressive.” She was losing her patience. She ducked under his arm. “Theo, get up.” She stood at the foot of the bunk looking up at his nest of chestnut hair. “I need you... old boy.”

“Lucky boy.” Eric ambled back to his typewriter. “I wish a pretty girl like you needed me.” He snorted. “I doubt Theodore knows how to get out of the gate. Are you sure you wouldn't like to change horses?"

"I'll take my chances with the worn-out brumby." She reached up and nudged Theo. "Saddle up, my friend. I have a job for you."

"Oh, alright." He sat up in bed and then threw his legs over the side of the bunk. Wearing only thin long johns, he climbed down the ladder.

Eliza looked away. But it was too late. His body-hugging union suit had already set her cheeks aflame. She stepped out of the room before the fire spread southward.

Wearing his uniform—thank the Lord—Theo joined her in the corridor.

"Have fun, kids," Eric called after them. "Papa will be here slaving away at the typewriter when you get back."

When they were out of earshot, Eliza pulled Theo aside. "We need to get into Peachy's cabin."

"Are you mad?" Theo blanched.

"Someone on this train is a killer." She leveled her gaze. "And everyone is in danger until we find out who."

"I'm not going back into that room." His hand trembled as he brushed a lock of hair from his forehead.

"But—"

He held up his hand. "Absolutely not."

"Then I'll do it without you." She turned on her heels and left him sputtering.

"Wait." He dashed after her. He gripped her elbow. "Alright. I'll stand guard."

She stopped.

He stepped in front of her. "But I'm not going in." He swayed slightly. "All that blood." He leaned against the wall of the corridor. "I don't feel very well."

"You don't look so good either." It was true. He'd gone white as a sheet of music.

"Thanks." He put the back of his hand to his forehead.

"Come on." She took his hand. "Afterwards, we'll round up some pudding for you." His skin was clammy against her palm.

"The last thing I want is pudding." He leaned against her. "I'm not a child."

"Whiskey, then." She led him through the corridor to the first-class carriage.

When they reached Peachy's cabin, she stopped and pointed to the door lock. "Are you going to open it?" She pulled a bobby pin from her chignon. "Or should I?"

"Not that I don't enjoy watching you pick locks." Theo stretched a key from the chain at his waist and unlocked the door. "I'll stand guard." He tightened his lips. "But if someone comes, I'll claim I was just passing by and have no idea how you got in."

"Fair enough," she said, sliding the door open.

It was obvious Peachy's death was not an accident nor from natural causes. Unless you count a shot to the head and another to the chest as natural, which must be why the manager decided to leave the body in situ rather than move it to the cold storage car with Ivan's.

Taking shallow sips of air, she searched the dead man's pockets. In the jacket pockets, she found a gold lighter and matching cigarette case along with the key to his cabin. She grimaced as she reached into his trouser pocket. In the back was a comb and a receipt from the bar. From the front, she fished out another key and some pocket lint. She examined the second key. A large, gold key on a ring with another tiny key. Engraved on the hilt in baroque script were the letters *PPH*. It wasn't a key to the Orient Express. PPH. What did PPH stand for? She slipped the key ring into her own bespoke skirt pocket.

A rap on the door signaled trouble. She quickly stood up, adjusted her skirt, and pressed herself up against the wall behind the door. Her heart raced as she listened to Theo talking to someone in the corridor.

"Just on my way to the kitchen, sir," Theo said. "To start preparing for lunch service."

"The kitchen is that way." It was Monsieur Fournier. "Mr. Fitzroy's cabin is off-limits until the police board in Constantinople."

"Yes, sir."

"Scotland Yard has someone meeting the train."

"Yes, sir."

"Help me attach this tape across the door." Noises right outside the door indicated the manager was close. "It's from the reefer car. Insulating tape."

Eliza held her breath. Were they locking her in?

"Yes, sir." Theo cleared his throat. "I'm sure you're very busy. If you like, I can fasten the tape on my own before heading to the kitchen."

"I am rather busy." The manager made a sound somewhere between a moan and a gasp, like a hiccup of distress. "Two men died on my train." More pitiful noises. "What business do they have dying on my train? And murder!" His cries turned to whimpers. "What's going to become of me?"

"Don't worry, Monsieur Fournier." Theo's voice was reassuring. "When we arrive in Constantinople the police will take care of everything."

"Thank you, Mr. Sharp." He sniffled. "You're not such a bad egg after all."

"Neither are you." Theo coughed. "I mean, yes, sir. Thank you, sir."

Eliza put her ear to the door. Footsteps. Receding. Hopefully, the manager leaving. A sharp knock on the door.

"Hurry up!" Theo hissed from the other side of the door.

She slid the door open, looked up and down the hallway, and then stepped out. "What do you think these are for?" She dangled the keys.

"Thank you, Theo, for risking your job and distracting the manager." His tone was mocking. "While I illegally rifle through a dead man's things." He tilted his head. "You're welcome, Eliza. Apparently, there's nothing I won't do for you." He waved the roll of insulating tape.

"Thank you, Theo." She rolled her eyes skyward. "I couldn't do it without you."

"That's what I'm afraid of." He shook his head. "You're going to get us both kicked off the train or worse, arrested."

"Or worse." She tightened her fist around the keys.

"What do you mean, worse?" He picked at the tape roll.

"I mean a killer is on the loose and—"

"I shouldn't have asked." He held up a hand. "Help me tape up this door." He stretched a length of tape across the threshold. "You're lucky the manager didn't tape it shut with you inside." He puffed out a breath. "You could have enjoyed Peachy's company for the rest of the journey."

"No, thank you." She pressed on the edges of the tape. "And thank you." With a smile, she jiggled the keys.

"Keys." Theo's face brightened. "Maybe that's what he meant."

"Who?"

"Peachy." He crisscrossed the tape up and down the length of the door. "Just before he died." He shuddered. "He said, 'my manuscript.' And, 'key.'" He continued taping. "Maybe he meant those keys."

"Maybe." She examined the keys and then tucked them into her pocket.

He stretched out the last length of tape across the door. When he bent down, his cap fell off. "How about that whiskey?" he said, retrieving his hat and tapping it back on. "Meet me back at my cabin in an hour. I'll be done delivering lunch trays by then."

"I'd rather avoid Eric, if it's all the same to you." She turned up her lip.

"The bar car then. See you in an hour." He gave her a brisk salute and then trotted off.

She stood staring at the insulation tape. Another day until they reached Constantinople. She hoped she and Theo and the rest of the passengers survived that long.

* * *

An hour later, behind the bar, where Theo and Eliza sat huddled together on the floor, the world felt cocooned in quiet. Rows of crystal decanters stood like sentinels, their contents gleaming in hues of gold and ruby. The faint murmur of the train's wheels was as steady a companion as a metronome. The lingering scent of spilled gin filled the tiny space with hints of pine needles.

Theo had grabbed a bottle of Scotch whiskey and two glasses on the way down. He poured two fingers in a glass and handed it to Eliza. "Seems odd Ivan was poisoned but Peachy was shot." Forget about two fingers of whiskey. Still shaken from what he'd seen, he went for an entire fist. "Killers usually stick to their preferred weapons." He took a couple of gulps.

"In books, maybe." Eliza sipped her whiskey. "Killing is messier in real life."

"You think our killer boarded the Orient Express with an entire suitcase full of weapons." He really wanted a smoke. But for her sake, instead, he plucked a toothpick from his pocket and clamped it between his teeth. "Like the society ladies who bring a different gown for every night?"

"Possibly." When she tilted her head to stare at the ceiling, a lock of blonde hair escaped her chignon.

He stared at the wisp of hair. It looked like a strand of flaxen silk. A golden filament as inspiring as the goddess Calliope gazing down from Parnassus. He bit his lip. Gawd. He was hopeless. He reached out and gently brushed the gossamer muse behind her adorable little ear.

She caught his wrist. Her touch was cool and arresting. He stifled a gasp and stiffened. His hand frozen, waiting for her next move. He didn't dare look into her eyes. He glanced in the direction of her lips. Mistake. His heart was racing. He wanted her more now than he had when he'd run away from London to escape the oppressive longing that ruined his concentration, when a freckle on her neck could send him into a frenzy of poetic imaginings. The way she blew at her fringe when frustrated, or tightened her lips when concentrating, could inspire volumes. He was jealous of her fork when she ate, her glass when she drank, and the buttons on her coat as she fingered them. And now, those fingers touched his wrist. How tiny her little finger was. So pale and delicate. If only he could keep her tiny finger with him always. Just her finger. Or that lock of hair. Some tiny piece of her. Was he mad? Was she driving him mad?

He closed his eyes. No. He'd never be satisfied with only part of her. He wanted everything. Her mind, her curiosity, her frustrations, her concentration, her body... He shuddered. It was all or nothing.

"Why did you leave London?" Her question broke the spell. "I thought we made a good team. And we were in the middle of a game of chess. And you up and left. Why?"

He shrugged. What could he say? He couldn't tell her he left because he was falling in love with her, that seeing her was torture, because he knew she didn't feel the same way about him.

She still had hold of his wrist. "Was I so terrible and such a mean person—"

"No." He looked her in the eyes. Big mistake. "I don't think you're terrible." Her steely eyes pierced his soul. "I... I... I think you're wonderful." His cheeks burned.

"Then why did you leave?" She leveled her gaze and looked right through him. She might as well have stuck his finger in a light socket. "Was it our game? Were you afraid I'd win? Or..."

"Or..." he repeated. He took her hand in both of his and pulled it to him.

She pressed her palm to his chest. He sensed more than felt her energy course through his torso. "Your heart," she said softly and then gazed up into his eyes.

"Eliza," he whispered. Her name so familiar to him and yet as solemn as a prayer.

* * *

Wheeewhaawwheewaa. A sharp, whistling sound made her pull her hand away. She held her breath. Could the killer be returning to the scene of the crime? She glanced over at Theo and saw the terror she felt reflected on his face. She listened. *Wait.* That whistle. She recognized it. The French inspector.

"Eliza," Theo whispered. "Should we get—"

She held a finger to his lips. "Shhh..."

As footfalls grew closer, the whistling got louder. Clutching her knees, she sat as still as a statue, forcing herself to breathe. In and out. Forcing her own heart to slow down. The proximity of Theo didn't help. The heat from his body. The smell of cedarwood and lime... and something else. Something uniquely him.

Forget about him. Concentrate. Lack of focus could get you killed. She'd learned that lesson the hard way at the docks. The night she stumbled and it cost her partner his life. She couldn't let that happen again. There was a killer on the loose. She couldn't allow herself to get distracted. She pulled her knees tighter to her chest and perked up her ears.

A rustling sound replaced the footfalls and whistling. What was he doing? She was sorely tempted to peek her head up above the bar. Was he investigating the murders? Had he found some new piece of evidence? Did he believe Ivan had been poisoned with a neurotoxin? Did he know Peachy's manuscript went missing right before he died? She touched her pocket. Did he know about the mysterious key engraved with PPH? And what about the blackmail letter? The one Dorothy received before Ivan was killed. She'd acted surprised when Ivan boarded the train in Paris. Could she have known all along that Peachy and Ivan would be on the train? After all, they were all going to the same writers' conference. And as a result, she'd come prepared to kill.

Eliza wasn't about to spill the tea on Dorothy. Not until she got more answers. And there was the fact that Dorothy was her boss and she needed this job. As her sister Jane loved to remind her, hustling chess wasn't exactly a steady income.

Until he wound up shot, she'd suspected Peachy was the

killer. Probably because she didn't want to believe Dorothy could have done it. And she knew nothing of this Obsidian Cartel. Still, Peachy could have poisoned Ivan. It made sense if Ivan found out about Peachy's exposé and was threatening him. But if Peachy killed Ivan, then who killed Peachy?

The whistling started up again. It was right there. Right above them. On the other side of the bar. She grimaced. Should she jump up and show herself? She bit her lip. And make herself a suspect? No. Best to stay hidden.

The whistling was on the move. Footfalls approached the edge of the bar. She kept her gaze focused on the end of the bar. The tip of a shoe. And then a hand. The inspector came into view. He reached up for a bottle of whiskey and then a glass. He hadn't seen them. He chuckled and then sat the glass on the bar and uncorked the bottle. As he poured, he glanced in their direction.

Her heart leaped into her throat. What would he think of them huddled behind the bar like criminals? She threw her arms around Theo's neck and kissed him.

"Hey, you there!" The inspector's voice sent panic down her spine.

She tightened her embrace. "Go along with me," she said into his mouth as she kissed him again, harder this time.

"What are you two doing down there?" the inspector boomed.

"Eliza." Theo buried his face in her neck. "You smell good." He looked up into her eyes. Holding her gaze, he leaned closer and brushed his lips against hers.

"Hey there!"

They ignored him.

"I'm looking for Lena Grigor."

"Join the club," Eliza said under her breath.

"Have you seen her?" The inspector stood towering over them, gawking.

"No," Theo said, his voice hoarse. "Can't you see we're busy?" He kissed her again.

This was no fake kiss to avoid getting caught behind the bar. It was real. And true. And... She wove her fingers into his hair. His kisses stormed across the drought-stricken desert of her love life like a monsoon, both desperately needed and uniquely terrifying. She'd kissed men before. And women. She'd even been in love. Or so she'd thought. But this: the intensity of the heat spreading through her chest threatened to explode her resolve to keep things platonic. This was not the kiss on the cheek and pat on the head of an older brother or a friend.

"I see." The inspector laughed. "*Amour*." His voice sounded distant, like it was coming from another world.

She should stop. She should break away. But the more Theo kissed her, the more she wanted. She pressed herself against him like her life depended on it. "Theo. We shouldn't..."

The inspector's glass clinked against his bottle and his laughter receded.

"He's gone," she whispered. No need to keep up the charade. And yet, the pang in her chest told her giving it up would be painful. "He's stolen away with a bottle."

"Stolen away, like my heart." He took her hand and again pressed it to his chest. "Stolen away by the most beautiful thief."

The depth of longing in his dark eyes overwhelmed her. She jerked her hand from his chest and averted his gaze. There was a murderer on the loose. She couldn't afford to get distracted or someone else might get killed. Someone she loved.

11

THE FILM

Early the next morning, Monsieur Fournier announced breakfast would be served in the dining car. Everyone was required to attend. No exceptions.

Eliza rubbed her eyes. She'd hardly slept. When she wasn't distracted by her investigation into the killings, she'd been agitated by something far more dangerous. Namely, unsettling and uninvited dreams about Theodore Sharp. Her skin still tingled from the intoxicating dream that left her sweating into her pillow and finally woke her for good.

The train would soon arrive in Constantinople and the police wanted everyone assembled in one place. Passengers could stay and enjoy a final champagne brunch while coppers searched their cabins and the rest of the train from one end to the other. The passengers were instructed to bring their passports. If and when they were allowed to depart the train, they would be expected to stay in the city at the Pera Palace Hotel until the police were satisfied, at which time, their passports would be returned and they would be free to continue their travels. "Until then, please make yourselves at home and enjoy the hospitality aboard the Orient Express."

The dining car was tense with an unnatural stillness, the soft clink of silverware against the china sounding like a clock counting down the minutes to Constantinople. Bright morning light cut through the frost-edged windows, while the pale faces of passengers avoided eye contact over tepid coffee and half-eaten pastries. The air was thick with unsaid words and darting glances. Even the usually lively hum of the train seemed subdued, as if it, too, was holding its breath, waiting for what would happen next.

Eliza ordered a pot of strong coffee, hoping it would wake her up. While she waited, she removed a notebook and pencil from her handbag and proceeded to make a list of suspects. Atop one page, she wrote *Ivan Grigor* and atop the next she wrote *Hugo "Peachy" Fitzroy*.

In the Ivan column, her first suspect was Peachy, a true-crime aficionado and expert on poisons. If Peachy had been trailing Ivan to discover his secrets, that could be motive for Ivan to kill Peachy. But the other way around? Why would Peachy kill Ivan? Theo's handsy friend Eric had told her Peachy was afraid of Ivan. Had Ivan confronted him? Would he have killed him to protect his manuscript? If so, obviously, he hadn't succeeded. The manuscript was gone and Peachy was dead too. His untimely death wasn't the only problem with the Peachy theory. Whoever killed Ivan did it with premeditation, unless, of course, the killer never left home without his poisons the way most folks never left without their toothpaste or cologne. Still, Peachy had the know-how, if not also the means and opportunity, and a pretty good motive.

Next on her list, Eliza wrote Dorothy L. Sayers. If anyone had a motive to kill Ivan Grigor, it was Dorothy. He was blackmailing her and threatening to expose her secret baby, which Dorothy was convinced would ruin her. In addition, he'd dumped her long ago because he didn't believe in marriage and then conveniently changed his tune and married the beautiful Russian piano player and one-time circus performer, Lena. In Eliza's book, that was motive enough: using an anti-marriage ideology as an excuse and then turning around and marrying someone else. It made her want to give him a good ju-jitsu kick to the family jewels.

Speaking of jewels. What of the ruby brooch Ivan sold to Father Richard? And its twin she'd found in Ivan's luggage. What was Ivan up to with those jewels? And more to the point, was his wife, Lena, in on it?

Lena Grigor. The wife. Of course she was a suspect. As Eliza had learned during her training at Scotland Yard, the spouse was always a prime suspect in any murder case. Certainly, Lena had the opportunity. She was sitting with her husband at dinner the night he keeled over. But what was her motive? Between a husband and wife stretched an eternity of motives. Most of them hidden. Some just below the surface required only a scratch to reveal and others in a well of revenge and regret so deep, they had sunk into the molten core of the earth. She smiled. She was beginning to sound like one of those dippy writers. Waxing poetic about murder. And yet, Lena had eaten the same meal as her husband. So, if the killer had poisoned the food, then why did Ivan die while Lena was still alive?

Where was she anyway? No one had seen Lena since the train left Nilš. And yet, Eliza had watched out the window at Nilš Station: the last time the train had stopped. And no one got on or off the train except for the whistling French train inspector. So where was Lena hiding and why? A shiver ran up Eliza's spine. What if she wasn't hiding, but had been hidden?

The third victim. Killed for the same reason as her husband. For the same reason as Peachy. What if the three of them were involved with this Obsidian Cartel? And the killer either hid her body or threw her from the train. What a gruesome thought.

Even if Lena had killed her husband, why would she kill Peachy? Was Peachy's book going to incriminate her, too? If Ivan was involved with the largest organized crime operation in Eurasia, then perhaps Lena had tired of her husband's illegal activities. Maybe she wanted him to get out of the crime racket. And maybe she didn't want Peachy announcing to the world that her husband was a crook.

Eliza's mind was abuzz with theories.

Then again, it was possible that the Obsidian Cartel had arranged for both Ivan's and Peachy's convenient demises. Since Peachy knew about Ivan Grigor's illicit activities, the higher-ups in the Cartel may have decided to do away with both men. Two birds with one stone, except in this case, it was poison and a handful of bullets. Ivan could have done any number of things to cross the Cartel. He was blackmailing Dorothy; what was there to stop him from embezzling from his criminal brethren or at least skimming a bit of cream off the top? Honor among thieves was a myth. There could have been any number of thugs after Ivan if he'd crossed the Cartel.

Peachy, Dorothy, Lena, the Obsidian Cartel. Who else might have wanted Ivan Grigor dead? What she needed was more concrete evidence. Not more theories, or more suspects.

There was an outside chance Father Richard Burrows or even Agatha wanted him dead. Father Richard was livid that he'd been duped by Ivan with the fake ruby brooch. Was he angry enough to kill? Men had killed for less. It seemed a long shot, but even so, she wrote Father Richard at the bottom of the list of suspects. Anyone else on the train from the passengers to the staff could have been involved. She wondered if Eric Blair knew more than he let on. More likely the other way around; he said more than he knew. He'd been almost giddy reporting on the unseemly activities of passengers and peers alike. If he were the killer, he'd probably be announcing it from the rooftop with a bullhorn.

If only she knew where to find the murder weapon: the gun that killed Peachy. If she could fingerprint everyone aboard and get prints off the gun, then she could identify the killer. Peachy's killer at least. And the poison. It had to be stored and delivered somehow. The vial or bottle or syringe must be on the train somewhere. Unless... unless the killer threw them overboard. She shuddered as she thought of Lena. Also missing, along with the murder weapons. Could the killer have thrown Lena's body from the moving train? She grimaced.

As she toyed with her pencil, she suddenly felt a warmth over her right shoulder. She turned and gazed up into Theo's smiling face.

He held a small tray.

"Reading over my shoulder?" She flipped the notebook shut.

"You should probably be more careful." He laid a cup and saucer in front of her and poured coffee from a silver pot. "You don't seriously think Dorothy is a killer?" He chuckled as he dropped three lumps of sugar in her cup and then filled it to the rim with cream.

"You remembered." She picked up the tiny teaspoon and swirled it around the cup before taking a sip. "Perfect."

He glanced around and then took a seat across from her. "Why would Dorothy kill Ivan and Peachy? What possible motive would she have?" He shook his head. "Ridiculous.

Dorothy isn't dangerous. I mean, her bark is worse than her bite."

"I wonder." She fingered the handle of her cup. "Don't you writers always say anyone could commit murder under the right circumstances?"

"And what are the right circumstances for Dorothy?" He removed his cap and fiddled with the band.

Let's see. Jilted lover. Secret baby. Blackmail letter. She held her tongue.

"She's at the top of her game." When he leaned forward, that adorable, unruly lock of hair fell across his forehead.

Eliza reached for it, and then thought better, and dropped her hand in her lap. Sitting across from him was distracting enough. She'd best not touch him.

He brushed the stray hair from his forehead. "Why would she risk—"

"Mr. Sharp!" It was Monsieur Fournier.

"I'd best get back to work." Theo replaced his cap and picked up the serving tray. "When we get to Istanbul, wait for me at the station and we can go to the hotel together."

She nodded.

"Mr. Sharp!"

"Coming." Theo winked at her and then trotted off toward his bellowing boss.

Agatha entered the dining car with an air of quiet resolve, her usually composed demeanor betrayed by the faintest flush in her cheeks. Father Richard was at her side, his tweed jacket rumpled as though hastily thrown on. His secretary trailed behind. Conversations faltered as heads turned, curiosity rippling through the tense room like a dropped stone in still water. Agatha approached Eliza's table.

"May we join you?" she asked, pointing to Father Richard.

"Of course." Eliza scooted her chair closer to the table to make room for Agatha to pass behind. "Where's Dorothy?"

"She won't come out of the cabin," Agatha whispered.

Eliza furrowed her brows. "Why not?"

Unflinching under the weight of so many eyes, wordlessly, Agatha offered a polite nod and settled into the seat near the window. Father Richard followed suit with the dutiful precision of a shadow and sat across the table. And his secretary took a seat next to him. The soft clink of china resumed, but the hum of whispered speculations lingered in the air, thick as the aroma of fresh coffee. Did the other passengers suspect Agatha of murder? Or merely of having the audacity to befriend a man of the cloth? Or, like so many others these days, were they merely awed by the great author's presence? She was becoming quite a celebrity.

Admittedly, after two deaths in two days, nerves were frayed and everyone was on edge.

"Why won't Dorothy come out?" Eliza repeated.

"Shh." Agatha glanced around. "Leave her be." She put on a smile. "It's a jolly nice day outside." She looked out the window.

After more superficial pleasantries, Agatha and Father Richard tucked into coffee and croissants, while the secretary smoked a cigarette. Eliza picked at the pastry on her plate. When should she brooch the subject of the ruby brooch? She took a sip of her coffee. No time like the present. "Might I see your brooch?" Her tone was as nonchalant as if she'd just asked Agatha to pass the salt. "The ruby dog pin Father Richard bought off Mr. Grigor?"

Agatha's cheeks turned pink. "Whatever for?" she sputtered as she pulled her handkerchief from her pocket.

"It might be important." Eliza twisted her napkin in her lap. "For the investigation of our two dead men."

Agatha unfolded the hanky to reveal the pin and then pushed it across the table. "It's seen better days, I'm afraid." She glanced over at Father Richard and gave him a weak smile.

From her handbag, Eliza withdrew the twin she'd found in the secret compartment of Ivan's suitcase. She laid it on the handkerchief next to Agatha's pin.

Father Richard snatched it up. "What the devil?" He turned it over in his palm and then tapped the gemstone on the table. "This is the real one." A look of recognition lit up his face. "This is the one he sold to me." He held it out to Agatha. "I'm sure of it. I wouldn't have been duped by that fake." He pointed at the sad duplicate brooch whose gold was flaking and ruby was chipped. "He must have switched them after I bought it."

"Could be." Eliza fingered the fake. "Was that his racket? Sell real jewels and then switch them for fakes?"

"He made a fool out of me." Father Richard reached for the brooch. "Damn fake." As if exacting his revenge, he pressed the thick end of his knife against the fake ruby and it crumbled.

"What in the world?" Agatha picked a tiny piece of film from the paste powder. "What's this?" She examined it. "Why it looks like a bit of microfilm."

"May I see it?" Eliza held out her hand.

Agatha dropped the tiny coil into her palm.

It was microfilm alright. She uncoiled it and held it up to the light. The black-and-gray images were so tiny, she'd need a magnifying glass, maybe even a microscope, to read them. Drat. Too bad she'd left hers back in London. How could she have known she'd need it aboard the Orient Express?

"Hold up your water glass," she said, giving instructions to her dining companions.

Agatha obliged.

"Hold it steady." Eliza stretched the film and pressed it against the glass. The light coming through the water backlit the film. Enough to see the tiny letters and numbers, but not enough to actually read them. "Do any of you have a magnifying glass?"

Her companions shook their heads.

"How about a mirror?" She let the film recoil in her palm.

"I have one in my shaving kit." Father Richard beamed. "I'll go get it."

Eliza glanced around. "Maybe we should find a more private place to—"

Father Richard's secretary ground out her cigarette in an ashtray. "I'll stay here."

"Microfilm," Theo interrupted. He stood next to the table holding a bottle of water. "Where did you get it?"

"It was inside Agatha's dog brooch." Eliza scooped up the remains of the paste jewel along with Agatha's handkerchief. "We're going back to Agatha's cabin to find a way to read it." She slipped the hanky and its contents into her jacket pocket. "Care to come along?" She nodded at the bottle. "Be sure to bring that. Unless you have a magnifying glass."

"Monsieur Fournier said everyone is to stay in the dining car until we arrive at Istanbul," Theo said.

"We can't very well examine this film in public with a murderer among us." Eliza glanced around. "Anyway, what is he going to do? Arrest us?"

"A distinct possibility." Agatha folded her napkin and laid it on the table. "Shall we?" She stood up. "Jolly exciting. A real murder investigation."

"Too bad it requires a real murder."

Eliza took Theo's hand and led the way out of the dining car. Luckily, Monsieur Fournier was nowhere to be seen.

* * *

Back in Agatha's cabin, they found Dorothy hiding out. Did she still fear her blackmailer even though he was dead? Theo didn't believe she was hiding from the police. Whatever the case, she was pleased to see everyone, especially given the excitement of the microfilm and the experiment they were about to conduct.

Theo adjusted the glass bottle with painstaking care, his pulse hammering almost as loud as the train's wheels against the tracks. The sloshing water refracted the dim lamplight, casting strange shadows onto the strip of microfilm spread across the small table. Eliza leaned in and, holding Father Richard's shaving mirror in one hand and a lit candle in the other, she angled the light so it reflected off the bottle and through the film. Her brow furrowed with an intensity that made his chest ache, as if she were solving the mysteries of the universe rather than deciphering the scratched letters on a microfilm.

"There!" she said, her voice filled with excitement.

Agatha, perched primly on the edge of her bunk looked on with a curious expression. "Please, do try not to catch our cabin on fire."

Theo swallowed hard, acutely aware of Eliza's shoulder touching his own. "If anything combusts," he whispered, his voice tight, "it won't be the cabin."

"And careful with my mirror, if you please," Father Richard said, leaning against Agatha.

"Where did you get this microfilm, again?" Dorothy leaned against the door. "Explain it to me. It was hidden in Agatha's brooch. Why? What does it mean?"

"That's what we're trying to determine." Eliza glanced at him, and for a heart-stopping moment, her eyes caught his.

Theo bent closer to the film, pretending to study the smudged letters. "A schedule," he said, his tone clipped. "Names. Dates. A list." His hand brushed hers as he adjusted the bottle. The warmth lingered longer than it should and he froze.

"What kind of list?" Her breath was warm on his neck as she spoke.

Finally, he looked up into her eyes again. "I don't know." The light from the gas lamp danced on her pupils.

"What does it say?" Agatha asked.

"Can you read it?" Dorothy chimed in.

"Shouldn't we give it to the authorities?" Father Richard said.

"Let me see." Eliza leaned closer and stared at the film, her breath fogging the glass. "I've seen this before."

"Where?" Theo's eyes went wide. "When you worked for the Met?" Although she rarely talked about her time with Scotland Yard, he knew it had made an impression on her. And she'd obviously learned a lot about forensics.

"No." Her face was a mask of worry. "Before that. At the War Office."

The War Office. She never talked about her work during the war. He knew she'd worked with the codebreakers in Room 40. He'd heard about it from his college roommate, the son of Captain Hall, Eliza's adoptive father. She'd only ever admitted to working as a Girl Guide at the Old Admiralty. Still, he knew better. He could tell from her silence and the furrows on her forehead whenever anyone mentioned the war. And he knew better than to mention her time at the Met. Whatever happened to her there was even worse.

"I need to call Jane." She straightened.

"Your sister?" Theo furrowed his brows. "Why?"

Eliza plucked up the microfilm and tucked it into her pocket. “This is bigger than we thought.” She sucked in a breath. “Much bigger.”

Over the last two years, he’d memorized and then rehearsed her every freckle and asymmetrical detail of her, attempting the impossible: to capture her in words. And yet, even in his worst nightmares, he’d never seen her looking like she did now.

Pale. Drawn. Eyes wide.

In a word: haunted.

12

THE INTERROGATION

Eliza fanned herself with her notebook. The dining car was suffocating. Not because of the heat—although the little brass fans mounted to the walls seemed more decorative than functional—but because of the weight of unspoken accusations that hung in the air thicker than the haze of the cigarette smoke curling from Dorothy's ashtray. The passengers were on edge, their words clipped as though afraid that saying the wrong thing might turn the spotlight on them. One of them was a murderer. But which one?

Eliza tucked her notebook discreetly beneath a napkin. She'd quit writing notes about the case. Too risky with Monsieur Fournier hovering nearby flapping his wings and looking over her shoulder. Instead, she studied the others, her gaze darting from face to face. Across the table, Theo stared into his coffee, the tips of his fingers tapping out a restless rhythm on the edge of the saucer. The tension of their arrival in Constantinople and the awaiting police must have made Monsieur Fournier too anxious to bark orders. He didn't chastise Theo or command him back to work.

When Theo caught her looking at him, he raised an eyebrow. "Who among us"—his voice was barely audible over the hum of the train's idling engine—"is a killer?" He glanced around the dining car.

She didn't answer. Instead, her eyes flicked toward the French couple seated two tables down. The woman was pale, her hands trembling as she pretended to sip from an empty cup. Her companion had given up the charade altogether and was staring out the window, his jaw tight. They hadn't spoken a word to each other since the announcement that the police would be boarding soon. Eliza filed that away for later, although she had no idea who they were or their relation to the two dead men. Watching the other passengers, she realized any one of them could be the killer. And there were dozens. All of them suddenly looking more suspicious than the next. Near the door, a burly man with a walrus mustache kept shifting in his seat, the buttons on his waistcoat straining with each deep breath. He dabbed at his forehead with a monogrammed handkerchief and muttered something under his breath. His tablemate, a gaunt, birdlike woman in a drab, gray dress, shot him a look so sharp, it could have cut glass. And where was the mysterious monocled man? He was nowhere to be seen.

Agatha, Dorothy, and Father Richard and his secretary sat at a four-top table across from Eliza and Theo's smaller table for two. The women writers had their heads together and whispered conspiratorially, occasionally glancing over and nodding. What would the police think if they found out about the blackmail letter and Dorothy's secret? And what about Father Richard's very loud and public threats against Ivan for selling him fake jewelry? Then there was Eric Blair pretending to be something he wasn't. Tramping around Europe. If that wasn't suspicious, she didn't know what was. Why would anyone pretend to be poor? She knew from experience that poverty wasn't romantic, but an unfortunate condition to be avoided at all costs. And he'd even got Theo involved in the stupid scheme.

The train jolted forward and then stopped again. A collective hush fell over the dining car. Another jolt and the train made its slow approach to the station. Outside, the sprawling skyline of Constantinople loomed closer, its domes and minarets silhouetted against a dusky sky. The glittering water of the Bosphorus came into view as it reflected the golden light of the late-afternoon sun. Clusters of red-tiled rooftops tumbled down toward the bustling harbor, where ships and ferries crisscrossed like insects stuck to the surface of a shining web.

Every creak of the train creeping into the station was amplified by the silence inside. The thick tension in the dining car hung in the air along with the dense smoke from Dorothy's cigar; yes, Dorothy had the unpleasant habit of an occasional cigar.

The train squealed to a stop. Eliza held her breath. The moment of truth. She had to find a way to get off the train and call her sister and tell her about the microfilm.

The microfilm hidden in the ruby wasn't just any list of names. They were code names for British agents. Eliza had recognized many of them from her work as a Girl Guide in Room 40 during the war. She'd met some of them: Dillwyn Knox, Biffy Dunderdale, Sidney Rielly, Vera Atkins, and Fiona Figg. It was not a list of criminals from some jewel-smuggling network or the Obsidian Cartel. It was a list of British espionage agents who had been working across Europe during the war. Some of them were still in the field spying on Germany and Russia and protecting British interests across the globe. If this microfilm fell into enemy hands, it would mean death to the people on this list. People who were Eliza's acquaintances, even friends.

Thunderous footfalls from the corridor startled her. The sound of boots: heavy, deliberate, and getting louder. The dining-car door slid open with a screech that made everyone flinch. A man stepped inside, tall and broad-shouldered, with a droopy, gray mustache that covered his entire mouth. Behind him, two uniformed officers flanked Monsieur Fournier, who clutched his cap in both hands as if it were a lifeline.

"Good afternoon," the tall man said, his deep voice slicing through the silence. He scanned the room, his eyes lingering on each passenger in turn. "I am Detective Inspector Orhan. You will all remain here while we conduct our inquiries." His eyes landed on Eliza. "No exceptions."

She stiffened. Theo nudged her under the table. She risked a glance his way and found him watching the inspector with a look that was half-curiosity, half-defiance. Again, the inspector's gaze landed on their table, and for one nerve-wracking moment, Eliza thought he was about to interrogate them. Instead, he moved on, addressing the entire car. "The cooperation of everyone here is essential. If you have nothing to hide, you have nothing to fear." His voice hung in the air.

Should she offer her services as a former copper? Her lips twitched. She knew from experience the police rarely welcomed help from laypeople who fancied themselves armchair detectives, especially when those people were women.

Detective Inspector Orhan quietly conferred with Monsieur Fournier. The longer they talked, the more the manager's cheeks reddened and hands fluttered. If the inspector didn't dispense with him soon, the poor man looked as if he might have a fit. Where was the French train inspector? The one who'd caught her and Theo behind the bar? Wasn't he in charge of the investigation? Why weren't the police consulting him? Wasn't he sent to initiate an investigation after Ivan Grigor's death? Isn't that why he boarded the train at Nilš?

"Excuse me, sir," Eliza said, raising her hand. "I don't mean to be impertinent or step out of line." She cleared her throat. "But I may be of assistance... I mean, if I can be of any assistance, I'm happy to help." She clutched her notebook in both hands.

"Everyone will get their turn." The inspector scowled, refusing to make eye contact.

While a uniformed officer stood guard at each end of the dining car, one by one, one of the officers called out passengers' names, starting with the burly man followed by his gaunt companion. Clutching a clipboard to his chest, Monsieur Fournier whispered a name into the police officer's ear and then the copper repeated it in a loud, tinny voice. The two of them led one of the passengers away and brought them back, sometimes a few minutes later, sometimes, half an hour later. Every time the inspector reappeared in the dining car, a hush fell like a curtain and everyone sat in nervous anticipation, waiting for their turn. Wringing his hands, Monsieur Fournier trotted back and forth behind the policeman. Each time one of the passengers returned from questioning, all eyes fell upon them, scrutinizing their faces for traces of what to expect. When they took their seat among the others, their friends whispered questions hoping for reassurance, until one of the guards shouted, "Quiet" and gave them the evil eye.

When the copper called her name, Eliza's heart leaped into her throat. She followed him back to the office, a compact space with a mahogany desk bolted to the floor and a leather desk chair behind it. A brass lamp with a green glass shade cast a spotlight on a leather-bound ledger and a stack of blank telegrams. Next to a small, curtained window hung a timetable and below it, a map of the route. Detective Inspector Orhan was seated behind the desk and motioned for her to step closer. He took a tiny notebook from the desk and flipped it open. From her vantage point, his hands were illuminated while his face was in shadow, creating an eerie sense of duplicity, as if the hands were operating independently of the rest of him.

Without looking up, Detective Inspector Orhan asked her name, her nationality, and the purpose of her trip. He recorded her answers in his notebook. When he got to questions about the two dead men, he stared her straight in the eyes, as if his gaze alone was a type of polygraph test; she'd heard of such a thing: an American invention, a machine to detecting lies. Having lived on the streets of London among thieves and cons, she knew a few things about lies. And while her time with the Metropolitan Police had made her more honest, it hadn't made her more trusting. She kept her answers to the bare minimum. It was obvious from the way the detective inspector glared up at her that he didn't want her help. And until she got a chance to ring Jane about the list hidden in the ruby, she wasn't about to divulge more than what was already common knowledge:

Ivan Grigor keeled over in the bar car after eating a heavy dinner complete with wine and cocktails. Hugo "Peachy" Fitzroy was found shot and his cabin ransacked. He was writing an exposé on Grigor which was rumored to contain enough incriminating evidence to put Ivan Grigor in prison. Yes, Lena Grigor went missing at about the same time as the second death. Yes, Ivan Grigor sold jewelry to a few passengers, including Father Richard. Yes, Agatha Christie was a famous novelist well-versed in poisons. No, she didn't threaten to poison passengers in the name of research. Eliza didn't mention the flaky brooch or the microfilm or her makeshift toxicology or Theo's strange obsession with Lena Grigor's piano music.

After forty minutes of answering questions, Eliza's palms were sweating. When the detective bent to write in his notebook, she wiped her hands on the back of her skirt. Nothing like an interrogation to make you feel guilty.

"You may go now," the detective said, still writing.

"Thank you." She cleared her throat. "Before I do, I'm wondering if you've consulted with the French train inspector who boarded at Nilš." She tilted her head, trying to get a glimpse of his notes.

"What French inspector?" He glanced up at her.

"He came on board to investigate Ivan Grigor's death." She squinted at him. "He asked a lot of questions and then disappeared. I just wondered if—"

He held up a hand. "Back up. Tell me more about this inspector." His mustache twitching, he hovered his pen over his notebook. "You say he was French? Describe him. What did he say to you? When was the last time you saw him?" Suddenly, he couldn't take his eyes off her. She'd obviously hit a nerve. She'd thought something was odd about that French inspector.

"Don't you know of him?" A lightbulb went off in her brain. The mysterious train inspector boarded at Nilš, right after Ivan was poisoned. He disappeared again after Peachy was shot. He couldn't have killed Ivan, unless he did so by proxy. But he could have murdered Peachy.

"I'm asking the questions, if you please." The detective tapped his pen on the desk. "What does he look like, this French train inspector?"

She described his belted uniform, his beady eyes and

beaked nose, and his crusty tone. The detective quickly scribbled in his notebook. The flash of his eyes told her something wasn't right. The French train inspector was indeed a suspect. She knew it. But why? Why would a train inspector kill Peachy Fitzroy? Her mouth fell open.

Unless he wasn't a train inspector at all, but a member of the Obsidian Cartel. "I suspect he's not really a train inspector." Blimey. That would explain the ransacked cabin. The killer was looking for Peachy's exposé, the incriminating manuscript that promised to reveal their operations to the world. And what about Lena? Had the imposter dispatched her, too? Eliza shuddered, imagining Lena's body strewn along the railway tracks some place in the Bulgarian countryside.

* * *

Theo watched as Eliza took her seat across from him. Although her expression was inscrutable, he knew her well enough to know something was wrong. It was the way she jerked her head and blew at her fringe. He thought back to their chess game. Whenever he'd taken one of her pieces, she blew at her fringe. Two years ago, and still, he was haunted by the gesture, along with the way she pinched the top of the bishop between her thumb and index finger and rocked it back and forth, deciding whether to make the move. God, he was hopeless.

"How was it?" he whispered.

"Educational." She pursed her lips and then glanced around.

Both uniformed officers shushed them at the same time.

He wished he could compare notes to get their stories straight. Eliza had offered to help Detective Inspector Orhan with the investigation. She was none too pleased when he waved her away. So, had she clammed up and refused to tell him what she knew? Or had she wowed him with her brilliance and railway forensics? *Educational.* What did she mean by that? Had she learned something from the detective? Or had she learned something about him? If Theo's experience was anything to go by, it seemed as if Eliza could see right through his skull and into his thoughts. Hopefully, he kept his heart more protected. If she saw what was there, surely, she'd bolt.

"Theodore Sharp." The officer called his name.

Theo adjusted his jacket and stood up. As he followed the copper back to Monsieur Fournier's office, it occurred to him that Eric had made himself scarce. He hadn't seen his roommate since yesterday. Had he somehow managed to get off the train without the police seeing him? He had been eager to get to the International Writers' Conference. Then again, maybe he was eager to get away from the police interrogation. They'd tangled with the police in Paris a few times. Dressed as tramps, scrounging for work and food, the coppers weren't always friendly, either. Eric took it in his stride. More than that, he wore it as a badge of honor. So where was he now? Usually, he'd delight in throwing caution to the wind by heckling the authorities. He loved nothing more than a couple of nights in jail to give him grist for his writerly mill. One such stint was more than enough for Theo, who'd been too distracted by the foul odors and pitiful bodily emanations to write anything. Even if he could have, who wanted to read about such filth and degradation? Didn't people read to escape the horrors of life rather than wallow in them? Theo was all for verisimilitude, but he had to draw the line somewhere: namely, sharing a toilet with someone who hadn't bathed since the nineteenth century.

When Theo entered the manager's office, the curtains were drawn and all he could see of the detective sitting in the corner was the glowing ember of his cigarette. Theo glanced around for a chair. Besides the one behind the desk currently occupied by Detective Inspector Orhan, there were none. Hands behind his back, he leaned against a wall panel and waited. With every pulse of the ember, his anxiety increased. Did the detective expect him to speak first? After another minute of silence, he couldn't stand it. "You called for me?" He shifted his weight.

"Tell me about your friend, Eliza Baker." The detective leaned forward and crushed his cigarette into an ashtray on the desk. The way he'd said "friend" set Theo's teeth on edge.

What could he tell the detective about Eliza? He'd known her for half of her life and still didn't really know her. Sure, he could tell when she was upset or angry. But she kept her softer emotions hidden under a thick armor of mistrust and betrayal. He'd learned to tread carefully lest she sense a chink in her armor and bolt. She'd accused him of running away. But he'd left to avoid the heartbreak of watching her slip further out of reach, like a train racing away from the station loaded with secrets he'd never be invited to share. He'd told himself it was for the best, that she deserved someone who could match her fire and chase her storms. But deep down, he knew the truth. He hadn't left because he didn't care. He'd run because he cared too much, and it terrified him. Eliza Baker was a chess game he couldn't win. And still, he couldn't stop playing. For the last two years, even three hundred miles away, his thoughts were drawn to her white-hot light despite the real possibility that their reunion might incinerate him.

At this very moment, standing in front of the police detective, he was driven to distraction by the lingering smell of her perfume on his jacket. He'd tried to outrun her. To bury himself in work... and other women. But it was no use. She was the constant, the inescapable pull of gravity in his otherwise drifting world.

Theo pushed himself off the wall and took a step closer to the desk. “What would you like to know?” Talking about Eliza was like walking on a razor’s edge. He ran his hand through his hair, wondering where to begin.

13

ISTANBUL–CONSTANTINOPLE

The dining car was stifling and stuffy. Weary passengers who had been waiting for hours to disembark wilted into the upholstery. The stench of sour perfume mingled with cigar smoke and the smell of fear. Eliza's stomach growled and she realized she hadn't eaten since breakfast. Would they ever be allowed to leave? She stared out the window, watching the sun setting behind a kaleidoscope of color. She'd been looking at the same stained-glass window all day. An arabesque pattern of white and red surrounding lush greens and blues resembling a river running through a meadow with a burst of yellow and orange exploding out of its center. As the light changed, so did its hues and textures.

The platform bustled with activity, but it had become a blur in Eliza's peripheral vision, like a watercolor left out in the rain, smudged and indistinct as she focused on a dog standing near the edge of the platform. A small beagle with a black face, white muzzle, and tan eyebrows. The floppy, black ears rimmed in tan reminded her of Queenie, her own sweet beagle back home. She missed Queenie. She did a double take, then bolted upright in her seat and pressed her hand against the window. The woman holding the end of the dog's leash came into view.

Eliza knew that red-and-black, herringbone trench coat and jaunty, gray fedora atop a neat, blonde bob. "Jane." Her sister's name came out as an exclamation of surprise. "What is she doing here?" Eliza glanced around the dining car, looking for a way out. She'd been waiting for the chance to telephone Jane and now here she was, standing right outside on the platform. Desperate to get to her sister, she rushed to the end of the dining car closest to where Jane was standing outside.

"My sister," she said to the officer. "She's waiting for me on the platform." Not exactly true. Eliza had no idea why her sister was waiting on the platform or what she was waiting for. But she was determined to find out.

"No one allowed off the train until the DI says so." The officer's tone was all business.

"But my sister—" She pressed her palms together, practically pleading with him.

"Sorry." He pointed at where she'd been sitting.

"But—"

"Please go back to your seat." He took her elbow.

With a frustrated sigh, she resisted the urge to make a break for it, yanked her arm away, and trudged back to the table.

"What's Jane doing here?" Theo asked, folding and unfolding a napkin.

Her lips twitched. It wasn't a secret that Jane worked for MI5, British Intelligence. But her assignments were always classified. Rarely, when she needed help on a difficult assignment, she'd confide in Eliza. After the war and then Eliza's short-lived career with Scotland Yard, she was in no hurry to get involved in espionage. She knew just how dangerous it could be. Not that she feared for her own life. If only it were that simple. No.

She worried that she'd slip on the job and someone—someone she loved—would get killed.

Eliza glanced out the window looking for Jane. But she was gone. Vanished into thin air and there was nothing Eliza could do to find her. "I don't know," she said finally. Could Jane's assignment involve the microfilm and list of British agents? If so, how did MI5 know about it? Had someone else informed them? Someone on the train. Who else knew? Agatha, Dorothy, Theo, and Father Richard. And of course, whoever had hidden it inside the brooch. Ivan Grigor or his wife, Lena?

Eliza fiddled with the handle of her empty teacup. MI5 was suspicious of the writers in the Detection Club. When Eliza first went to work for the club, Jane had asked her to keep her eyes and ears open. Apparently, MI5 suspected one of the writers, probably Agatha Christie, had access to classified information. From what Eliza had seen, the mystery writers had access to nothing more classified than overactive imaginations. That and a knack for being in the wrong place at the wrong time, depending on your perspective, of course. For them, witnessing murders and poisonings might count as stellar opportunities for first-hand research. Still, Eliza hadn't seen anything that made her suspect espionage.

What of Father Richard? He said he was an archeologist on his way to a dig in Ur. Could he secretly be working for MI5? Or Ivan Grigor, for that matter? Peachy claimed Ivan was a member of the Obsidian Cartel, but could he have been a British undercover agent who had infiltrated the Cartel? Given the paranoid state of global espionage, anything was possible.

A commotion at the end of the car turned all heads. A blur of trench coats and black boots boarded the train. A few seconds later, a wet tongue was licking Eliza's hand.

"Queenie!" She lifted the beagle onto her lap.

"Queenie." Jane's voice was stern. "Get back here." A swirl of red-and-black herringbone blew toward them. "Thank God you're safe."

"What are you doing here?" Scratching behind Queenie's ears, Eliza gave her sister a quizzical look. "I assume you're here for the murders."

"Hello, Jane," Theo said, tipping an imaginary cap. "Nice to see you again."

"Likewise." Jane nodded and then pulled up a chair from a nearby table. "What do you know about the murders?" Her voice was low and hushed.

"Get us off this blasted train and I'll tell you." Eliza fed Queenie a stale crust of croissant left over from breakfast, which, her grumbling stomach reminded her, was hours ago. "Preferably over dinner."

* * *

An hour later, Eliza was sitting with her sister and friends in a lovely café looking out at the Bosphorus River through arched windows framed by hand-painted tiles and enjoying an egg and tomato omelet called *menemen* along with a very strong Turkish coffee. Agatha took delight in a local dumpling called *manti*, while Dorothy practically swooned over a bowl of mussels. Theo and Jane opted for kebabs served with baked potatoes and plates of olives, cheese, and fresh vegetables and herbs. Queenie moved around under the table, accepting handouts from anyone who'd give her a morsel.

They were only allowed out of the station because Jane took responsibility for them in her capacity as a representative of MI5 and British security. The rest of Jane's team was still questioning other passengers in the dining car, including Eric

Blair, who'd finally turned up and was just obnoxious enough to offend most everyone he talked to for more than five minutes. The detective had questioned him for at least thirty-five. No doubt his claims to know everything made him an indispensable witness. Father Richard Burrows and his secretary had stayed at the railway station in the hopes that Detective Inspector Orhan would permit them to catch their train to Ankara where they would transfer to a motor coach to continue to the dig at Ur. Given the circumstances, Agatha seemed in no hurry to get to Ur. A double murder on the Orient Express had been sufficient to distract her from her recent divorce. Indeed, she was probably taking notes for her next murder mystery.

Everyone, except Jane, tucked into their dinner with such gusto, you'd think they hadn't eaten for a week. Only after they'd ordered pudding and another round of strong coffees did Eliza consent to Jane's interrogation. The others knew Jane was there on behalf of the British government to investigate the death of British citizens. Only Eliza suspected their deaths had something to do with the microfilm list of British agents. Apart from Eliza, and presumably Jane, the others had no clue what the list of names meant. Or if they did, they were very good actors and didn't let on.

Eliza repeated everything she'd told Detective Inspector Orhan. Then she told Jane about her experiments on the train with the black tea testing for toxins, and the secret compartment in Ivan's suitcase, the real and fake ruby brooch, and the microfilm. At the mention of microfilm, Jane raised an eyebrow and narrowed her eyes in a warning. With a sigh, Eliza bent down, removed the microfilm from her boot, and slipped it into Jane's palm.

Then she recounted her list of suspects for the murders, "present company excepted." And she didn't mention Father

Richard's threats toward Ivan for selling him a fake or the blackmail letter Dorothy received from Ivan that threatened to expose her secret baby. She needed to get Jane alone to find out the significance of the list and why Jane was really sent to meet the Orient Express. Jane admitted to being in Constantinople to investigate Ivan Grigor's death. She didn't say what Ivan meant to British Intelligence.

The waiter brought dessert: baklava and Turkish rice pudding. Eliza closed her eyes, enjoying the magical combination of honeyed pastry and bitter coffee. Dorothy took a double helping of both. Their love of sweets was something they had in common. After her childhood on the streets, Eliza never turned down pudding.

"What about Lena Grigor?" Theo asked, balancing a bit of baklava on his fork. "I swear there was something odd about her music." He popped the sweet into his mouth.

Jane blanched. "We're looking for her now. Poor thing." Her eyes darted back and forth. "What do you know about her music? If you don't mind telling me, of course."

"My hunch is it was a code of some sort." Theo took a sip of coffee. "Does this mean anything to you?" He showed her a piece of paper.

"What's that?" Agatha asked, plucking another square of pastry from the center plate. "Sounds like musical notes." She gently placed the baklava on her own plate and licked her fingers.

"Right," Theo said, wiping his hands on his napkin. He pulled a piece of sheet music from his pocket. "Look." He pointed at the notes. "I think it's code." He slid his finger across the letters he'd written above the notes.

Jane's cheeks reddened and she held her spoon in mid-air. Theo must have hit upon something.

"B-A-G-B-A-G," Dorothy said. "D-A-D-D-A-D." Dorothy jabbed the air with her finger. "I've got it. Baghdad Café." She beamed. "It's a location. Here in Constantinople. Or should I say, Istanbul." She pulled a guidebook from her handbag. "I read about it." She flipped through the pages. "See." She held the book open and set a finger above a paragraph about the Baghdad Café.

Eliza leaned in for a closer look. The café was on Bağdat Caddessi or Baghdad Avenue, a road connecting Istanbul with Anatolia during the Byzantine and later the Ottoman periods, according to the guidebook.

Jane threw her napkin on the table, which set Queenie to barking. "I need to get to the Baghdad Café." She jumped up, tugged on her trench coat, and jerked a bank note from her handbag. "Eliza dearest, I'll meet you back at the Pera Palace Hotel later." She handed the money to Eliza.

"I'm coming with you." Eliza dropped the note on the table and added another of her own.

"Me too," Theo said, following suit. He drained his coffee and stood up.

"It's too dangerous," Jane said, shaking her head. "Please, I've got to go alone."

"At least tell us what's happening." Agatha's bright eyes were full of wonder. When it came to adventure, the woman was fearless.

"Yes," Dorothy joined in. "We're pretty good detectives, if I do say so myself." She wiped her napkin across her mouth. "We might be able to help."

"What do you expect to find at the Baghdad Café?" Eliza asked, although she knew the answer. She was a pretty good detective, too. And if Lena Grigor had sent a coded message in her music indicating the Baghdad Café, there was a good chance that was where they would find the missing woman. Providing, of course, she was still alive.

* * *

The only rooster at a hen party, Theo trailed behind the women. He'd only met Eliza's sister once. It was uncanny how much they looked alike, which only made their differences even more pronounced. Whereas Eliza was blunt to a fault, Jane was gracious even when interrogating suspects. Eliza marched through life, pushing forward as if the world was her adversary, every move a strategic gambit in a championship game. Jane, on the other hand, seemed to float gracefully on the surface while secretly rooting out the enemy. Eliza would just as soon kick her opponent in the head as sneak up on them. And if you made her feel pressured in any way, she became like a trapped animal who would do whatever necessary to escape, which was why he had to be careful. He dared not press himself on her or she'd chew her own arm off to escape—not to mention one of his.

As he stepped onto the tram, he caught a glimpse of a familiar figure. At least he thought he did. A tall man wearing a cape fluttered toward the back of the carriage and disappeared into a pack of bodies filling the tram. Where had Theo seen him before? In Paris? London? Or on the Orient Express?

The tram jolted forward with a metallic groan, its wooden frame swaying as it lurched over uneven tracks. Theo gripped the brass pole, his fingers brushing the smooth, worn surface polished by countless hands. Outside, the city unfurled like a living tapestry. Narrow, cobbled streets wound between ancient, stone walls and crumbling, Ottoman-era houses, their wooden shutters flapping lazily in the breeze. The air was thick with a heady mix of roasting meat, sea salt, and the faint acrid tang of coal smoke.

As the tram clattered closer to the heart of the city, the hum of life grew louder. Street vendors lined the sidewalks, their carts spilling over with bright pomegranates, stacks of bread, and glistening olives. Children darted between the legs of hurried men in dark coats and fezzes, their laughter mingling with the occasional call to prayer drifting down from a nearby mosque. Theo leaned out the open window, catching the faint sparkle of the Bosphorus in the distance, the setting sun glinting off its rippling surface like shards of glass. The strait seemed impossibly vast, stretching between two continents, its waters busy with bobbing ferries, sleek yachts, and the occasional hulking steamer.

The tram's bell clanged sharply as they approached a bustling intersection. Here, the city seemed to converge: Men arguing over the price of textiles, women balancing baskets of fish on their hips, and the rhythmic clang of a blacksmith's hammer echoing from an alleyway. The cacophony made Theo's head spin, but it was invigorating too. There was an energy to Istanbul, a chaotic symphony of old and new, East and West, that inspired him. How would he describe what he saw? How could he translate into words the juxtapositions and contradictions that made this city so beautiful, both familiar and strange? If only he could find the key to turning raw experience into language, the Rosetta Stone of the heart.

As the tram rattled downhill toward the ferry terminal, the scent of the sea grew stronger, mingling with the aroma of grilled fish from nearby stalls. He caught a glimpse of the ferry waiting at the dock, its deck crowded with passengers clutching bundles and bags, ready to cross to the Asian side. The tram squealed to a halt, and Theo stepped off, the world tilting slightly beneath his feet. When he turned back and held out his hand to help Eliza off the tram, he saw him again. The caped man, deboarding through the rear exit and disappearing into the crowd. An uncanny sense of déjà vu washed over him, intensified by the sound of waves hitting the rocky shore.

Ahead, the Bosphorus stretched wide and blue, its waters promising a new adventure—and perhaps, a key to the mystery of Lena Grigor's coded musical score. With any luck, they'd find the solution to the murder mystery there, too. On the other side. At the Baghdad Café.

14

THE BAGHDAD CAFÉ

Sporting a worn, wooden sign that gave nothing away, the Baghdad Café was tucked into a side street off bustling Baghdad Avenue. Inside, the dim light of gas lamps and faded mirrors created a hazy atmosphere that blurred the edges of the room. Persian rugs in rich reds and blues covered the floor and muffled their footsteps. Patrons lounged on low divans, some sipping coffee from delicate cups, others bent low over backgammon boards or reading foreign newspapers. The smoke curling lazily from long-stemmed hookahs added to the café's dreamlike ambiance.

In her mind, Eliza began cataloging details: The frayed velvet on the divans, the cloying haze of tobacco smoke hanging low in the air, and the persistent click of backgammon pieces mingling with the lilting strains of music from the baby grand piano in the far corner. Queenie tugged lightly on her lead, nose twitching as if she, too, were on the hunt for something, or someone.

Eliza glanced over her shoulder at the rest of the group. Theo had already gotten that faraway look in his eyes. He was scanning the room, but she could tell his thoughts were spinning out a dozen plausible theories before they'd even begun to dig. Agatha, ever the adventurer, was studying the café with a keen interest, her lips curved in a lively smile as if she might leap into action at any moment. And Dorothy, well—Dorothy was Dorothy, bustling past the rest of them like she owned the place, her booming voice already demanding to know who was in charge.

"Dorothy, for heaven's sake," Eliza muttered, her tone sharper than she'd intended. "Maybe try not to be so conspicuous." Impossible, she knew. Dorothy was a large woman with an even larger personality. Eliza adjusted Queenie's lead and followed Dorothy further into the café. The beagle was sniffing furiously now, tugging insistently toward the corner where the pianist sat playing a melancholy melody. Eliza felt Jane sidle up beside her. She turned to her sister, whose blouse, skirt, and hair remained impeccable despite the long train journey. Jane's face was unreadable.

"Thinking of hustling a game of chess," Jane said under her breath. "You could make your train fare home and leave me to handle this situation."

Eliza shot a look at her sister, who had miraculously arrived in Constantinople for some shadowy assignment tied to the murders aboard the Orient Express. She wasn't convinced the coded message from Lena's music that led them to the Baghdad Café came as a surprise to Jane. "I didn't realize MI5 took such an interest in dead jewel smugglers," Eliza said, her voice low. "And why did they send you, of all people?"

Jane scanned the room with practiced ease. "You'd be surprised what we take an interest in." She glanced at Queenie, who had stopped at an empty table and was sniffing furiously. "Queenie's onto something."

The dog jerked at the leash. Eliza frowned. Queenie was trained—most of the time—and she rarely acted without reason. The beagle gave another sharp tug, her nose pressed to the floor under the corner table. "What is it, girl?" Eliza crouched down and reached under the table. Her hand brushed against something small and cold. She pinched it between her fingers. A gold cufflink. She picked it up and studied the design, a yellow gold scarab on turquoise enamel encircled by a band of delicate pearl. She turned it over in her palm, her mind racing. She knew this cufflink. It belonged to Ivan Grigor. What was it doing here?

"Anything?" Theo asked, appearing at her side.

"A cufflink," Eliza said flatly, slipping it into her pocket. "Exactly like the ones Ivan Grigor was wearing when he boarded the Orient Express."

"Let me see." Jane opened her palm. "Please."

Eliza obliged. "How did it get here?"

"Someone planted it here," Jane said, handing it back. "To lead us on a wild goose chase."

"Possibly." Eliza slid the cufflink into her pocket. But unlikely. More likely, Jane knew exactly what it was doing here and was trying to throw them off the scent. It couldn't be the cufflink Ivan was wearing on the train... unless someone had taken it off his dead body.

"The simpler explanation." Theo grinned. "Ivan Grigor was here and dropped it. Occam's razor is sometimes effective."

"I prefer facts to razors," Eliza shot back, straightening up. "And the fact is, Ivan was wearing these when he died. So, he couldn't have dropped it." She smirked. "Unless like Lazarus, he rose from the dead."

He shrugged.

She raised her eyebrows. "Someone else dropped it. Or left

it here." She paused. "And if this cufflink belonged to Ivan, perhaps it was left by his killer."

Queenie yipped.

"Taken off his dead body for some reason."

Theo got a funny look on his face. "Does that music sound familiar?"

"Come on." She weaved her way through the tables. The pianist had just finished another sad song. She stood at the back of the instrument and watched as the pianist's hands appeared and disappeared beneath the lid of the baby grand. He turned the page on his music. She couldn't believe what she saw. Her breath caught. At the top of the page, *Lena Grigor* was inscribed in bold, black ink. "Look," she whispered, nodding toward the sheet music. "It's Lena's composition."

Theo stared at the pianist. "What if she left it as a breadcrumb?" He leaned closer. "A trail to follow?"

"Or she left it for someone." With a glass of arak in hand, Agatha joined them. She must have the hearing of a bat. "Another secret, coded message." She was clearly in her element, her eyes sparkling as she surveyed the café. "I saw the waiter bring it to him. Maybe Lena left it for the pianist, or for whoever's supposed to collect it."

Eliza's gaze darted to the waiter, a petite man weaving gracefully between tables, balancing trays of coffee cups. "Let's split up," she said, handing Queenie's lead to Jane. "Agatha, Dorothy, do your usual: charm people, ask questions. Jane, keep an eye on the waiter. Theo and I will deal with the pianist."

"Don't get too far ahead of yourself, dearest," Jane said, her voice soft. "If this ties back to Ivan"—she put her hand to Eliza's ear and whispered—"and the microfilm"—she took a step back and gave Eliza a knowing look—"it's bigger than you think. And more dangerous."

"Don't forget about the Obsidian Cartel." Eliza's tone was curt. It wasn't that she didn't respect Jane or wasn't glad she was here. It was MI5 she didn't trust. Nothing like government bureaucracy to gum up the works. "If we wait for you to file a report back to London"—she smiled— "we'll be here until next Christmas."

Jane's lips twitched, but she said nothing.

With Theo in tow, Eliza circled around the piano. The pianist's dark eyes flicked to her, sharp and assessing, before returning to the music, his fingers dancing over the keys with ease.

"That's a lovely piece," Eliza said, her tone measured. "Who is the composer?" She took a step closer to the musician's stool.

The man's hands faltered for a fraction of a second, an almost imperceptible mistake, but Eliza caught it. He looked up at her fully now, his face carefully blank. "No English." He shrugged.

She crossed her arms and then repeated her question in French. Theo joined her and leaned in to get a better look at the sheet music.

The pianist's expression tightened but he shook his head. He knew something—of that, she was certain.

From across the café, Queenie gave a sharp bark. Had the dog found another clue? Eliza glanced around.

Jane had followed the waiter to a corner table, where he'd paused to exchange words with a man in a tailored, gray suit. Queenie seemed especially interested in the waiter. Or was it the tray of kebabs he was delivering?

At the other end of the room, Agatha was gesturing animatedly, holding court with a group of bemused patrons while Dorothy stood, arms akimbo, shaking her head.

Eliza turned back to the pianist, her voice low but firm. "Where did you get that sheet music?" She tried German this time. "*Wo ist Lena Grigor?*"

The man's hands stilled on the keys, his face betraying the slightest flicker of fear. He shook his head, said something in Turkish, and went back to playing. But now his hands were trembling slightly.

"Do you mind if I take a quick look at your sheet music?" Theo asked, pointing.

The man snatched the music off the piano and stared at Theo with wide eyes. Obviously, he understood English better than he was letting on.

Theo reached over and, with one finger, tapped out the melody from the song the pianist had been playing. As he did, he named the notes, "A-G-A-D-A-G-A." He looked over at Eliza. "It repeats those letters."

Clutching the music to his chest, the pianist slid off his stool and darted behind a curtain. Eliza dashed after him. As soon as she parted the curtain, she knew she'd made a mistake. The kitchen was small and crowded and steamy. Four men wearing white aprons and cooks' hats stared at her. They were big and didn't look happy about an intruder in their kitchen. She glanced around the narrow room just in time to glimpse the pianist slipping out the back door. She could foot-fight her way through the room, but she didn't want to set off an international incident. Especially since the biggest of the bunch was wielding a butcher's knife.

"Sorry." She grimaced and ducked back into the café.

Her sister and her friends were huddled at the bar. Queenie sat at attention next to Jane's feet. Eliza joined them.

"A-G-A-D-A-G-A," Theo said. "Do you think it could be code?"

"For what?" Agatha asked. "Agad aga. Agada ga. Aga Daga." It sounded like a tongue-twisting nursery rhyme.

"Look," Dorothy said, pointing to a page in her guidebook, which was laid out on the bar. "Aga Daga." She picked up the book and read, "This ancient ruin is steeped in legend, from its origins as a sacred site for the worship of Cybele to its time as a secluded Ottoman retreat. Wander past crumbling archways and hidden cisterns. Locals say it's haunted. If you're lucky, you might hear whispers on the wind." She looked up and chuckled. "Sounds delightful."

"Let's go," Agatha said. Obviously, she'd forgotten all about getting to the dig in Ur. Nothing like a good treasure hunt to enliven the spirits. Hopefully, the treasure wouldn't turn out to be Lena Grigor's corpse.

"Where are we going?" Eliza asked as she bent down to pet Queenie. The dog nuzzled her hand.

"The sheet music," Theo said. "A-G-A-D-A-G-A." He fiddled with his cap. "That refrain repeated over and over. We think it could be another coded location."

"Right." Dorothy waved her guidebook. "I remembered reading about the Aga Daga ruins."

"Perhaps, Lena Grigor is hiding there." Agatha clapped her hands together. "On the run from the police."

"Or worse, from the Obsidian Cartel," Eliza said under her breath.

"Or maybe your friend Lena Grigor is leading you a merry chase," Jane said, shaking her head. "If those are codes in the sheet music, they aren't very sophisticated."

"Sorry they aren't up to the standards of MI5." Eliza slipped her hand through the end of Queenie's lead. "But right now, they're all we've got to go on." She suspected Jane was trying to shake them by downplaying the clues.

"Breadcrumbs," Theo said. "Musical breadcrumbs."

Eliza spotted it lying on the floor like the gauzy skin shed by a coral snake. Around the foot of a chair in a back corner, a red, scarlet, silk scarf. She dashed over and picked it up. She recognized it. The scarf Lena was wearing on the train. Yes, Lena had been here. And the scarf proved she'd been here recently, after she'd left the train.

Waving the scarf, Eliza said, "At least we have evidence that Lena was here. And recently, too." Whatever the Baghdad Café was hiding, she was determined to find out. "Someone here must have seen her." She scanned the crowd. "Let's ask again."

Using all the languages at her disposal, she circled the café, asking the waitstaff and the customers if they'd seen an attractive Russian woman wearing the scarf. None of them had. Or if they had, they wouldn't admit it. When she questioned the man behind the bar, he reached for the scarf and insisted it belonged to his cousin. She held it to her chest. She wasn't about to relinquish it. It was hard evidence.

She'd collected all the evidence the Baghdad Café was willing to give up, so she led the group back to the ferry, and then to the trolley and back to the Pera Palace Hotel, where they'd had their luggage delivered from the train. They'd been instructed to stay at the hotel until the police were satisfied none of them were killers.

An hour later, she was standing in front of a large, stone building, which sat at a dignified angle, jutting into the intersection of East and West. Stepping inside, she was transported to another world where chandeliers dripped crystal above heavy, velvet draperies, chairs, divans, and ottomans that swaddled visitors in shades of red. Enormous, ornate ceilings, arched windows, and blue glass domes gave the place the feel of an enchanted cave. Mouth open, Eliza gawked upward in awe. Resisting the temptation to stand there soaking in the scene, she asked for her key.

"Meet back here in the lobby in fifteen minutes," she said to the others and then headed straight to her room to change for the trek to Aga Daga. They had to hurry to make it there and back before sunset. As she slid the key into the door lock, she noticed the engraving on the room key. In baroque script, the letters PPH. Just like the key she'd nicked from Peachy's cabin. The key she still had hidden in her luggage. After they returned from the ruins, she knew where she was going next. To Peachy's hotel room.

She surveyed the hotel room. It was nicely appointed with mahogany furniture, including a writing desk, and burgundy drapes and matching bedspread. Eliza hurriedly changed out of her skirt into the new knickerbockers she'd purchased in London before the trip. The woolen trousers were loose fitting and quite liberating. She rolled the long socks over her calves and then pulled on knee-high boots. She slipped on a thigh-length, woolen jacket that matched the knickerbockers and topped off the ensemble with a matching pith-style hat. Wearing trousers was exhilarating. She stopped in front of the mirror and gave a quick ju-jitsu kick. Yes, these would do nicely. She wanted to be prepared for the excursion to the Aga Daga ruins. What they would find there was anybody's guess.

* * *

An hour later, Theo stood at the edge of the ruins, brushing dust from his sleeves. The crumbling remains of Aga Daga felt ancient, older than the city sprawling beyond the Bosphorus, older than the tarnished minarets in the distance. The wind stirred up dry leaves and turned them into whirling dervishes dancing atop the stone steps. A Byzantine column half-swallowed by time jutted from the earth at an awkward angle. Beyond it, the black mouth of a tunnel yawned beneath the hill. He left the others poking around the ruins. Boots scraping against the loose gravel, he headed for the hill.

"Where are you going?" Eliza called after him.

"The tunnel," he said, without looking back.

Lena's music had brought him here, each note leading deeper into the mystery. And now he stood before the remnants of time, both sacred and forgotten. What did this place mean to those who had come before him? What was it like one hundred years ago? Two hundred? A thousand? He stopped to stare at a gnarled fig tree. "What wonders have you seen in the last hundred years?" he said under his breath.

And the huge rocks beside the entrance to the tunnel. Were they witnesses to human beings, in their own ways, century after century, reaching for God? To turf wars and lovers' trysts. The river below, the cavern up ahead, the very earth itself. These were the constants, indifferent to the tides of man washing up on their shores. The fig tree didn't care what robes a man wore, or which god he worshipped, or who he loved and what he fought for. The fig tree didn't declare war on the olive tree because its fruit was different from his own.

Theo thought of Tennyson: "Nature, red in tooth and claw." And yet, of God's creations, it wasn't the beasts who were cruelest. It was man. Only man killed his fellows merely for being different from himself. Only man enslaved his neighbors and used nature to justify his lust for power and riches. The deaths of Ivan and Peachy and their ties to the Obsidian Cartel weren't far from his mind.

"Wait for me!" Eliza's voice brought him out of his reverie. In her knickerbockers, she looked like Nellie Bly, ready for a trip around the world—either that or a round of golf.

"You're looking sharp." He repressed a grin.

"I feel sharp." She caught him up and pressed a pointy finger into his arm.

"Indeed." At her touch, the repressed grin escaped. "Where do you think it leads?" He nodded toward the tunnel.

"Let's find out, shall we?" She took his arm.

The wind whistled through the trees, howling a warning. As they approached the tunnel's mouth, a shadow moved along the inside wall. The crunching beneath their feet was accompanied by another sound. A clanging.

He glanced around. "What's that noise and where is it coming from?" It sounded like metal on metal. Was it the wind?

He slowed his pace. Eliza didn't. If anything, she picked up speed. She disappeared into the darkness and the noise stopped abruptly. In silhouette, he saw her kick at something. As if in slow motion, she whirled around, her legs like a propeller, her boots making contact with a shadowy form. Thwack. The sounds of shuffling gave way to groaning. Heart racing, Theo sprinted into the cave. As his eyes adjusted to the darkness, a metal case came into view. Crumpled next to it was a man. He couldn't make out his face. Eliza stood over the man, holding a gun. Where did she get that?

"What's going on?" He dashed to her side. "Who's that?"

"Our old friend, the French train inspector." Eliza kicked at him with the toe of her boot. "Not very nice to greet your old pals with a gun, though." She waved the weapon at him. "You might as well finish what you started and hammer the lock off that case." Using the gun, she motioned toward the metal case. "Go on, then. Get it open."

The man crawled to his feet, picked up his hammer, and glared at Eliza.

"Well?" Eliza pointed the gun at him. "What are you waiting for?"

He raised the hammer. But instead of striking the lock, he threw it at Eliza. It hit her in the head. With an eerie scream, she crumpled to the ground.

"Eliza!" His heart in his throat, Theo stared down at her.

The man ran further into the tunnel and disappeared.

Gritting his teeth, Theo fell to his knees. He gently brushed the hair from her face. "Eliza." He lifted her head. She was breathing. In the dim light, he couldn't see if she was wounded. He felt a sticky wetness on his hand where he was holding her head. Blood. "Eliza, please." He took her hand and squeezed it. He closed his eyes and channeled all his strength, the entirety of his life force, into her hand. "Please," he repeated. *If there is a God, please let him spare her.*

A loud roar echoed through the tunnel. The smell of petrol hit his nose. In a flash, a motorcycle thundered past, nearly running them over. So that was why the fiend ran into the tunnel instead of out. He had a motorcycle stashed back there. The man exited the tunnel in a cloud of exhaust.

Theo coughed. One arm under Eliza's shoulder and the other under her knees, he scooped her off the ground. As he did, he grabbed the gun and slid it into his pocket. He held her tightly to his chest. "Eliza, Eliza, Eliza." Every time he whispered her name, it was as if he were praying.

15

THE PERA PALACE HOTEL

Eliza woke up and put her hand to her head. It hurt. And there was a rather large sticking plaster attached to her forehead. When she opened her eyes, the room was blurry. Where was she? What happened?

Someone licked her hand. "Queenie." The warmth of her best friend next to her was reassuring. "Where are we?"

"We're at the Pera Palace Hotel," said a familiar voice.

"Theo?" She turned her head and fixed her attention on his blurry face.

"I'm here." Theo's sweet smile came into focus.

"What happened?" When she tried to sit up, the room started spinning. She sank back into the pillow. "Where's Jane?"

"Jane and DI Orhan went back to the ruins." He squeezed her hand. "As for you..." He told her about their encounter with the impostor French train inspector at the Aga Daga ruins. The tunnel. The metal case. The foot-fighting and the gun, which he'd turned over to D.I. Orhan. The hammer. The hit on the head. And the motorcycle escape. "Are you alright?" His cheeks turned the color of dusty roses. "I was beside myself with worry."

"I'll be okay." She touched her head and winced. The way her head was pounding, she wondered if she would be okay. "Where's Dorothy? And Agatha?" Queenie nuzzled closer and she reached out to pet the beagle's head.

Theo's lips twitched. "They went back to the ruin with Jane to fetch the chest."

"What!" Eliza sat up. She regretted it. She held on to the headboard for support. "Was that wise? What if the fiendish fake train inspector comes back? This time with evil associates?"

Queenie barked.

"Jane and D.I. Orhan are professionals. Agatha and Dorothy are writers."

"I tried to talk them out of it." Theo shrugged. "But they thought it was a terribly exciting adventure. And once the doctor said you'd be alright, they set out."

"In the dark!" She swallowed hard, not sure if her nausea was caused by the head injury or the shock of hearing that her sister along with her boss and England's most famous mystery writer had set out on a dangerous mission... without her.

Queenie must have sensed her agitation. The dog wriggled up closer to her face and started licking her nose. Tightening her lips and turning her head to avoid a messy kiss, she hugged the beagle and pressed her down at the same time.

"I'm afraid you've been out cold for a while." Theo smiled weakly. "They set out first thing this morning."

"Oh my." She tried to process everything. "How long have I been out?"

He glanced at his watch. "About thirty hours."

"Oh dear." She closed her eyes and leaned back into the

headboard. "And the investigation?" She caressed Queenie's soft ears.

"No one has seen hide nor hair of Lena Grigor." Theo tightened his lips. "I fear the worst."

"What about the murders?" She put a hand to her forehead and pressed on the plaster to counter the pain. "Any news?"

Theo shook his head. "The official statement from the railway lines is Ivan Grigor's death was a heart attack. The local authorities are doing an autopsy now." He sighed. "Obviously, Peachy Fitzroy was shot. And D.I. Orhan is checking ballistics on the gun you took from the man in the tunnel to see if it's a match."

"The French train inspector." She picked at the edge of the blanket. "I'm betting he doesn't work for the railway at all." She shifted in the bed, which caused Queenie to shift too. "He's probably an operative of the Obsidian Cartel. Maybe an assassin."

"We will know soon enough." Theo stood up and went to the window. He turned back to her. "What do you think happened to Lena?"

"I don't know." She shuddered to think of Lena's body thrown off the Orient Express somewhere between Nilš and Constantinople. They needed more information. She remembered Peachy's key—the one engraved with PPH that she'd found in his pocket—and threw the blanket off. Queenie barked in protest and jumped to the floor. "We need to search Peachy's room." When Eliza realized she was wearing only her smalls, she clutched the blanket and pulled it back up to her chest. Queenie sat on the floor looking up at her with those sweet, chocolate eyes.

"Your clothes were covered in blood." Theo's cheeks turned almost as red. "So, Jane sent them to be cleaned." He whirled around and looked out the window again. "Would you like me to leave so you can rest?"

"I'd like to get dressed and go investigate Peachy's hotel room." She took advantage of his turned back and slipped out of bed.

"Why would Peachy have a hotel room?" Theo twisted his head around. When their eyes met, he whipped back around to face the window. "He's dead."

"The key I found. It is a key to a Pera Palace Hotel room." She went to the cupboard. Queenie followed close on her heels. "Just like the keys to our rooms." She looked inside for her suitcase, which was sitting on a luggage stand. "He told us he liked to write at the hotel." She opened the case and pulled out a skirt and then a blouse. "I think he must have kept a room here," she said, buttoning her blouse. "This is where he worked on his exposé." She stepped into the skirt and pulled it up around her waist. "And if I'm right, we may find clues to identify his killer." She grabbed her boots and returned to sit on the edge of the bed. Queenie followed and sat at her feet. "Who knows, maybe we'll find Lena Grigor?" With Queenie in hot pursuit, she returned to the cupboard and plucked a couple of sample tubes from her case and slipped them in her pocket. The prospect of sleuthing brightened her spirits—and did wonders for her headache. Better than BC powders.

"Good heavens." Theo turned from the window. "You think Lena and Peachy were... were... collaborators?" Was he suggesting they were lovers? She hadn't thought of that. But a love triangle would be a darn good motive for murder.

She shrugged. "Anything is possible." She bent to pet Queenie. "You be a good girl and stay here. Uncle Theo and I have a job to do."

Queenie sat at attention.

"Good girl." Eliza gave the beagle a biscuit from her pocket. "We'll be back soon."

The biscuit between her teeth, Queenie trotted across the room, jumped onto the bed, and growled, one paw protecting her bounty.

* * *

The Pera Palace Hotel keys did not have the room numbers on them. Probably for security reasons. But Eliza had no trouble persuading the clerk to give her the number for her "Uncle Peachy's" room, where she claimed to have left her college textbook for the honor's English class she needed to finish and graduate Oxford. Theo might have been more believable in the role as a student of literature, but the clerk was a young man, and she knew from experience that a pretty smile and a toss of blonde curls worked better than either sincerity or eloquence where young men were concerned. When she showed the clerk the key, and said she'd forgotten the room number, he was only too happy to oblige.

"Room 333," he said with a broad smile. "Is there anything else I can help you with, miss?"

"No, thank you." She returned his smile. "You've been very helpful."

When they reached the lift, Theo gave her a sideways look. "Were you flirting with him?" He pushed the button.

"Of course!" She flipped her curls over her shoulder.

"You had the poor chap eating out of the palm of your hand." He shook his head. "No wonder you have men swarming around you like flies."

"In your metaphor"—the door opened and she stepped inside—"am I manure or honey? Both attract flies."

"Definitely sweet." He followed her in.

There was something about being alone in a lift that intensified proximity. She was forcefully aware of Theo standing next to her. She had to actively focus on not looking at him. When she did glance over, he caught her gaze and her cheeks warmed. Why? They were just good friends. Right? Pals? She'd grown up with him. Nothing more, she reminded herself. It was absurd to even entertain. She inhaled the scent of him. Cedarwood, lime, and something else. Something uniquely Theo. Something that caused a tightening in her chest.

The lift door opened on the third floor. And not a moment too soon. The heady scent of Theo might have made her do something she would regret. She stepped out and, key in hand, headed up the hall looking for room 333.

She wasn't sure why, but she knocked on the door. Maybe it was the *DO NOT DISTURB* sign. She didn't expect anyone to answer. Still, it seemed prudent. After a few seconds, she inserted the key in the lock. The door popped open. "Voilà." She was right. The key was to Peachy's room. By the look of it, he'd been living in the Pera Palace Hotel for some time. Books and magazines were piled everywhere, an ashtray on the table overflowed with butts, and a pair of slippers sat cockeyed near the bed. The suit jacket thrown across the back of a chair gave the impression Peachy had just popped out to buy cigarettes and would be back at any minute.

Stepping over discarded clothes and magazines, she crossed the room and peeked into the cupboard. Not all his clothes were on the floor. A nice dinner jacket hung next to a starched, white shirt and black trousers. At the back of the cupboard, she found a small case. It was locked. She carried it to the writing desk and, using one of her hairpins, jimmied the lock. Inside, a neat stack of envelopes was tied up with a royal-blue bow. She examined them. Whoa. They were old letters to Peachy from Dorothy.

"His first volume," Theo said, holding up a book. "The one on poisons." He flipped through the pages.

"Look what I found. Letters from Dorothy." She waved the packet of letters. "Probably some pretty juicy stuff in here." Which was precisely why she put them back in the case without reading any of them. If they didn't find any other clues, and she wanted to read them later, she knew where to find them. For now, she wouldn't intrude on the privacy of Dorothy's past. Although she was curious. Was Peachy blackmailing Dorothy, too? Maybe she should keep the letters. Return them to Dorothy before the police found them.

"You're not going to read them, are you?" He lifted an eyebrow. "I'm not feeling good about rummaging through a dead man's things."

"We're not rummaging." She replaced the letters, closed the case, and sat it by the door to take to Dorothy. "We're investigating a murder, remember?"

"Shouldn't we leave it to the police?" Still holding the book, he came to her side. "I'm surprised they haven't been here already."

"Exactly why we should not leave it to them." She pushed the clothing aside and peered into the back of the cupboard. "Well, what have we here?" A small safe was tucked into the corner. She bent to get a closer look. "You don't happen to have a torch on you?"

"No." He poked his head into the cupboard. "But I have a match." He stuck the book under his arm, fumbled in his pocket, and withdrew a box of matches.

The steel rotary combination lock reflected the flickering light. "You don't happen to know how to crack a safe, do you?"

She'd had a good deal of experience picking locks but not cracking safes. The infractions of her youth were petty crimes. She'd never robbed a bank or a hotel safe. The safe instructions indicated it was a four number combination set by the guest.

"I'm afraid I've lived a rather dull life." He chuckled. "That is, until I met you."

"What year was Peachy born?" She fiddled with the dial.

"Ouch!" He waved his hand and dropped the match. "No idea, sorry."

"He is probably about the same age as Dorothy." She turned the lock this way and that. "What year was she born?"

"Well, she's in her mid-thirties, so around 1894?" He leaned closer. "Why?"

"If Peachy is like most, he would use a familiar four-digit code." She spun the dial again, listening for a click. "Like his birth year."

"Clever." He watched over her shoulder. She could feel his presence but tried to ignore the heat behind her. He moved away and she felt his absence even more acutely. "I think I know how to find out."

Now she turned to see what he was doing. Flipping through the book again. "Born 1892," he said gleefully. "It's here in his author bio."

"Now who's clever." She smiled. "Let's try 1892," she repeated to herself as she turned the rotary to the right and then the left and then the right again. "Very clever indeed." With a satisfying click, she'd cracked the safe. "Can you light another match?" Her pulse quickened as she slid her hand inside the dark hole. Why was she anxious? It wasn't like he kept a snake in there.

Scratch. Hiss. The smell of sulfur. And the cupboard glowed in the dim light of Theo's match. She grasped a thick envelope and pulled it out. For good measure, she ran her hand around the inside of the safe to make sure she hadn't missed anything. Other than the envelope, it was empty. Clutching the treasure to her chest, she stood up. "I bet this is his manuscript." She weighed the heft in her hand. "Must be a couple hundred pages at least."

"A copy of his exposé?" Theo backed out of the cupboard to give her room to pass.

She exited the cupboard. "If so, then why was he distraught when his manuscript disappeared from the train?" She took a seat at the writing table.

"The Obsidian Cartel?" Theo shrugged. "Maybe, if it fell into the wrong hands..." He grimaced. "If that's why he was killed, it could be dangerous."

"Since when is reading dangerous?" She rolled her eyes. "You crime writers sit around dreaming up clever ways to kill people. But the results are nothing more than words on a page."

"You'd be surprised." Theo cocked his head. "In one way or another, words are the inciting incidents for most crime."

"What about deeds?" She grabbed a letter opener off Peachy's desk and sliced through the crease of the flap. "What about, sticks and stones may break my bones but words will never hurt me?"

"A cruel word from an esteemed colleague or precious paramour"—he lowered his voice—"can hurt worse than the deepest cut from a blade." He got a strange look on his face, as if a blade had been thrust between his ribs. His lips twitched. "I should know."

She sighed. "I hope you're not going to start calling me cruel again." Before he'd left for Paris, he'd said she was cruel.

She wasn't cruel. Just honest. What Jane called bluntness, she called honesty.

"I wasn't..." His voice trailed off. He closed his eyes and exhaled. "So, what's inside? Is it the exposé?"

"Let's take a look, shall we?" The manuscript was fat and the envelope was tight. Carefully, she maneuvered the pages out of the envelope. "Blimey." The first page read:

> The Obsidian Cartel: Smuggling, Spies, and the Syndicate's Secret Weapon, by Hugo Fitzroy

The kind of title that could get someone killed. She sized up the manuscript. Geez. It was long. She didn't relish reading through three hundred pages looking for clues. "You're the writer," she said, holding it out to Theo. "You read it."

He took it with both hands. "Gladly."

"I'm going to take another look around." She relinquished her seat to Theo and resolved to go over every inch of the room with a fine-toothed comb.

* * *

Theo tried to concentrate on Peachy's manuscript, but Eliza's snooping around the room was distracting, especially since she had a large sticking plaster on her forehead. It didn't help that the exposé had too much backstory about Ivan's and Lena's early years to keep momentum going forward. He didn't need to know that after immigrating to England from Russia, Ivan worked as an attaché to the embassy and then moved to a position at the Bank of England, where he sponsored annual trips to the circus for Save the Children.

So far, Ivan Grigor sounded like a saint, not an operative of the Obsidian Cartel. Maybe Peachy wanted his reader to be invested in the protagonist before bringing him down with a twisty revelation about his criminal activities.

Lena's story was more colorful. Ivan met her at the circus where she worked as a snake charmer and trapeze artist, along with playing the piano. The elegant woman, it seemed, had hidden talents. *Hidden* being the operative word at this moment. Where was she? And why had she left sheet music and a scarf at the Baghdad Café?

The sound of a sharp exhale made him look up from the pages. Eliza was crawling on all fours, heading for the bed. "What in the world?" He stood up. "Should you be doing that?" He really should get her back to bed. Why had he allowed her to get out of bed in the first place? He sucked his teeth. Unfortunately, Eliza didn't need his permission. She did what she pleased and she was as stubborn as an ox. "You should be resting and—"

"I'll rest when I'm dead." She cut him off.

"Let's hope it doesn't come to that." He sighed. "The doctor said—"

"Blast the doctor." Her head disappeared under the bed.

Click. Keys jangled just on the other side of the door. He jerked his head in the direction of the sound and stuffed the pages back into their envelope.

"There's someone at the door." Clutching the manuscript, he lunged to the side of the bed. "Get under!"

She scooted under and he slid beneath after her. The sound of the door opening made his heart skip a beat. He put his finger to his lips. "Shhh." He shimmied away from the edge of the bed and to the center. His body was next to hers. He rolled to face her and pulled her closer so they couldn't be seen from the room—hopefully.

Voices entered the room, followed by footfalls. The click of high heels. A woman's voice. He pricked up his ears. The voice sounded familiar. He put his lips to Eliza's ear and whispered, "Lena?"

Eliza's hair smelled like springtime. He closed his eyes and put his arms around her. For all he knew, he was about to be executed by the Obsidian Cartel and all he could think about was Eliza's hair. The plaster on her forehead was rough against his chin and the envelope pressed into his chest. He held onto her for dear life and listened to the voices of the interlopers in Peachy's hotel room. If Lena was working for the Obsidian Cartel and discovered them under the bed, at least they'd die together.

"Look in the safe," Lena said. "He told me he had a second copy. We've got to find it."

"Someone's beat us to it!" The man's voice was familiar too. "The safe is empty."

Lena's heels tapped against the marble floor. "Then we're too late," she said. "The Cartel got here first."

Did that mean she wasn't part of the Obsidian Cartel? Unless she meant another cartel. Perhaps Obsidian's competitors.

"So it seems," the man said.

"Who is he?" Theo whispered.

"Did you hear something?" Lena said.

Theo clamped his mouth shut and held his breath.

"No," the man replied.

"I guess I'm just jumpy," Lena said. "Mr. Fitzroy's book is my death sentence."

Theo exhaled.

"Why do you say that?" the man asked.

"Because I've read it." There was fear in her voice.

What? Lena read Peachy's manuscript? When? On the train? Did he show it to her? Or is she the one who pinched it from his cabin?

"And it incriminates you?" the man said.

"Let's just say Mr. Fitzroy's tell-all tells more than I'd like my enemies to know." The sound of her heels clacked across the room. "In fact, every one of the Cartel's associates throughout Europe and beyond will want my head once that information gets out. How ironic." She scoffed. "If I survive Ivan's threats and venom only to die at the hands of his associates. And for what? To have everything ruined by Mr. Fitzroy's exposé."

"Should we give you a security detail?" he asked.

A security detail. Was the man with the police? *Wait. Is that D.I. Orhan?*

"I'll make contact with Jane Archer and she'll see to it." Lena's voice was hushed. "If I live long enough to come out of hiding."

"Jane." Eliza gasped.

Theo put a finger to her lips. He'd heard Jane had married last summer. Archer must be her married name.

"Did you hear that?" Lena asked.

"What?"

"Never mind." Papers rustled. She must be looking through Peachy's magazines. "The walls are thin. Either that or I'm hearing things."

The slap of a magazine hitting the floor startled Theo and he winced. He tightened his embrace around Eliza.

"You're as jumpy as a cat in a dog park," the man said. "Let's get you back to Tepebasi before someone sees you."

Tepebasi: the historic district near the Pera Palace Hotel.

The door clicked shut and silence fell over the room like a blanket. The sound of Theo's pulse beat in his ears. He loosened his grip on Eliza and rolled over on his back. "Whew. Close call." He took a deep breath and held the envelope to his chest. "What does your sister have to do with this?"

"I'm not sure." Eliza flattened herself on her stomach and scooted out from under the bed. "But I have an idea."

He followed her out, crawled to his knees, and then stood up. "This must contain some pretty damning evidence." He waved the manuscript. "I only got to the part where Ivan meets Lena at the circus—"

"What did she do at the circus?" Eliza squinted at him.

"Snake charmer, trapeze artist, piano player." He shrugged. "A bit of a Jacqueline-of-all-trades."

"Snake charmer?" Eliza brushed off her skirt. "What kind of snakes?"

"Ah, poisonous ones." His lips twitched. "Cobras."

"The neurotoxin." Her eyes went wide. "That's it!"

"Neurotoxin?" Did she think Lena poisoned Ivan with snake venom? How absurd.

"You finish reading." She ripped the sticking plaster off her head. "I'm going to find Jane."

"Should you do that?" He pointed to the gash on her forehead. "Maybe you should rest."

Ignoring him, she marched to the door, opened it, and then turned back to him. "And Theo, read fast."

"But... but..." Gulping like a fish out of water, he watched her leave, helpless to stop her.

16

THE BLOODHOUND

Armed with Queenie and the red, silk scarf, Eliza stepped out of the Pera Palace Hotel. She braced herself against the evening air, which was sharper than she expected. The cold sent a sting through the fresh wound at her temple, and she sucked in a breath as the ache pulsed behind her eyes. She pressed her fingers lightly to her forehead beneath her hat: damp. Blood, or maybe sweat. She couldn't tell. Maybe Theo was right. She shouldn't have ripped off the plaster.

At her side, Queenie sniffed at the scarf in Eliza's hand. Her velvety ears twitching with interest, the little beagle had already taken in the scent back in the room. Eliza prayed Lena's perfume, faint as it was, would still be enough to guide her.

"Find her, Queenie." She loosened the leash. The beagle let out a short huff, then put her nose to the ground and pulled forward.

Eliza followed, her steps uneven on the cobbled street beneath her feet. Her dizziness had lessened since she'd first woken, but the pounding in her skull hadn't. She had refused the laudanum the doctor had left for her at the hotel—she needed her mind sharp—but she was beginning to regret it. Maybe she should have at least had some aspirin powders.

She divided her attention between the crowded streets and focusing on Queenie.

The beagle led her down Meşrutiyet Avenue, her small frame determined as she pulled toward the tram tracks. A tram clattered past, its whistle piercing through Eliza's skull like a knife. She flinched at the sound and stumbled, nearly pitching forward onto the stones. A passing bookseller caught her by the elbow, his face a blur of concern. "*Hanımefendi, iyi misiniz?*" He repeated in English, "Miss, are you alright?"

"I'm fine," she lied, wrenching herself free, her heart hammering with something dangerously close to panic. The hammer must have hit her head harder than she knew. In addition to the concussion, it had shaken her confidence.

She blinked hard, trying to focus on Queenie, who had barely hesitated, still tracking something, weaving past a group of French tourists lingering outside St. Anthony of Padua Church. The scent of incense curled from the arched doorway, sweet and cloying, masking everything else. Eliza swallowed against the nausea clawing up her throat and forced herself to move faster, her bare fingers tightening on the leash.

Queenie turned sharply down a side street, her tail wagging with certainty. Eliza's stomach twisted. The path was darker here, shadowed by the tall buildings on either side. She risked a glance behind her; was someone following them? The sensation of being watched prickled along her spine, but when she turned, the street was filled only with the regular faces: a man reading a newspaper, a woman adjusting the flowers in her cart, a group of boys playing with a ball.

She shook off the feeling. *Focus. Find Lena Grigor.*

Queenie led her past the edge of a café terrace where a

pianist played a lazy tune for a boisterous crowd. The notes sounded warped, as if they were drifting from underwater. The concussion. It was distorting her perception. But now was not the time to dwell on it.

The beagle pulled toward an iron-railed staircase leading up to a stately building whose grandeur had been softened by the patina of sea air. Gilded balconies wrapped around upper floors. The name *Büyük Londra Hotel* was carved into the stone above the entrance. Eliza exhaled sharply, her grip tightening on Queenie's leash. A parrot on the second-floor balcony squawked a greeting, making her jump.

Queenie sat at the base of the steps, her tail thumping against the stone, looking up expectantly. The scent had led them here.

Eliza swallowed past the dryness in her throat, steadying herself before pushing open the brass-trimmed doors.

If Lena was inside, they would find her.

Unfortunately, the nagging sensation of being followed told her she wasn't the only one searching.

Stepping inside, Eliza was greeted by the scent of old wood polish, faint cigar smoke, and a lingering trace of amber perfume. A heavy brass chandelier, its crystals dulled with dust, swung gently above the lobby, which was filled with well-worn, plush armchairs, their velvet faded in places by years of use. The wooden reception desk had deep gouges on its legs from the cleaning staff hitting it with the Hoover. A woman behind the reception desk gave her an odd look. And a man looked up from his newspaper. But no one said anything as she and her little dog walked across the lobby.

She stuffed the scarf in her coat pocket, but not before giving Queenie another sniff. "Come on, girl." She gave the leash a gentle tug. "Let's find Lena."

The dog led her to a stairwell and then stopped and looked up at her. She opened the door and waited for Queenie to lead the way. Her nose to the ground, the beagle picked up speed as she climbed the stairs. Nothing could distract her when she was on a scent. On the second-floor landing, the dog stopped and turned in circles. After a few confused seconds, she pawed at the door.

The dimly lit hallway stretched long and narrow, its plush, red carpet muffling her footsteps as she followed Queenie. Ornate sconces cast flickering shadows on the faded wallpaper. Heavy, wooden doors with brass numbers lined the corridor, each leading to a guest room. If Queenie was right—and she usually was—then behind one of these doors, they would find Lena Grigor.

The little beagle padded softly up the hallway, her nose twitching as she followed an invisible trail only she could perceive. Eliza stayed a few paces behind, letting Queenie work. The hallway smelled faintly of polished wood and old books, with a lingering trace of pipe smoke from some long-past visitor. But Queenie wasn't interested in any of that.

Near the end of the corridor, the dog paused, nostrils flaring, head tilting slightly. Then, with renewed focus, she picked up her pace, trotting to a closed door on the right. She sniffed at the gap beneath it, gave a quiet whine, then scratched lightly at the wood.

"Good girl, Queenie," Eliza whispered and bent down to give her pal a congratulatory pat. She straightened and adjusted her hat. The moment of truth. She took a deep breath and knocked on the door. She waited. Nothing.

"Lena, I know you're in there." Holding her fist in mid-air, she listened. She heard shuffling inside. "Lena, it's Eliza Baker, from the Orient Express." She knocked again. "I just want to talk to you." She waited and listened again. Silence. "About Hugo Fitzroy's manuscript."

The door flew open. Startled, Eliza took a step back. Tail going a mile a minute, Queenie sniffed Lena's boots.

Lena glanced down for a fraction of a second and then pulled Eliza inside. "Get in here before someone sees us."

The hotel room looked unoccupied. Quite the opposite of Peachy Fitzroy's room at the Pera Palace. The bed was neatly made, the draperies pulled, and not a single personal item anywhere to be seen. Then again, Lena Grigor had simply vanished off the Orient Express. Neat trick. And now here she was in Constantinople, having avoided questioning by Detective Inspector Orhan or MI5.

"I won't ask how you found me," Lena said, scowling at Queenie. "The question is, why? What do you want with me?" She gestured to a small sitting area in one corner of the room and then crossed over and dropped into an overstuffed chair. "And what's this about Mr. Fitzroy's manuscript?"

Eliza followed her and sat down in an adjacent chair. "Everyone is looking for you." *Including the Obsidian Cartel.* She could tell by the look on Lena's face she didn't need to say it. It was obvious Lena was in trouble. "What were you doing in Peachy, Mr. Fitzroy's room at Pera Palace?"

Lena furrowed her brows. "How did you know about that?"

"I was there." Eliza snapped her fingers and Queenie trotted over to the side of the chair. She pointed at the floor and the dog lay down and put her head on her paws but never took her eyes off her mistress. "Why were you there?"

Lena exhaled sharply, eyes flicking toward the door as if she expected someone to barge in at any moment. Then, with a reluctant sigh, she sank back into the chair. "I needed something." She folded her arms tightly across her chest. "Something Hugo left behind."

Eliza tilted her head. "The manuscript."

Lena scoffed, shaking her head. "Not the manuscript. Something inside it."

Eliza didn't react, though her mind was already turning over the possibilities. Lena was being careful, too careful. The way she spoke, the way her eyes darted around the room, the way her hand twitched toward the small satchel at her feet. This wasn't just guilt. This was fear. "What? What inside it?"

Lena shook her head and looked toward the window.

Eliza waited a beat, then changed tactics. "How long were you in the circus?"

Lena flinched.

Eliza smiled. "You didn't think I knew, did you?" She tapped a finger against the arm of her chair. "Snake charmer, wasn't it? Working with cobras, whose poison contains deadly neurotoxins."

Lena's eyes darkened.

"I can see you under the big tent. Every time a snake struck at you, the audience gasps, never realizing you'd built up an immunity to the venom over years of careful exposure." Eliza's voice was measured, her words deliberate. "Yes, you and Ivan ate from the same plate the night he died. But you'd built up an immunity to the venom and that's why you survived when he didn't. Because you knew exactly what kind of poison to use. And exactly how much."

Lena's hands clenched into fists on her lap. "You don't know what you're talking about."

Eliza sat on the edge of her seat. "Don't I?"

Lena's nostrils flared, but she stayed silent.

"Ivan was blackmailing you," Eliza said, pushing further.

"He found out something. Something dangerous. And you knew if he talked, you were dead." She squinted. "So, what was it, Lena? What did Ivan know that made you so desperate?"

Lena's jaw tensed. She stayed quiet for a long moment, then finally whispered, "He found out I wasn't just his wife."

Eliza stilled.

Lena exhaled slowly, her gaze flicking toward the door before she spoke again, her voice barely above a whisper. "He discovered that I was working against him."

A chill ran down Eliza's spine. "You're a spy," she said carefully.

Lena shook her head sharply. "Don't say that. You don't understand." She wet her lips. "They're everywhere, Miss Baker." Her voice was raw. "If they find out—if they even suspect—I won't make it out of this city alive." She was trembling.

"If you're not working for the Obsidian Cartel..." Eliza sat back, absorbing the full weight of Lena's fear. "Who are you working for?"

Glancing around the room again, Lena hesitated. She leaned forward and whispered, "Your sister."

Eliza inhaled sharply. "Jane?"

Lena nodded. "She is my contact." She let out a humorless laugh. "Funny, isn't it? You and I circling each other, neither of us realizing we're on the same side."

Eliza shook her head in disbelief. "Jane never told me."

"She wouldn't. She couldn't." Lena's expression turned grim. "Ivan found out. He intercepted messages, found things he wasn't meant to see. He gave me a choice: Cut ties with MI5 and work for him, or... suffer the consequences." She exhaled. "You can't imagine what he was capable of." She picked at the worn, velvet arm of her chair.

"The coded music." Eliza tilted her head. She couldn't believe Jane hadn't told her. "I should have known."

Lena gave a wistful chuckle. "Jane sent a low-level operative to spy on you and—"

"Spy on me!" Geez. Didn't Jane trust her to take care of herself?

"Not spy exactly." Lena shifted in her seat. "Keep an eye on you. Protect you."

"I see." She tightened her lips. The creepy monocled man from the train. She was going to have to have a talk with Jane.

"After Ivan threatened me, I had to let MI5 know I was in danger." Lena sucked in a breath. "I only hoped your babysitter could get my message to your sister in time." Her expression twisted. "Ivan was many things—a thief, a smuggler—but he was more than that. He had ties to the Obsidian Cartel. He helped move their stolen goods across Europe. And he sold information." She paused. "About British Intelligence." One of her eyes twitched. "Jane wanted me on the inside, feeding her information. I was supposed to stay close, gather intel on what they knew."

The microfilm.

"But then..." Lena licked her lips. "He found out."

Eliza's pulse quickened. "And he tried to use it against you."

Lena gave a hollow laugh. "You think Ivan would just turn me in? No. He wanted leverage. Otherwise..." She trailed off, her expression tightening.

Eliza finished the thought. "He would have handed you over to the Cartel."

Lena nodded.

Eliza exhaled. "So, you killed him first."

Lena's voice was barely a whisper. "I didn't have a choice."

Eliza watched her carefully. "And now you're here, hiding

from the Cartel." She shifted in her seat. "But how did you get off the train without anyone seeing you?"

"An advantage to being small." She chuckled. "I hid under a cart in the restaurant car before it was switched in Nilš." She waved her hand. "Once the Orient Express was underway again, I simply took the next train to Istanbul, as we prefer to call it."

"Why risk coming here?" Eliza narrowed her eyes. Tilting her head, she thought a minute. "Because you're still looking for something." She glanced at Lena's bag. "Something at the Baghdad Café." She watched for Lena's reaction.

Lena's eyes went wide. "How do you know about the café?"

She smiled. "Your coded message." She didn't mention it was Theo and Dorothy who worked it out.

Lena blew out a breath. "The café is where Ivan met his Cartel contacts." She fiddled with a button on her blouse. "My cousin works there." She paused. "It's also where I was to meet Jane." Her eyes filled with tears. "I got there early and waited. But when one of the Cartel's thugs showed up, I made my escape." When she closed her eyes, a tear ran down her cheek. "I left one of Ivan's cufflinks and another piece of coded music." She suddenly stood up. "Tell your sister I have to leave Istanbul. I can't wait any longer for MI5 to extract me, as they say."

"You still haven't told me why you came here in the first place." Eliza gazed up at the petite Russian. "Was it to meet Jane? Or something else?" Why would MI5 arrange to meet Lena in Istanbul if it wasn't safe? Why not someplace else? Why was Lena in Peachy's room? What was she looking for? And who was with her? "Something Hugo Fitzroy had. Something you need."

Lena's mouth pressed into a thin line. She walked to the window and looked out.

"Let me guess." Eliza sat back. "It's not the jewels or the money. It's not the manuscript. It's information."

Lena's fingers twitched.

Eliza narrowed her eyes. "Something he wrote. Something hidden inside the pages."

Lena finally spoke, her voice low and urgent. "Hugo had a list."

Eliza's breath caught. The list of British agents, most of whom were still in the field.

"A list of names," Lena continued. "Contacts. Associates. Operatives who worked with Ivan: some of them in the Cartel, some of them spies embedded in governments. He was going to use it to expose them. That's why they killed him." Her lip trembled. "That's why my cousin and I went into Hugo's room. To look for the list inside his manuscript."

They killed him. The Cartel. Eliza's mind raced. The man with her in Peachy's room was not Detective Inspector Orhan, but her cousin. The barman from the café. And the list she needed was not the list from the microfilm. But another list deadly to the Cartel. A list they'd do anything to get their hands on. "And you need it to stay alive. The list of Cartel operatives." She thought a minute. "You plan to exchange that information for your life."

Lena nodded once.

Eliza processed this. Hugo Fitzroy's exposé had been more than just a tell-all; it had contained dangerous information. The kind of information people would kill for.

Before she could say another word, a noise outside the door made them both freeze.

Someone was coming. Lena didn't waste any time waiting to find out who. She sprinted to the window, jammed it open, and leaped out.

Eliza dashed to the window and looked out. Queenie ran after her, barking like mad. Somehow, like a cat, Lena had landed on her feet and hit the ground running. In a flash, she disappeared down the alley and was gone. Leaving Eliza to deal with the threat on the other side of the door.

* * *

Theo clutched Peachy's manuscript like a relic pried from a tomb. Sitting at the writing desk in Eliza's room, one finger tracing the words, he read it as quickly as he could. He wasn't the world's speediest reader. And usually, his goal was comprehension over speed. But Eliza had commanded him to read fast, and as always, he was keen to please her. More backstory. Sigh. *Come on, Peachy old boy, get to the good stuff.*

After Ivan Grigor attended that fateful circus performance with the group of his beneficiaries from Save the Children, he and Lena the snake-charming acrobat and pianist had started up a hot and heavy romance. Theo winced at a mention of Dorothy Sayers and how Ivan had jilted her, claiming he "wasn't the marrying type," only to wed Lena Novikov three months later. No wonder there were so many pages. It read like a penny dreadful.

He flipped the page. Finally. The next chapter was entitled *The Obsidian Cartel*! A thunderous declaration, as if the mere utterance of the name should strike a reader paralyzed with dread. Theo pressed his lips together, bracing himself as he read on.

> The Obsidian Cartel: An unseen leviathan that drifts through the corridors of power, its many arms entwined with the throats of kings and criminals alike. It does not announce

> itself with fanfare or fire, but with the silent suffocation of inevitability. To resist it is to fight the tide, to beg the sea for mercy as it claims you, inch by inch, breath by breath.

Theo exhaled through his nose. *Good Lord, Peachy, could you be any more dramatic?* He could practically hear the man's voice: over-enunciating, reveling in his own cleverness. But Theo knew better than to dismiss it outright. Beneath all the florid nonsense, there was truth. As he read, he put the pages he finished inside the top drawer of the writing table for safe-keeping.

The Obsidian Cartel, he learned, once he'd scraped layers of Peachy's pulpy indulgence, was a menacing network of ruthless criminals, entrenched in every echelon of power, moving unseen, their presence known only through the ruin they left behind. He read on. The next paragraph bludgeoned him back into horrified amusement.

> Their laughter—a sound more chilling than the cries of orphaned children upon finding their homes reduced to smoldering embers—echoes across the desolate avenues of shattered dreams! They move as wraiths, draped in shadows woven from the night itself, their hearts barren landscapes where love and mercy go to die!

Theo pinched the bridge of his nose. "Good lord, Peachy," he muttered under his breath. "Was a single metaphor not enough?" He turned another page, skimming past overwrought descriptions of shadows that *breathed like living things* and men whose eyes *held the weight of unspeakable sins*. Then, finally, something concrete. What he'd been waiting for. Ivan Grigor's role in the Cartel.

"Ivan Grigor: Known to the Cartel as the Black Bishop, a man whose hands have never touched a blade, yet who has orchestrated more deaths than the sharpest dagger. He speaks, and the world bends. He is not a king, nor a god, but something worse: a man with no country, no allegiance, and no limit to his patience."

The Black Bishop. Theo's fingers tightened around the page. So it was true. Peachy was threatening to expose Ivan Grigor's connection to the Obsidian Cartel.

He scanned further, pulse quickening as another detail emerged. The ink was slightly smudged where Peachy's restless fingers must have traced over the words.

> The Cartel has no face, no singular master. But Ivan Grigor, he is the hand that turns the wheel. He does not kill. He does not steal. He simply decides who will.

Theo sat back, the weight of the words pressing against him. If Peachy was right about Ivan, then he'd been playing a far more dangerous game than they had realized. And when Ivan found out what Peachy was writing...

A shuffling in the hallway made him start. Theo's gaze flicked to the door. The doorknob rattled.

"Eliza?" He stared at the door.

Peachy had known too much. And it got him killed.

"Room service." The deep voice came from the hallway.

Theo stood up and went to the door. His hand on the knob, he swallowed. And hoped he wasn't about to make the same mistake.

17

THE ROBBERY

Back at Pera Palace Hotel, Queenie jerked her leash away and bolted up the hallway.

"Ouch." Rubbing her hand, Eliza dashed after the little dog. The leash burn exacerbated the soreness from her quick knife-hand to the assailant's jaw. Presumably the grisly man who charged into Lena's room was a thug from the Obsidian Cartel. She chuckled. She'd shown him a thing or two, including a swift kick to the privates.

Trailing her leash, Queenie stopped in front of the door to Eliza's hotel room. "What's got into you?" She fished for her key. The little dog started scratching at the door and barking.

"Alright, alright." Eliza used her key in the lock. "We're going inside. Be patient." Was the dog expecting a special treat for finding Lena? She deserved one, to be sure. Of course, finding Lena and keeping her were two different stories. Eliza had searched the alley, and up and down the adjacent streets, with no luck. Even Queenie couldn't follow her trail this time.

The door swung open. Queenie pushed past and darted into the room.

"What's the rush?" Eliza followed her in. She stopped in her tracks. "Oh no!"

Theo lay on the floor, his hair matted with blood, a page of the manuscript crumpled in his palm.

"Theo!" She ran to him and dropped to her knees. "Theo." Her heart raced as she put two fingers to his neck. "No." Tears sprouted in her eyes. "No. No. No." Her heart was pounding so hard, she couldn't tell if he had a pulse or not. She bent down and put her face next to his. Was he breathing? She put her hand on his cheek. It was warm. She held her hand under his nose.

Thank God. He was breathing. "Theo, wake up." She gently shook him. How long had he been unconscious? "Wake up." She brushed the hair from his face. "Come on." She bent closer and kissed him. "Don't you dare die on me."

Queenie pushed in and started licking his face.

His eyelids flickered. He groaned.

She exhaled. "Thank you, Jesus." She sat down on the floor next to him. "Are you alright?"

"Eliza, stop with the sloppy kisses, please." He dragged his arm over his face to block Queenie's licking. The dog whimpered and wagged. "And when was the last time you brushed your teeth?"

She smiled. He must be alright; he was teasing her—either that or he was delirious. She unclipped Queenie's leash from her collar.

"What took you so long?" He opened his eyes and propped himself up on an elbow. "I do hope you judo-chopped my assailant?" He flashed a weak smile. "Is he tied up in the bathroom?"

"I'm afraid not." She caressed his cheek. "What happened?"

"The Obsidian Cartel is now providing room service." He

smirked. "And I made the mistake of answering the door." He sighed. "I'm such an idiot." A cloud passed over his countenance. "They got Peachy's manuscript, I'm afraid." He looked up at her with sad eyes. "I'm so sorry."

"Don't worry about that now." She stood up and held out her hand to him. "Let's get you cleaned up." When she pulled him to his feet, he wobbled slightly. She took him around the waist. "Here, sit down." She led him to an overstuffed chair in the sitting area. "I'll get a cloth and some alcohol."

"Alcohol!" He grimaced. "Won't that hurt?" He touched the sore spot on his scalp where it was caked with blood. He got a funny look on his face and pulled his hand away. "Oh dear," he said, staring down at his red fingers.

"Don't be such a baby." She squinted at him. "I took a hammer to my head and you don't see me whining about it."

"There's no doubt." He shrugged. "You're tougher than me." He folded his palms in his lap. "Nurse me, then. I'll be brave."

She chuckled. "We're a pair to draw to."

"Draw?" He furrowed his brows. "A picture?"

"Poker." She raised her eyebrows. "Another one of my ill-gotten talents. Cards." She went to the bathroom and turned on the tap.

"Goodness." He grinned. "You're a woman of many talents."

Once the water was warm, she soaked a towel and wrung it out. Then she fetched a bottle of alcohol from her sample kit. Carefully, she dabbed at the wound on the back of Theo's head.

"Ouch!" He jerked his head away.

"Unfortunately," she said, holding his chin with one hand and dabbing the wound with the other, "nursing isn't one of them."

"Obviously," he said through gritted teeth.

"There." She stood back and admired her handywork. The

blood was gone and the cut on his scalp was dry. "Good as new." She smiled. "Once that nasty bump heals." She tossed the soiled linen into the bin and returned the alcohol to her case. "Now." She sat on the edge of the bed. "Tell me what happened."

"Did you find Lena?" His eyes widened, as if he'd just remembered she'd gone after the missing woman.

"You first." She opened her palms. Queenie trotted over and jumped up on the bed. She patted the little dog's head and, after a couple of circles, the beagle curled up next to her.

"Yes, boss." Theo scowled. "I was reading the manuscript. Room service knocked on the door. Then he knocked on my head." He shrugged. "Not much to tell. A tall man dressed as a porter. I didn't get a good look at him before he whacked me. But I think it was that blasted French train inspector again." He touched his head. "He knocked me out and then stole Peachy's manuscript." He bent to pick up a crumpled page from the floor. "Except this page." His face brightened. "And this." He opened the drawer to the writing table and pulled out a stack of pages.

"Good on you," she said, clapping her hands together. "Hopefully, you saved the juiciest part."

"Not hardly." He tightened his lips. "Mostly backstory and purple prose." He tapped the pages. "Although the Obsidian Cartel sounds like the nastiest of the nasty. And Ivan Grigor was their 'Black Bishop.'" He made quotes with his fingers.

"Black Bishop. Goodness. But we suspected as much." She stood up. "Any sign of Jane?"

Theo shook his head.

"Come on, Queenie." She retrieved the dog's leash.

Wagging her tail, Queenie jumped off the bed.

"Wait!" Theo stood up too. "What happened with Lena? Did you find her?"

"Queenie found her." She bent to give the beagle a pat and reclip the leash to the collar. "Didn't you, girl?"

"So, what happened? Where is she? Is she alright?" Theo ran his hand through his hair and then grimaced.

"She's fine." At least she hoped so. "We found her nearby at the Büyük Londra Hotel." Eliza patted Queenie. "She admitted to poisoning Ivan using cobra venom in his meal." She raised her eyebrows. "And she escaped the train crouched into a compartment in the kitchen car when it was switched out at Nilš."

"But how could she poison him without poisoning herself?" Theo squinted at her. "She ate everything he did."

"Self-immunization through taking small amounts of venom." She smirked. "Over a long period. Her circus act."

"Mithridatism." His eyes shone with realization.

"Mithri-what?" She shook her head. He was always coming up with fancy words.

"Legend had it that King Mithridates IV was so afraid of being poisoned, he took small doses to immunize himself." Theo smiled. "Mithridatism." His expression turned serious. "Did you take her to the police?"

Eliza blew out a breath. "She jumped out the window and ran off."

"Self-defenestration," he said.

"Queenie and I had to incapacitate a rather nasty fellow who showed up at her room." She demonstrated her knife-hand. "A few good ju-jitsu moves and a nice ankle bite, right Queenie?" She bent down and scratched behind the beagle's ears.

"You and your foot-fighting." Theo's eyes were wide. "What about Peachy? Did Lena kill him too?"

"No," she said, gently tugging on Queenie's leash. "I'm willing to bet that was the work of the Obsidian Cartel." The dog came to her side and stood at the ready. "In fact, I'd go one step further and wager it was our old friend the French train inspector, who conveniently boarded the train at Nilš, bumped off Peachy, and then disappeared." She smirked. "Until our reunion in the tunnel."

"By Jove!" Theo beamed. "I think you're onto something."

"Any word from D.I. Orhan about ballistics from the gun?"

A knock on the door startled her. She gave Theo a questioning look. He shrugged. Queenie ran to the door, tail wagging, and yipped.

Eliza went to the door and opened it. She knew from the tone of Queenie's excited yip that it had to be Jane.

Jane wasn't alone. She had Agatha and Dorothy in tow.

"We've had the most exciting adventure," Agatha said, clapping her hands together. "The treasure box in the tunnel at Aga Daga—"

"Jewels," Dorothy said. "A treasure chest of jewels."

"Stolen jewels," Jane said, patting Queenie's head.

Eliza blinked. A lightbulb went off in her brain. "The robbery in Paris. It was in the newspaper." She paced the length of the room. Queenie trotted behind her. "Ivan boarded the train in Paris."

"Yes," Theo said, stabbing the air with a finger. "Right after the jewel heist at Chanel. I read about that robbery in the French newspapers just before I boarded."

Eliza stopped and turned to face her sister. "Coincidence?"

"What do you think?" Jane raised her eyebrows.

"But if Ivan carried out the Chanel heist, how did he get the jewels to the tunnel at Aga Daga?" Eliza started pacing again. "He died mid-journey."

"The Obsidian Cartel," Theo said. "Obviously, he had an accomplice."

Jane started to say something but stopped herself.

Eliza stood staring at her sister. "What do you know that you're not telling us?" She thought of the state of the Grigors' cabin. Like Peachy's, it was torn up, as if someone was looking for something. She was pretty sure the Obsidian Cartel was looking for Peachy's manuscript. In the case of the Grigors' cabin, it must have been the stolen jewels. She realized then that the metal case full of stolen jewels wasn't there when she'd searched either Ivan's or Peachy's cabins. Whoever took it had already made off with it by the time she had the chance to search. She tried to remember the timeline. Did the case disappear after Ivan's death or after Peachy's? Did Lena take it when she escaped the train? Or was it gone already?

Queenie sat at Jane's feet and barked up at her as if demanding she answer Eliza's question.

"I see whose side you're on," Jane said, petting the beagle.

"Why don't we go to the dining room?" Agatha said. "I'd like to sit down and get a bite to eat."

"I'm parched." Dorothy removed her hat. "I could use a drink to wash down the dust."

"Good idea," Theo said, touching the back of his head. "A nice whiskey as an analgesic."

"Do you have a headache, dear?" Agatha asked. "I have powders in my room."

"I'll tell you all about it over cocktails." He rolled up what was left of Peachy's manuscript and tucked it into his jacket pocket. "Then Eliza can tell us about her recent adventures, too." Theo gestured toward the door. "Shall we?"

“Tit for tat,” Eliza said. “I’m not giving out any information until I get some in return.” She met her sister’s gaze.

“Very well.” Jane let out a little chortle. “Whiskies and whispers it is.”

* * *

Theo stepped into the grand dining room of the Pera Palace Hotel, momentarily arrested by its opulence. The high, vaulted ceiling gleamed under the glow of crystal chandeliers, their light refracting across gilded moldings and the deep, mahogany paneling. He thought of his mother and how much she adored the Pera Palace. Blowing out a breath, he admitted it to himself. He missed her. Them. His parents. He winced. What would his father say about him working as a waiter on a train, carrying trays and scrubbing toilets? Or tramping around Europe? Or attending a writers’ conference, for that matter? A pang of guilt struck his chest.

In her last letter, his mother had said his father was ill and asked him to come home. She’d also enclosed *a little extra for a rainy day*. He dare not tell her that his idea of a rainy day was a double murder aboard the Orient Express and a hit on the head from a Russian gangster.

The host led them to a table near the window. Crisp, white tablecloths adorned each table, set with polished silver and delicate porcelain, while waiters in sharp, black uniforms moved with quiet efficiency, their gloved hands balancing trays of fine Anatolian wine and steaming platters of lamb and saffron rice. The scent of spiced coffee and warm bread mingled with the low murmur of conversation. Theo adjusted his cuffs, feeling an odd sense of displacement, as if he had stepped into one of the grand illusions found in the pages of his favorite mystery novels. One of Agatha's or Dorothy's, perhaps. He glanced around the table and smiled.

Taking dinner with a group of ladies, the only gentleman in the bunch, would send shivers of disapproval up his father's aristocratic spine. Even so, perhaps Theo owed the old man a visit. How would he feel if his father took a turn for the worse and, God forbid, died when they weren't on speaking terms? The guilt would crush him. Plucking an olive from the dish the waiter just delivered, he wondered whether he truly loved his father. He didn't particularly like him. So, what was this pull on his heart? Was it love or guilt? And when it came to familial relations, how could you really tell the difference?

He chewed the olive absently, its briny bite sharp against his tongue, and then sat the pit on the saucer. His father's expectations weighed on him like a lead-lined overcoat, pressing down with the accumulated gravity of generations: An inheritance not of wealth, but of duty, stitched together with obligation and lined with the cold silk of disappointment.

"Don't you agree?" Eliza's voice brought him out of his reveries.

"Agree with what?" He cleared his throat and then snatched another olive off the plate. Only then did he notice the table was filled with more delicacies. Kofta, dolma, and two types of kebabs, along with saffron rice and another plate of feta cheese and flat bread.

"That the fake French train inspector is the most likely candidate." She tilted her head and a blonde curl fell across her cheek. He resisted the temptation to brush it away.

"Candidate for the Cartel operative." He nodded. It was true. The fake inspector could have taken the jewels from Ivan's cabin after he boarded in Nilš, then snuck off the train, and then later hidden them in the tunnel at Aga Daga. Then again,

Lena could have been the accomplice. Just because she was a beautiful woman was no reason to rule her out. Ha! That would be just the kind of trick a writer might use. Play on the reader's prejudices to set up a big reveal.

"And Peachy's killer," Agatha added.

"But not Ivan's." He loaded his plate with one sample of each dish. "Since the fake inspector didn't board the train until Nilš, right, Eliza?" He took a bite of dolma. The chewy grape leaves outside and the soft rice and ground lamb inside made a perfect combination.

"Right." Eliza put her tulip-shaped glass down on its saucer with a clatter. "I paid a visit to Lena Grigor this afternoon."

"Where is she?" Jane demanded, her spine straightening like a soldier's on parade.

"Calm down." Eliza held up her wrist. "She was at the Büyük Londra Hotel." She rubbed her hand. "Until a couple of Obsidian Cartel thugs showed up and she jumped out the window," she said, shaking her head. "We lost her."

"We?" Jane asked.

"Me and Queenie." She ripped a piece of bread in half and popped it into her mouth.

"And the thugs?" Jane raised an eyebrow. "Don't tell me." She tutted. "You dispatched them with your bare hands."

"In a manner of speaking." Eliza bit into the bread with gusto, as if demonstrating how she ground the thugs to mincemeat.

"And what did Lena have to say for herself?" Dorothy asked, sipping a cup of sweet tea. "Why did she disappear like that? And how did she disappear like that?" She blushed. "I hope she doesn't share her husband's penchant for blackmail," she said between clenched teeth.

"Blackmail?" Theo asked. Weren't two murders and a jewel heist enough?

"Never mind."

"But—"

Eliza gave him a warning look and he took the hint.

"About Lena," Jane said. "I really need to find her." She lowered her voice. "She's in grave danger."

Eliza showed off her bruised knuckles. "Tell me about it." She shoveled a couple of dolmas onto her plate. "Maybe Detective Inspector Orhan has found her by now."

"Why do you say that?" Jane's tone was steady but her expression was one of alarm.

"Because I rang him when I got back to Pera Palace to tell him Lena confessed."

"Confessed!" Agatha nearly spit out her cocktail. "How exciting."

"Confessed to what?" Dorothy asked. "Murder, theft..." She lowered her voice. "Blackmail?"

"She poisoned Ivan with snake venom," Eliza said, munching on a dolma.

"But she ate the same meal." Agatha tilted her head. "How intriguing."

"Yes." Eliza dropped two more sugar cubes into her tea and stirred. "She made herself immune by taking small doses of the poison herself over a long period of time." She took a sip. "Pity they don't have milk or cream."

"Pity," Agatha agreed.

"Ohhh!" Dorothy said. "Sounds like a wonderful plot for a novel. I like it." She smiled. "I'm thinking *Strong Poison*, where the victim and killer share a meal and that becomes the killer's iron-clad alibi." Her face lit up. "Very clever."

"Very deadly, more like." Eliza scowled. Theo knew how she

felt about writers rejoicing in death and planning clever ways to bump people off. And he had to admit, Dorothy's tone was more than a little gleeful.

"Ivan was a hateful man." Dorothy sniffed. "I'm sorry about Peachy, but I can't say I'll miss Ivan Grigor." She fiddled with her napkin. "Too bad Peachy won't get to present his work at the conference." She smiled weakly. "He was so proud of that manuscript."

Theo patted his pocket. "At least I managed to save the first couple chapters."

"Wonderful." Dorothy's countenance brightened. "Let me see it." She wiggled her fingers at him.

Begrudgingly, he pulled the pages from his pocket and handed them to her.

She put on her spectacles. He and the others watched in silence as she devoured the text. After a minute, she looked up. "Marvelous." She smiled. "I'm going to read this tomorrow at the conference."

"Do you think that's wise?" Jane asked.

"Jane's right. It's too dangerous." Eliza's brows furrowed. "Two men are dead because of that book and Lena is running for her life."

"Listen to them, dear," Agatha said. "We wouldn't want you to put yourself in harm's way." She grinned. "Although it does sound thrilling. And a fitting tribute to your friend."

"I agree." Dorothy gave one quick nod of her head. "I'm not going to back down because of some black-market bullies."

"Bullies?" Theo scoffed. "We're not in the school yard. The Obsidian Cartel are cold-blooded killers." He reached for the manuscript. "No, we can't risk it."

Dorothy yanked the pages away from him. "What's the fun in life without a little risk?"

"Are you mad?" Eliza said.

"Maybe I am." Dorothy chuckled. "But Peachy was a dear friend and I plan to honor him." She tossed her napkin onto the table. "Tomorrow. At the conference." She stood up. "I'll bid you good evening. I must go prepare my remarks and decide what part of this lovely book to present."

Eliza sighed. "It's your funeral."

For Dorothy's sake, he sincerely hoped she was wrong.

18

DOROTHY'S PRESENTATION

The ballroom of the Pera Palace Hotel had been transformed for the writers' convention. Rows of chairs faced a raised platform at the front, where a long table held water glasses, neatly stacked papers, and a brass reading lamp casting a pool of light. Chandeliers overhead bathed the room in a golden glow, their crystals sparkling and tinkling as waiters wafted to and fro. The air was thick with cigarette smoke and an occasional murmur from the audience.

Eliza fidgeted in her seat, awaiting Dorothy's presentation with equal parts dread and admiration. At the podium, the hideous Eric Blair recounted tales of working for the Imperial Police in Burma, caught between empire and the scorn of the natives, before resigning to write, which began with his tramping around London and Paris, simultaneously repulsed by the conditions of the poor and proud of his joining them. The audience seemed to alternate between mild amusement and horrification. For Eliza's part, the sound of his thin voice reminded her of him pawing at her and, needless to say, got on her nerves. She glanced at Theo, who had a derisive smirk on his face. She refused to look at the stage while Eric was speaking. Instead, she scanned the audience, looking for trouble.

When Eric finished, the master of ceremonies, a Mr. Ahmed Hasim, announced a short break. Eliza took the opportunity to move to a spot against the wall for a better view of the ballroom.

The crowd was a restless mix of international writers, critics, and journalists. French poets slouched in their chairs, smoking lazily as they murmured among themselves. A German historian, neatly dressed and precise, adjusted his pince-nez while flipping through his notebook. A Russian exile, his coat too fine for his frayed cuffs, leaned forward intently, watching every movement on the stage. Turkish novelists and playwrights sat together, their conversation low and rapid. A few Americans stood near the back, taller and louder than the others, their laughter cutting through the hum of foreign tongues.

Scanning the room, Eliza barely heard any of it. She wasn't here for the talk of books. She was watching for danger.

Ten minutes later, the master of ceremonies returned to introduce the guests of honor. Dorothy and Agatha took to the stage, while he continued heaping praise on the two grand and brilliant English mystery writers.

Dorothy sat behind a table at the center of the stage. If she was nervous, she didn't look it, except perhaps the way she was clutching the pages of Peachy's manuscript: the words that had cost him his life. Agatha sat beside her, her hands clasped tightly, her expression unreadable. Theo stood at the edge of the stage, leaning against a railing, one hand in his pocket, his casual posture betrayed by the sharp focus in his eyes.

Eliza's stomach twisted. She suspected that someone in this

room wanted those pages buried, and they were ready to bury anyone who got in their way.

When the master of ceremonies finally finished his extended introduction, he waved in Dorothy's direction. With an air of dignity and the slightest hint of trepidation, she stood up and approached the podium. Her eyes flashed as she looked out at the audience. Carefully, she laid the papers on the podium and then put on her glasses. She cleared her throat. "Thank you for being here this evening." She smiled. "I'm honored to be one of the keynote speakers." Her smile faded. "I'd planned to read my latest Lord Peter Wimsey story"—she sighed—"but last week, I lost an old friend, a dear friend, Mr. Hugo 'Peachy' Fitzroy." Her hand trembled as she picked up the stack of papers. "So, I want to dedicate this reading to him. And to honor his memory and his work, I will read from his unpublished exposé, which is entitled, *The Obsidian Cartel: Smuggling, Spies, and the Syndicate's Secret Weapon*."

Gasps and whispers stole her thunder.

Like a displeased schoolmarm, she stopped and peered over her spectacles at the crowd.

Eliza curled her fingers into a tight ball. This whole performance made her uneasy. Why tempt fate? After two murders, didn't Dorothy know better? She held her breath and waited for her employer to begin reading Peachy's tell-all.

After the murmurs died down, Dorothy adjusted her glasses and started up again.

"There are names that history dares not record, shadows that move between the lines of written power, unseen yet omnipresent. Among them, none loom larger than Ivan Grigor, the Black Bishop of the Obsidian Order: a man who commands no armies yet topples empires with a whisper." Dorothy paused and glanced around the audience for effect.

Eliza stared at the stage. Theo wasn't exaggerating about Peachy's purple prose.

"His reach is infinite, his justice cruel, his patience that of a predator watching from the dark. To speak his name is to invite misfortune; to cross his path is to court oblivion."

But Peachy had exaggerated the dominion of Ivan Grigor. Eliza knew Ivan and he was no Black Bishop with unseen powers. If anything, he was a sad pawn in a larger game, one he'd obviously lost.

"He does not kill with his own hands, nor stain himself with the vulgarity of violence; he merely decides who will perish, and the world obeys."

The hall was rapt, everyone on the edge of their seat, so quiet, you could hear a pin drop. Eliza scanned the crowd. Maybe her nerves were for nothing. Maybe Dorothy was right and no one would dare make a move in the large, crowded ballroom with her in the spotlight for all to see. Maybe the Obsidian Cartel preferred to operate in darkness, slipping on and off trains passing in the night.

In the back of the ballroom, waiters delivered wine and canapés for the reception after Dorothy's presentation. Eliza watched as men and women in servant's livery set up a long reception table adorned with flowers. Silver trays gleamed under the chandeliers, the scent of freshly baked bread mingling with the heavier perfume of the guests. The scene was perfectly ordinary—too ordinary.

As Dorothy read, Eliza focused on the staff, her gaze skimming over their crisp uniforms, their movements practiced and efficient. Most were young men, Turkish or Greek, their expressions blank with the quiet professionalism of hotel service. A few women in black dresses and white aprons arranged glasses with nimble fingers, their voices hushed as they whispered final instructions.

One of the waiters caught her eye. He was taller than the others, his uniform immaculate, but something about him felt wrong. It wasn't just the way he moved—too stiff, too controlled—but his face. Despite his black beard, a shadow of familiarity prickled at her memory. She knew him. Her breath caught. Oh no. He wasn't a waiter. And he wasn't here to serve canapés. A cold dread settled in her stomach. No. No. No. The French train inspector. "No. No. No." Heart racing, she cut across the room, sprinting to the back of the hall. "Stop!"

She caught the flicker of movement: His hand dipping beneath the silver tray he carried, fingers wrapped around something dark and metallic.

"Everyone down!" she shouted.

In a flash, her training kicked in and she lunged at him. Her hand locked around his wrist just as he drew the pistol. His grip loosened and the gun slipped free, clattering onto the table and knocking over a vase of flowers in a spray of petals and water. He slammed his elbow into her ribs. Pain jolted through her side, but she gritted her teeth and held on, pivoting her weight to trap his arm in a lock.

"Eliza!" Theo's voice broke through the pounding in her ears.

The assassin wrenched free with a sudden burst of strength and drove his fist toward her face. She dodged, but the blow grazed her temple. She covered her face with her arm and struck back. With a knife-like precision, she snapped her foot and kicked him in the ribs. He blocked with his arm, then staggered back, one hand scrambling for the gun. She grabbed the front of his jacket, twisted her hips, and threw him. The force sent him crashing onto the marble floor with a thud. He groaned but recovered fast—too fast. He jumped up and lunged for the table. As if in slow motion, she watched him snatch up the gun and lift the barrel.

"No!" Eliza lunged again. But he'd already fired, the deafening crack splitting the air.

Gasps and screams erupted from the crowd. Chairs scraped against the floor as guests bolted for cover. A waiter dropped his tray and glasses shattered against the hard floor.

On the stage, Dorothy stumbled back, her eyes wide with shock. The wooden podium splintered where the bullet struck, fragments flying.

Eliza's heart clenched. The bullet had missed Dorothy by mere inches.

Another movement: a figure in red silk, cutting through the chaos like a knife. Blimey. It was Lena Grigor. She'd appeared out of nowhere, her dagger flashing as she struck. The blade slashed through the air, slicing the gunman's sleeve before he managed to jerk away, narrowly avoiding a deeper cut.

"You thought you'd seen the last of me, didn't you, Boris?" Lena smirked. "I'm not so easy to kill."

He snarled and aimed the gun straight at her.

Eliza lunged at him.

Another shot rang out. But this time, it wasn't his. It came from behind them. Eliza spun around toward the source.

Jane stood near the table with her pistol raised and her stance solid. "Drop it," her sister ordered, her voice like ice.

Boris hesitated, eyes flicking between Lena, Jane, and Eliza. In a desperate move, he hurled the gun at Jane. She ducked, but the distraction was all he needed to twist away and sprint for the exit.

Theo was faster. He slammed into Boris from the side, tackling him hard against the reception table. Trays crashed to the floor, wine bottles shattered, and cutlery clattered as they struggled. Theo grabbed for the assassin's arms, trying to pin him, but Boris fought like a wild animal, landing a brutal elbow into Theo's ribs. Theo cried out.

Without thinking, Eliza darted forward, grabbed Boris's arm, and twisted it behind his back. He roared in pain, but before she could fully subdue him, he jerked back violently, yanking her off balance. Pain shot through her shoulder as she hit the floor, her breath knocked from her lungs. Broken glass dug into her palms as she scrambled up, but Boris was already on the move. He was heading for the stage.

Eliza lunged for his legs, trying to trip him, but he danced out of her grip.

Moving like a striking cobra, her red, silk dress shimmering, Lena stepped into his path. The blade in her hand gleamed as she slashed low, aiming for his inner thigh. He twisted, barely avoiding the cut, and threw a punch. Lena dodged his fist.

"Tsk. You're getting sloppy, Boris, darling."

Eliza scrambled to her feet.

A gunshot cracked through the ballroom.

Eliza flinched.

Lena froze, the knife raised above her head.

The shot hit the ceiling, a warning. "Don't move," Jane ordered, her voice flat and steady.

Boris hesitated. For a second, Eliza thought he might surrender. Then, with a desperate growl, he pushed Lena to the floor and rushed to the stage.

Eliza's heart lurched. In hot pursuit, she sprinted after him, scanning for a weapon as she went. She grabbed a champagne bottle off a waiter's tray. "Thank you," she said as she breezed past. She sensed Theo and Lena coming up behind her.

Like a battering ram, Boris slammed into Dorothy,

knocking the manuscript from her hands, sending Peachy's pages flapping across the stage like wounded birds. Agatha gasped and grabbed for Dorothy, pulling her back.

Yelping, Dorothy held her hands in front of her face. Agatha kicked at the assassin, who reached out for Dorothy's neck. He got his hand around her throat and squeezed. Her eyes bulging, Dorothy scratched at his face.

Quick as lightning, Eliza came around behind him and brought the bottle crashing down over his head. In an instant, Theo and Lena were at her side. The bottle shattered and Boris staggered, glass in his hair, blood trickling down his face. Theo gripped his shoulders. "You're not getting away this time."

Jane closed the distance. In a single, precise movement, she pressed the barrel of her gun to Boris's temple. "Enough," she said, the sharpness in her voice cutting through the air.

Silence fell over the ballroom. Boris stilled, his chest rising and falling in ragged pants. Blood dripped onto the floor.

Eliza took a deep breath, her pulse pounding in her ears.

The guests had scattered to the edges of the room, whispering in stunned voices, staring at the wreckage: the broken glass, the overturned tables, the manuscript pages strewn across the floor. Dorothy stood frozen on the stage, clutching Agatha's hand, her face pale. Agatha swallowed hard, her eyes darting between the assassin and Jane's unwavering gun. Lena stood close to Theo, her hand on his sleeve.

A commotion in the back of the ballroom turned all heads. Detective Inspector Orhan and several uniformed police officers marched up the aisle. "We'll take over now," he called as he strode to the stage.

Eliza exhaled. When she turned back to face the podium, she glimpsed Lena disappearing behind the curtains.

"Cuff him," D.I. Orhan said to one of his mates.

When Boris tried to jerk out of Theo's grasp, Jane jabbed him in the side with her gun. "Hands out in front of you."

He tightened his lips but held out his hands. A copper snapped the handcuffs around his wrists. "Come on, then." He gave Boris a little shove.

"Well done, Mrs. Archer," D.I. Orhan said to Jane.

"It's Agent Archer," Eliza said. "Special Agent." She winked at her sister.

Jane holstered her gun under her jacket. "Thank the British government."

The police led Boris out of the ballroom. When the coppers were gone, Eliza and her friends heaved a collective sigh of relief. A chorus of animated voices rose from the audience members who hadn't already fled.

Theo brushed shards of glass from his jacket. "Well." He rubbed his ribs and winced. "That was exciting."

"A bit too exciting," Agatha said, a tremor in her voice. "If that bullet had hit two inches higher..." She winced. "Are you alright, dear Dorothy?"

Nodding, Dorothy wiped her brow with her handkerchief. "I will be after a stiff drink."

A flash of color in her cheeks, Jane glanced around the stage. "Where's Lena?"

Theo's head jerked. "She was here a minute ago." He looked around. "Standing right beside me."

"She disappeared behind the curtains right after D.I. Orhan arrived." Eliza pointed. "Since we now know she poisoned her husband, I'm guessing she's not keen on an encounter with the coppers."

"Dammit." Jane sighed. "I should have known she'd fly."

"Should we go after her?" Eliza asked. "Maybe we can catch up to her."

"If we don't, the Obsidian Cartel will." Jane bit her lip. "My job here isn't done until I bring Lena in."

Eliza sidled up to her sister. "Is she really working for you?"

"Yes," Jane whispered through clenched teeth.

Eliza whistled.

Theo let out a low breath, running a hand through his hair as his eyes swept the stage again as if Lena might reappear from the shadows. But the curtains hung still. The only movement was the slow, uneasy shifting of the shaken guests.

Eliza stared at Jane, her stomach twisting. The scent of gunpowder still clung to the air, mingling with the sharp tang of spilled wine and crushed flowers.

Lena was gone. Again. Out there, somewhere in the twisting alleyways of Constantinople, slipping through the night like a ghost. Was she running to escape, or running straight into the arms of the Obsidian Cartel?

Eliza followed Jane's gaze toward the heavy curtains, still rippling slightly from where Lena had vanished. Caught on the edge of the heavy fabric, one of her signature red, silk scarfs fluttered like a dying ember before it slipped free, drifting to the floor.

* * *

After the chaotic scene in the ballroom, Theo was glad to be sitting at a corner table in the dark hotel bar. As he sipped his whiskey, he watched Eliza and Jane, their heads together, conspiring, the sisters so much alike and yet so different. Both had blonde hair, the same icy-green eyes, and rosebud lips, but despite the gun holstered under her jacket, Jane was somehow softer than Eliza. Yet, it was Eliza's edginess that attracted him to her: That *je ne sais quoi* he struggled to put into words. How did you describe a feeling that transcends the physical world? Sure, he felt it in his body. And how. Yet, the beauty of his connection to her went beyond physical attraction.

He thought of his publisher's reaction to his latest manuscript, the one inspired by his last adventure with Eliza. After Theo had sent in revisions, the team at Bloodworks Books claimed it was too "cliché and melodramatic." "The love story is too intense," his editor had said of the first draft. As if any true love story wasn't intense.

That was just it. How to describe what he felt without resorting to cliché or melodrama? What his editor didn't understand was that it wasn't just describing Eliza or love that balled him up. It was describing anything. Anything at all. Language was the problem. Or more accurately, the gulf between words and experience. How to translate the world into words. That was his conundrum. The conundrum of every writer.

He swirled the whiskey in his glass. How could he do justice to the amber liquid whirling like a tiny storm, catching flashes of gold from the bar's brass fixtures? How could he capture the way the heat of it burned low and steady in his chest, the way it mirrored the fire Eliza sparked in him: sharp, heady, impossible to ignore?

He set the glass down with a muted clink and watched as Jane leaned in, murmuring something to Eliza. Eliza's brow furrowed in concentration, her fingers tapping idly against the table. Theo knew that gesture: She was working something out, piecing together a puzzle in that sharp mind of hers. He wanted to bottle that focus, that relentless curiosity, the way her eyes flashed when she was on the verge of discovery.

How could he translate that into words?

Not just love, but *her*: This restless, brilliant, maddening woman who infuriated and fascinated him in equal measure. The woman who could throw a man twice her size but still hesitate before touching his arm. The woman who could see through any lie but refused to acknowledge the truth staring her in the face.

He fingered his glass and let out a slow breath.

Maybe that was why language always fell short. Because no combination of words, no clever turn of phrase, no poetic flourish could ever fully contain the depth of a moment: the heat of a glance, the weight of silence, the ache of wanting something just out of reach.

And God help him—and Bloodworks Books be damned—but he wanted her.

More than whiskey. More than words. More than landing a bestselling novel.

Alright, that last one might be a tie.

Out of habit, he reached into his pocket for the soothing smoothness of his well-worn fountain pen. To his surprise, his fingers landed on the sharp corner of a folded piece of paper. He withdrew it. "What the heck?" He unfolded it. A piece of sheet music.

"What is it?" Eliza asked.

"Looks like another piece of Lena's music." Quickly, he grabbed his fountain pen and started transcribing the musical notes into letters. "Another coded location, perhaps?" He scribbled on the page, reciting as he went, "B-E-G-E-C." He looked up. "That repeats for a few bars. Then, G-A-C-E-F." He made a note. "Then C-A-F-E. With each phrase repeated three times." He scanned his friends' faces. "Ring any bells?"

"Isn't Begeč a town in Serbia on the Danube River?" Agatha said, picking at a bowl of olives.

"May I?" Jane reached for the music.

He held it out of her reach.

"You'll give it to me, if you please." She snatched it out of his hand. "Unless you want your ringing bells turning into death knells."

"C-a-f-e must be café," Dorothy said, a pleased note in her voice.

"A café in Begeč, then?" Agatha's face was bright and her cheeks rosy. "I'd say it's called Gacef. Gacef Café."

"Forget you've ever heard of such a place," Jane said sharply. "If you know what's good for you, you'll not mention this to anyone."

"Gacef Café in Begeč," Eliza said with a smirk.

"Erase it from your mind," Jane said. "Scrub it from your ears."

"Why?" Eliza tilted her head.

"Because if you don't..." Jane lowered her voice. "Lena Grigor will die."

Tapping his pen against the table, Theo glanced over at Jane and the sheet music, with its black ink stark against the white paper. Outside, a faint church bell tolled: A low, solemn knell rolling across the rooftops, swallowed up by a howling wind.

19

THEO'S PRESENTATION

Later that night, while lying in bed, Queenie, who was sleeping next to Eliza, stirred, alerting her to her sister's departure.

"Wait!" Eliza jumped out of bed. "Wait for me." She didn't bother getting dressed or even throwing on a dressing gown. Instead, she dashed out into the hallway in her night dress.

Halfway down the hall, Jane was clad in fedora, trench coat, and low-heeled Oxfords. Obviously, she was on a midnight mission. "Where are you going?" Eliza called after her.

Jane swiveled around. "What are you doing out of bed?"

"I'm coming with you." Eliza caught up to her.

"No, you're not." Jane scowled. "This is my mission, not yours."

"You're going to Gacef Café in Begeč." She reached out and took her sister's hand. "Aren't you?" She squeezed. "At least tell me where to look for you if you don't come back." She gave her sister her most sincere and pleading look.

"Alright, alright." Jane sighed. "I'm going to meet Lena, but it's absolutely essential you don't tell a soul."

"Look, I know about the list of agents on the microfilm, the one in the fake brooch." Eliza kept hold of her sister's hand. "I know Peachy's book contains another list. A list of Obsidian Cartel operatives. What's Lena's role in all this?" She tightened her grip. "Is Lena Grigor really working for you?" Her mind raced as she tried to reassemble the pieces of the puzzle, only now with Lena Grigor working for MI5. "That's what she told me."

"Not here." Jane glanced up and down the hallway. "Come on." She pulled Eliza back into their room. Once inside, she patted the edge of her bed. "Sit down," she said in her army-general voice. "If I tell you, you have to promise not to follow me."

Eliza nodded.

With a squeak, Queenie jumped up onto the bed. Eliza sat down next to her furry friend and gave the beagle a good ear scratching while she waited for Jane to spill the beans.

Jane sat on the other side of the little beagle and stroked the dog's back. "This is highly classified," Jane began. "I shouldn't even be telling." She shook her head. "In fact, I don't know why I am."

"Because I'm your sister." Eliza raised her eyebrows. "Not to mention, I'm the one who found Lena and got her to confess to poisoning her husband."

"Yes, well." Jane sucked in air. "Ivan Grigor may not have been the ogre or tyrant your Mr. Fitzroy made him out to be, but he was bad enough." She twisted the end of a lock of hair. "Lena has been deeply undercover as Ivan's wife for years."

"She married him for MI5?" Eliza whistled. Now that was commitment.

Jane proceeded to explain how Lena's musical code aboard the Orient Express was a call for extraction, which she'd used after Ivan learned she was working for MI5.

"Intended for my babysitter, no doubt," Eliza interrupted.

Jane got a funny look on her face but cracked on with her story. Ivan was blackmailing Lena and threatening to kill her if she didn't feed false information to British Intelligence about the Obsidian Cartel. Unbeknownst to him, Lena used paste jewelry to smuggle out the information the Cartel had got its hands on, information about British agents in the field. But when Agatha admired Lena's paste brooch and Father Burrow wanted to buy it for her, Ivan couldn't resist pulling the bait and switch on the priest. "Two birds with one stone, he'd told Lena after he sold the priest the real one and then switched it for the fake one."

"The fake one with the microfilm in it," Eliza said.

"Exactly. And her plan to deliver the brooch to her contact in Istanbul at the Baghdad Café was scuttled." Jane pulled a biscuit from the pocket of her trench coat and presented it to Queenie, who was only too happy to gobble it down. "And you know the rest."

"No wonder my little girl has gained weight," Eliza said, teasing. In truth, she was glad her sister had a soft spot for her furry best friend. She gave the dog a pat. "And now Lena is running for her life."

Jane sucked her teeth. "Now that Ivan is dead, the Cartel suspects Lena. Not only that. They think she has Mr. Fitzroy's list of their operatives and is ready to turn it over to us." She stood up. "Which is why they want her dead." She tightened the belt on her coat. "And why I've got to get to her before they do."

"We're coming with you—"

"No!" Jane held up her hand. "You promised."

Eliza stood up and went to fetch Queenie's leash.

"No. You're not coming." Jane narrowed her eyes.

"Yes—"

"Look, you don't understand." Jane raised her voice. "If you come with me, or follow me, or otherwise show up in the general vicinity of Gacef Café or the city of Begeč, or anywhere in Serbia for that matter"—she stood face to face with Eliza—"I'll lose my job. Do you hear me? I'll get sacked." Her cheeks were as red as two freshly cut beets. "Is that what you want?" She had her fist on her hips. "And then who would feed you and Queenie?"

That was a low blow. Eliza blinked.

"Do you understand?" Her tone was softer now and therefore scarier. "And not a word to anyone."

Eliza nodded.

Jane glared. "Not even your beau, Theo."

"He's not my beau." Her cheeks warmed.

"Just promise me you won't try to follow me." Jane sighed. "Please, Eliza. This once, just do as you're told."

"Oh alright." Eliza dropped back onto the edge of the bed. "I promise."

"Thank you!" Jane gave Queenie one last pat on the head. "You two be careful. The Obsidian Cartel is everywhere."

"We will." Eliza patted the bed, and with both tongue and tail wagging, Queenie joined her. "Won't we, my furry friend?"

"Alright. Stay safe." Jane went to the door. "I'll see you back at the flat."

"You'd better." Eliza couldn't lose her sister. Jane—and Queenie—were all she had in the world. "Don't do anything I wouldn't do."

"That does preclude much." Jane chuckled. "Goodbye, my loves." She slipped out the door.

"Wait!" Eliza's stomach twisted into a knot.

Jane peeked her head back into the room. "What?"

"Where can I find you? Just in case." She didn't give voice to the chorus of horrible images going through her head.

"You can contact me through the embassy." Jane paused. "But only in an emergency." She stepped back inside. "Don't worry. I'll see you back home in London very soon."

Eliza nodded. Saying a silent prayer, she slid back under the covers and pulled Queenie in with her. Jane was a grown woman and an MI5 agent, after all; why should she worry about her sister? Eliza's only living relative and the only person she trusted to watch out for her. The only person she trusted, period. The warmth of the little dog against her chest helped calm her. And, after many furry cuddles and caresses and an occasional lick on the nose, Eliza drifted off to sleep.

* * *

A sharp ray of sun coming through the curtains stabbed at her face and woke her up. She plucked her watch from the nightstand. Crikey. She'd have to hurry or she'd miss Theo's presentation at the conference. After the incident the night before, several participants dropped out, which left an opening for Theo, who gladly stepped in. He'd warned her he was going to read from the book he'd been working on for the last two years. The one he'd started before he left London. The one based on their first case together, if you could call it a case. Although they had cleared Agatha's name after she was wrongly suspected of murdering a fellow author.

Still, it wasn't like she was Scotland Yard or anything. At least, not anymore. She shuddered at the memory of her last day working for the Met: The day her partner, and best friend, sacrificed himself to save her from a homicidal woman with a gun. From that day on, she'd vowed never to let down her guard. Especially not when protecting someone she loved. She shuddered. They say time heals all wounds. But they're wrong. Wounds leave scars that will never heal.

She gave Queenie a gentle nudge. After the dog hopped down off the bed, Eliza threw her feet over the edge and stretched. Time to get a move on. No time for a bath or proper toilette. She threw on the same clothes she wore yesterday, took a quick look in the mirror, and smoothed her hair.

"Come on, Queenie," she said, bending to attach the leash to the beagle's collar. "Let's go see what Uncle Theo has to say." She gave the dog a pat. "Maybe you'll be in the story." She winced, remembering when she'd snuck a peek at Theo's manuscript. It was supposed to be a detective yarn but was equal parts love story. A love story about two characters solving a crime together, one an aspiring writer and the other a secretary for a writers' club. "Sound familiar?" she said to the dog. Too familiar. Anyway, wasn't he always going on about the protocols of detection fiction and meeting readers' expectations? Who wants a love story in their mystery? "Right, Queenie?"

Tail wagging, the little dog let out a loud bark.

"Time to face the music." She gave the leash a tug and off they went.

* * *

The ballroom was less crowded than the day before. Obviously, Theo wasn't as big a draw as Dorothy had been. Either that or writers were a bunch of scaredy cats put off by a few gunshots. Eliza smiled. Figures. Crime writers talk a good game. But when it comes to real crimes, they run.

Her empty stomach grumbled as she took a seat in the back row. Queenie sat at her feet. "Good girl," she whispered.

Theo was at the podium, shuffling papers. "I'm going to read from my unpublished manuscript, *The Mysterious Adventures of Emily and Leo.*" When he looked out into the audience, she could swear their eyes met. Impossible given the size of the ballroom and the distance between them. But seeing him up there on stage sent a jolt of electricity through her chest, nonetheless. The way he ran his hand through his hair, and the way his lips twisted into an apologetic half-smile, she knew he was nervous. His anxiety was contagious. She bit her lip and waited for him to start.

He cleared his throat, and then, voice trembling, he buried his head in his pages and began reading. Without looking up, he barreled through his story like a racecar driver with his foot to the accelerator.

Slow down. She squirmed in her seat. *Look up. Don't be so nervous.* All her willing him to slow down and make eye contact didn't do any good. He plowed on despite the restless sounds of people shifting in their seats and checking their watches. Poor Theo. She wanted to jump up and scream, *Pay attention. He's talking!*

Queenie sensed her annoyance and looked up at her with a whimper. Even the dog knew something was wrong. And Eliza thought her mortification would come from his words and not his performance. She didn't blame him. She wouldn't want to stand up in front of an audience and say anything. He was brave to get up there, she told herself. And these daft cows in the audience should respect that. A couple of women in front of her started whispering to each other. Eliza cleared her throat and when one of them turned around, she gave her the evil eye.

When Theo got to the part where Leo brushes a stray hair from

Emily's cheek and gazes longingly into her sparkling jade eyes, Eliza grimaced. When Leo's thoughts filled with unspoken desire that burned him like a branding iron searing the name Emily onto his soul, Eliza's cheeks prickled with heat. She didn't know how much more of this she could bear. She held her breath and imagined she was in the dentist's chair. Hopefully, it would be over soon.

Finally, Emily and Leo got back to solving the mystery and Eliza could relax. Thank the Lord. Still, at any moment, the intensity of Leo's passion threatened to break out of the confines of Theo's manuscript, and, like a ravenous lion, take a bite out of her dignity.

After what felt like an eternity, Theo looked up from the pages. "That's it," he said with a sheepish grin, which was met by weak applause.

Eliza stood up and clapped as hard and loud as she could. She wasn't about to let these snobby writers snub her friend. Queenie lifted her snout and howled. The audience roused and gave Theo a reluctant round of applause. The master of ceremonies announced another ten-minute coffee break. Murmurs broke out as the crowd stood and stretched.

Eliza waited for him to make his way down from the stage. His gaze locked on her, he strode up the aisle like a man who'd finally completed a dirty job he'd been putting off for months. Queenie's tail thudded against the floor as he approached.

"Well done," she said as he scooted onto the chair next to hers. "Congratulations." She patted his hand.

"Thanks." His cheeks turned crimson. "I'm just glad it's over."

So was she. She didn't tell him how glad.

"Where is everybody?" He glanced around. "Where's your sister?"

She sighed. "Jane went after Lena." She put a finger to her lips. "It's all very hush-hush, classified, and top secret."

Theo's countenance turned dark. "I hope your sister gets to her before the Obsidian Cartel does."

"Me too." She reached down and scratched behind Queenie's ears.

"What about Agatha and Dorothy?" he asked, his cheerful tone betrayed by the sadness in his eyes.

She scanned the ballroom. Surely, they didn't skip Theo's presentation. If they did, they'd better have a jolly good reason or she'd never forgive them.

* * *

The slap on his back came out of nowhere.

"Well done, lad," Eric Blair's voice drawled, thick with his signature smugness. Theo stiffened, forcing a smile as Eric's hand lingered just a second too long. "Your story could use a dose of reality and a meaningful theme. But all in all, not bad writing... ahem, for an amateur." Another left-handed compliment from the master.

"Thanks, lad." Theo glared at his erstwhile friend. "That means a lot coming from you." His words were smooth and polite: A practiced façade he'd learned growing up among the aristocracy.

"Talk about injustice." Eric shook his head theatrically. "A hack like you getting the glory and the girl." His teeth clicked together in mock disappointment.

Theo's pulse stuttered. *Had he got the girl?* His hand raked through his hair, an automatic gesture to buy time and mask the sudden heat crawling up his neck. "I wouldn't say that..."

The words died halfway out. He couldn't look at Eliza. Not now. Especially not with his face on fire.

Eric clapped him on the shoulder, leaning in just enough for his voice to feel personal—and pointed. "Just like in Paris, mate. You always got the good-looking ones." He winked and then let out a long, exaggerated sigh. "*C'est la vie.*"

Theo's stomach twisted. He stole a glance at Eliza and caught a flicker of surprise in her eyes. The damage was done. *Paris.* Damn Eric and his needling jokes. Why should it matter if she knew? It shouldn't matter, except it did. None of those girls could hold a candle to her. They were nothing but distractions, attempts to exorcise her from his soul.

"Those Parisian girls are—" Eric raised an eyebrow and paused for effect.

"Paris was nothing," Theo said, low and sharp, his gaze cutting toward Eric like a blade. "Some chapters are best left unwritten if you know what's good for you."

Eric's smirk thinned. He glanced at Eliza, obviously reading the tension on her face. "I'd best keep my mouth shut, eh?" His voice dipped to that mockingly conspiratorial tone. "Or are you worried I'll steal her away from you?"

"You're many things, mate." Theo's fists clenched in his pockets. "But I didn't figure you for a thief."

Eric's grin stretched wider. "Everyone has a bit of larceny in their soul."

Eliza arched a brow. "Real thieves know when to make a clean getaway." Her voice was cool as glass. And the look she gave Eric was just as sharp.

For the first time, Eric's grin faltered, just enough for Theo to savor the crack in his confidence. "Right," Eric said, clearing his throat. A beat of awkward silence hung between them. "Well, cheerio, then. I'd better get back to the train before

Fournier has a fit." He tapped his hat onto his head. "You'd better hop it too, my friend." He gave Theo a fake punch to the shoulder. "Unless you want to lose your job."

"I quit," Theo said, matter-of-factly.

Eric laughed. "I knew you couldn't cut it, old boy." He gave Theo another irritating clap on the back. "Real life is not for everyone."

"I'm going back to my real life." Theo tightened his lips. "Enough pretending to be someone I'm not."

"Here, here." Eric stabbed the air with a finger. "Spoken like the son of an earl."

"At least I know who I am." Theo blanched. Of course, he didn't know who he was, did he? That was the point. Like a moth between panes of glass, he was stuck between what he was and what he wanted to be.

"So, I'll see you back in Paris, then." Eric turned on his heel.

"I'm not going back to Paris." Theo glanced at Eliza.

Her eyes brightened. "You're not?" Her voice was soft and tentative.

He shook his head. "No."

"I'm going to hold you for next month's rent, my friend." Eric furrowed his brows. "You're not going to leave me holding the bag."

"Of course not." He pulled his wallet out of his jacket pocket and produced several bank notes. Enough to cover his share of the rent and more.

Eric snatched the bills with greedy fervor. "A gift from Daddy, no doubt," he said mockingly.

He might as well admit it. He couldn't live on what he made as a novelist. He swallowed his pride. "From my mother, if you must know." Theo stood tall and kept his voice even.

"Spoken like a true mummy's boy." With a loud guffaw, Eric strode off.

"Better than a snide bastard," Theo said under his breath. The tightness in his chest eased as Eric's figure disappeared into the crowd.

"Charming friend you've got there," Eliza said, cutting him a sideways glance.

He sucked in the breath that had been lodged in his throat since the conversation began. "You have no idea."

"I can't wait to hear all about your Parisian girls." She flashed a scornful smile.

"There's nothing to tell," he said to his shoes. *Oh, to hell with it.* He gazed into her bright eyes and took her hand in his. "Darling, Eliza. You're the only girl—"

A commotion storming up the aisle interrupted his confession. Waving a bunch of papers, Dorothy marched toward him. Eagerness in her step and anticipation on her face, Agatha was close behind.

"We've found something." Dorothy's voice was filled with excitement. "In Peachy's chapter. Another coded message."

"That's why we missed your presentation," Agatha said with more animation than regret. "We were caught up deciphering the code."

"Wait until you hear." Dorothy glanced around as if looking for more assassins. "We've got to warn Jane."

"Warn Jane what?" Eliza pulled her hand away.

Theo stuffed his hands in his pockets. Just like that, he'd missed his chance.

20

ANOTHER CIPHER

Eliza and the others followed Dorothy to a small room around the corner from the ballroom. The quiet tearoom was a private sanctuary away from the conference and the bustle of the hotel. If it weren't for the revelation that Peachy may have hidden a coded message in his manuscript, entering the dimly lit room with overstuffed chairs might have been comforting. A pocket of tranquility with heavy drapes muting the city's noise and casting long shadows on the polished, mahogany table and the air smelling faintly of bergamot.

Agatha and Dorothy took seats at the table. Under the soft glow of a brass reading lamp, Dorothy scattered pages of Peachy's manuscript, which spread between them like a shuffled deck of secrets. Agatha's expression was agitated and expectant, while Dorothy's lips were pressed into a thin, unreadable line.

"See." Dorothy pointed at a spot on the page.

Eliza stood over the table, scanning the pages. "I thought we combed through every inch of that already."

Agatha shook her head. "Not quite. Dorothy noticed the

underlined words: faint, barely visible under the lamplight." She put a finger on a word.

Eliza squinted at the pages. Sure enough, faint pencil marks traced under random words on different pages. At first glance, they seemed meaningless.

"Peachy was clever," Dorothy said, her voice tight. "Too clever to leave evidence lying around openly. This isn't emphasis; it's a code."

Theo leaned in. "A cipher?"

Dorothy nodded. "A basic acrostic but cleverly hidden in plain sight. First letters of the underlined words form a message." She took out a notebook. "We wrote them down and here's what we came up with."

Eliza's heart sank as Dorothy began reading:

"The Cartel runs deeper than you know. Lena's not the only one with ties to MI5. Trust no one, not even those at the top."

They stared at each other in silence.

Theo's voice was the first to break it. "You're saying." He paused. "Someone in MI5 is helping the Obsidian Cartel?"

Agatha's hands trembled slightly as she gathered the edges of the pages. "Peachy knew. He must have uncovered more than just Ivan's smuggling operation. This wasn't just about stolen jewels or blackmail; it's about infiltration at the highest levels of British Intelligence."

Eliza tried to steady her thoughts, but the weight of it all settled on her chest like a stone. "Boris, the fake train inspector wasn't just here for the jewels. And he wasn't just sent to silence Peachy before he could expose the Cartel's network." She tapped the table. "He had to make sure MI5 didn't get wind of the mole. The Cartel operative embedded in MI5."

"So it seems." Dorothy's jaw tightened. "And Lena: Her

betrayal was only part of the problem. The Cartel's reach is wider than any of us realized—all the way to the top."

Theo sank into the chair opposite Dorothy, rubbing his hands over his face. "So that's why you missed the presentation. You were busy solving the rest of the mystery."

Dorothy gave him a rare, apologetic glance. "We couldn't risk waiting. If someone else from MI5 is involved, every moment counts."

Agatha folded the pages carefully, her voice low. "At least Peachy didn't die for nothing. His final act was leaving us the truth."

"I've got to warn Jane." Eliza jumped up and paced the length of the tearoom. "She's in great danger." She bit her lip.

"Unless Jane is the mole," Dorothy said softly.

"No!" Eliza stopped and stared. "No. She wouldn't. I know her."

"Alright." Dorothy held up her hand. "But we have to consider all the options."

"Jane being a mole is not an option." Eliza grimaced. She knew her sister. Jane would never betray her country like that. Her mind was racing. But who would? She flipped through the names of the people she knew who worked in MI5. People Jane trusted. People the government trusted. One of them was a double agent. A traitor. A spy. Her palms broke out in a cold sweat. How could she get word to Jane? She pounded a fist into her thigh. She knew she should have gone with Jane. Then again, if she had, she wouldn't have learned about the coded message. "What can I do?" Her voice trembled. Her face was hot like she might cry. "I've got to get to Begeč."

"Why don't we try ringing Gacef Café?" Theo came to her side. "We could leave a message for Jane there." He gently touched her elbow. “That’s where she was going, right? To find Lena.”

Eliza nodded. “But we can’t very well ring and tell the hostess to tell the next blonde British woman who comes through the door that her life is in danger because someone she works with at MI5 is a mole.” She shook her head. “We need a way to contact her quickly but discreetly.”

“A telegram then,” Agatha offered.

Eliza’s lips twitched. “She told me, if necessary, I could contact her through the embassy.”

“I have an idea.” Theo went back to the table. “Loan me your pencil,” he said to Dorothy, who obliged. He dropped into a chair. “We must deliver the message in code. One Jane will understand.”

Eliza sat down next to him. “But how?”

Theo tapped the pencil against his chin, thinking. “It has to be something only she would recognize, something innocuous to anyone else but clear to her. What’s something only the two of you share? A phrase, a memory, a code word?”

Eliza swallowed hard, searching her memory. “Chess,” she said suddenly. “We used to play together when we were younger. Jane hated it because I always won.” She smiled. “Sometimes, we would leave each other coded messages using chess moves. At the church. With meet-up locations and warnings to watch for the coppers—simple notations, but if she saw one, she’d know it was from me.”

Theo’s eyes brightened. “Perfect. We’ll write a telegram using chess notation. To anyone else, it’ll look like a random game strategy. But to Jane, it’ll be a warning.”

Agatha leaned in. “What’s the message going to say?”

Eliza’s voice was steady now, determination replacing the fear. “We’ll use an opening she knows: the Queen’s Gambit, since that was her favorite. But we'll deliberately slip in an illegal move, one that breaks the pattern. It'll be our signal that something's wrong, that she's in danger. That's what we did as kids when the police were patrolling looking to pick up street urchins... and pickpockets." Her voice trailed off. She wasn't exactly proud of her days picking pockets and hustling chess on the streets. But those harsh days had given her grit, determination, and a few handy, if illicit, skills.

Dorothy nodded approvingly. "And include the Black Bishop. She'll understand you're referring to Peachy's manuscript where he called Ivan the Black Bishop of the Obsidian Cartel."

Eliza watched closely as Theo quickly scribbled down the moves, embedding the warning with precision. His handwriting was quick and sure, each stroke of the pencil filled with urgency.

Dorothy glanced at her watch. "You should arrange for the hotel concierge to deliver the telegram." She gathered the manuscript pages into a neat stack. "I've booked us on the one o'clock train back to London."

"What?" Eliza blinked. "That's less than an hour. Why didn't you tell me?"

"It was only during Theo's presentation." She gave an apologetic smile. "Which we're terribly sorry we missed." She fiddled with the handle on her handbag. "Detective Inspector Orhan cleared us to leave. So, I had the concierge get us return tickets." Dorothy stood up. "I don't know about you, but I've had enough of the writers' conference and intrigue. I'm eager to get back home to my pride of cats and my boozy rat and get to work on my next novel. *Strong Poison*, inspired by Lena Grigor." She grinned. "Perhaps I'll dedicate it to her." She brushed imaginary dust from her skirt. "I'll meet you in the lobby in thirty minutes and we can ride to the station together." She turned to Agatha. "Enjoy your dig, dear. I can't wait to hear all about it when you get home."

"I'm sure I will." Agatha smiled. "Now that the detective inspector has given us permission to leave, Katharine and Leonard are picking me up." She clapped her hands together. "Isn't that splendid? I can't wait to get my hands dirty."

Concentrating on Theo's coded telegram, Eliza was only half paying attention. As she reread the message, her throat tightened as she realized how much danger her sister could be in.

"Shouldn't you be sending that telegram?" Dorothy waved as if to shoo Eliza away.

Paralyzed with worry, Eliza sat there, blinking.

"Well?" Dorothy scowled down at her. "What are you waiting for? You'd best hop it."

"I just hope we're not too late," Eliza whispered.

"Don't worry, dear." Agatha placed a reassuring hand on her arm. "If Jane's anything like you, she's already two moves ahead."

"The best thing you can do is go home and wait for her," Dorothy said. "Here, take the tickets. I'll have the porter come fetch our luggage."

In a daze, Eliza took the tickets. "I suppose you're right." She hoped so, anyway. She felt so helpless. But Jane had expressly forbade her from following. If her sister said it would jeopardize the mission, risk Lena's life, and Jane's job, then she meant it. Jane was not one to exaggerate. "I'll meet you in the lobby, after I send the telegram."

"Here," Theo said, handing her a Turkish lira note.

"What that's for?" She looked up at him.

"Persuasion." He raised an eyebrow. "A tip to convince the concierge to hop it with your telegram."

She took the note. "Thanks." Her grip on the coded message was so tight, her fingernails dug into her palm as she made haste to the concierge desk. After she handed the concierge the note, and repeated her urgent plea, she dashed upstairs to pack.

As she gathered her belongings, stuffing her gloves into her valise and fastening the clasps, she told herself Jane was the careful one. Eliza may be calculating and decisive in a chess game, but Jane was the one in control when it came to life. She had to trust Jane to survive. She sucked in a breath. "She'd better survive, or I'll kill her myself."

Queenie barked and turned circles at the door.

"Goodness." She stood watching the dog. "What are we going to do with you?" Dorothy hadn't considered the little beagle when she purchased return tickets on the Orient Express. The train didn't allow pets of any kind.

"We're going to have to smuggle you aboard." She attached the leash to Queenie's collar. "We'll get Uncle Theo to help." He would know the secrets of the staff and how to get Queenie aboard. At least she hoped so.

She slipped on her traveling coat and reached into the pocket for the room key. Instead of the key, her fingers touched the sharp corner of a folded piece of paper. *What's this?* She withdrew it, and smoothing the paper between her fingers, she traced the hurried strokes of Jane's handwriting.

You must trust me, Eliza. No matter what you hear, no matter what happens, I need you to stay clear of this one.

Her chest ached. How many times had they exchanged

such reassurances, promising to look out for each other even when duty or danger pulled them in opposite directions?

A deep breath. Then another.

The truth settled over her like the cool weight of a London fog: stifling, but familiar. Jane had given her an order, and she had no choice but to obey. It wasn't cowardice. It wasn't abandonment. It was the only way to ensure they both made it through.

She folded the letter carefully, tucking it back into her pocket. Then she picked up her bag and waited for Queenie to follow. "Let's go home." She gave the leash a little tug and Queenie joined her in the hall. The door closed behind them with a decisive click.

They were going home. And Jane... Jane would find her way back, too. She'd better.

21

HOMEWARD BOUND

By the second night back aboard the Orient Express, the rhythmic clatter of the train on the tracks was a familiar lullaby. The first-class compartment was lavish. Far more than Theo was accustomed to lately. But after months spent tramping around Paris and living in a hovel, he felt justified in splurging. His mother's timely monetary gift had sealed the deal.

Besides, he had another reason for securing first-class accommodations: the small, highly illegal beagle currently curled up on Eliza's lap.

He leaned back in his plush seat, stretching his legs under the small table. Eliza set up the chessboard between them. A half-empty bottle of wine sat next to him, alongside a plate of biscuits that had been strategically repositioned to protect them from an opportunistic thief: Queenie.

"What are you doing?" he asked. Instead of putting the pieces in their starting positions, Eliza was arranging them just as they were when he'd bolted off to Paris midway through their last game. He sat up. "You remember."

"Of course I do." She smiled.

"I'm impressed. But why don't we start a new game?" He placed his hand on top of hers to stop her placing her king in its precarious position on the board.

"Why?" She grinned. "Afraid I'll beat you?"

"No." He returned her smile. "I was hoping we could start over." He took her hand in his. "That you might give me another chance."

"You're not going to run off this time?" She cocked her head and began resetting the pieces.

He lifted her hand to his lips, still gazing into her eyes. "Not unless you chase me off."

She laughed. "Let's see how the game goes, shall we?" She pulled her hand away and then moved her pawn in the classic Ruy Lopez opening. He answered with the Berlin Defense.

"How about a game of speed chess?" she asked. Of course, she would suggest speed. She was a master at moving fast.

"I'd rather we take our time." He wanted to savor every moment spent alone with her. "A nice, long, relaxing game, especially now we know Jane is safe."

"Yes." She stared at the board. "Thank God." Yesterday, at their first stop, Eliza had received a telegram from her sister. Jane had used the same chess notation for the Queen's Gambit, only correcting the error. "But I can't completely relax until I see her at home." Eliza's head gave a little jerk. "If there's a mole in MI5, someone at the top, then Jane won't be safe..." Her voice trailed off. "No. I won't relax until I find the mole. However long it takes."

"Jane can take care of herself," he said, hoping it was true. "Don't worry."

She nodded.

Queenie let out a sigh. The beagle was relaxed, or perhaps exhausted from her latest bout of thievery, one paw resting possessively over the remains of a stolen biscuit. Smuggling the dog aboard had required no small amount of ingenuity. First, with Eric's help, Theo had distracted the station staff while Eliza tucked Queenie into a traveling trunk, leaving the lid just loose enough for air. Then, once safely on board, Theo had retrieved her under the pretense of needing a "very private" moment with his luggage. The porter had been too well-trained to inquire further.

Now, with the danger behind them, Queenie seemed to have settled into the role of first-class passenger quite comfortably. He suspected that if anyone discovered her, she'd simply cock her head, wag her tail, and charm her way into a lifelong supply of steak from the dining car.

Eliza moved her pawn to D3. Repressing a smile, he countered with the Mortimer Trap. Would she fall for it and grab his pawn? He studied her. The intensity of her concentration only deepened her beauty.

"The clock is ticking." He tapped his watch.

Ah! She did it. She took his pawn.

"You always hesitate before making a losing move," he said as he swirled the last of his wine.

"I'm merely considering my options." She shot him a glare over the chessboard. "Unlike some, I don't act rashly."

"Is that so?" Theo grinned. "Because I seem to recall you running head long into an assassin only a few days ago."

"That was calculated." She waved her hand over the board.

"A calculated risk?" He refilled his glass.

"A calculated necessity," she corrected, finally shifting a bishop forward.

Rubbing his jaw, he studied the board. "We've had our fair share of calculated necessities on this trip."

Now, she tapped her watch. "Tick. Tick."

He moved his bishop to meet hers. "So, Ivan was blackmailing Dorothy, but to protect her own skin, Lena, his lovely but deadly pianist wife, killed him with snake venom, having conveniently built up an immunity over the years."

Eliza nodded. "And then Peachy got himself killed for writing an exposé on Ivan's smuggling network." She drained her wine. "Lena was supposed to retrieve the manuscript and turn it over to the Obsidian Cartel, but instead, she turned out to be working for British Intelligence and turned on Boris." She poured herself another glass. "And saved Dorothy in the process. Rather spectacularly, I might add."

"And somewhere in the middle of all this"—he moved his knight—"we nearly got shot, engaged in thievery of our own, not to mention successfully smuggling a dog onto one of the most prestigious trains in Europe."

"Not bad for our second case together," Eliza said, leaning back against the deep, velvet cushions.

Theo pretended not to notice how at ease she looked there. "Are you implying there will be more?"

Eliza lifted a shoulder in a casual shrug, but there was a glint in her eye. "I was thinking of writing a novel." She grinned. "About an up-and-coming mystery writer who bumbles his way into real-life detective work."

"Bumbles?" Theo scoffed. "I think you mean, masterfully navigates."

"Oh, absolutely. Masterful navigation." She smirked. "Just like this chess game, which I am about to win."

Theo glanced down at the board. Then back at her. "Oh,

Eliza," he sighed, shaking his head. "That's adorable." He moved his queen into place. "Checkmate."

Eliza blinked at the board. "No, no, that's not—" She leaned in, studying the pieces, then groaned.

Queenie, sensing an opportune moment, sprang into action. In a flash, the little dog's snout shot across the table, snatched the last remaining biscuit from Theo's plate, knocking over the remaining pieces, and then disappeared beneath the table.

"Queenie!" Eliza yelped.

Theo peeked under the table and burst into laughter, watching as Queenie wagged her tail furiously, biscuit clenched between her teeth, entirely too pleased with herself.

Eliza sat back with a resigned sigh. "Speaking of thieves."

"How about another game?" As he started setting up the pieces, he wondered what the future held for them. More murder cases? More chess? More smuggled beagles? He glanced at her, watching the way she tapped a thoughtful finger against her glass, eyes glinting in the low lamplight. A sharp pang hit his heart. Whatever mysteries lay ahead, he knew he couldn't —didn't want to—solve them without her.

She must have read something in his expression because her eyes faltered for just a moment, her fingers tightening around the stem of her glass.

Theo set his own down, slowly, deliberately. She was his greatest mystery. "You never answered my question," he said softly.

She raised an eyebrow. "Which one?"

He leaned across the small table. "Are there going to be more cases?"

Eliza didn't move away. If anything, she tilted her head slightly, lips parting as though to answer.

He held her gaze. And before he knew what he was doing, he took her hand in his. For a moment, everything else—the rumble of the train, their chess game, the Obsidian Cartel—fell away. The warmth of her hand as she gently squeezed his gave him hope. Just as she began to take his other hand in hers, Queenie launched herself onto the table between them with an excited yip, wedging her little body directly into the space where their hands had just touched. She gave his face a vigorous licking.

Eliza gasped, startled, while Theo let out a strangled laugh as Queenie squirmed happily between them, tail wagging furiously.

"Queenie!" Eliza scolded, though her voice was more amused than irritated.

"Nice move, Queenie." Theo sighed, ruffling the dog's ears in self-defense. "But not quite the kisses I was hoping for."

Eliza huffed a laugh and plucked the dog off the table and placed her on the bed. "You've got to learn better manners, my furry friend." She nuzzled Queenie.

"At least one of the Baker girls likes me." He winked.

"Yes." When she smiled at him, her eyes danced.

He let out a slow breath. He didn't dare give voice to his desires—even if he could—for fear of scaring her off. Yes, to what? His heart was racing faster than the train. To being together? To kisses? To love? He took another breath. "To the game?" He raised an eyebrow. "Or to more cases?"

A knowing smile tugged at the corner of her lips. "To both."

Queenie gave a sleepy sigh from the bed, clearly satisfied with her matchmaking efforts, and curled into a tiny ball.

"To our next game." He lifted his glass. "And our next case." *And a life of games, and cases, and...* He set up the board.

Without a word, Eliza reached for her glass and took a

contemplative sip, as if their moment of connection had never happened. But the glint in her eye told him otherwise.

Outside, the night blurred past the window, the rhythmic clatter of the train a reminder that soon, they'd be back in England. Back to real life.

She tapped the rim of her glass with a finger, then arched an eyebrow. "You never did say, Theo: What's your next move?"

He studied her and then the board. He picked up a knight and turned it between his fingers. "That depends," he said with a wink. "Are we still playing chess?"

"Why?" Her answering smile was enigmatic. "Did you have another game in mind?" She leaned forward, resting her chin on her hand.

Theo fingered the well-worn knight, considering her question. Chess and detection: two games they had been playing all along. The rules weren't always clear, the moves not always fair, but that was the thrill of it. Sometimes, they played against each other, sometimes, side by side. Either game required patience, strategy, and the nerve to take risks. What wouldn't he risk to keep her by his side?

He set the piece down with a quiet click. For now, he would settle for chess.

She held his gaze for a moment, then nodded, as if they had just struck an agreement.

Queenie lifted her head from the bed, ears twitching as if she'd been following the conversation all along. With a decisive huff, she flopped back down, curling into a tight ball, her tail draped over her nose. Whatever game they were playing—chess, detection, or something neither of them dared to name—Queenie had already decided the matter was settled.

The train rocked gently, the steady rhythm of the wheels on the tracks like a heartbeat. Outside, as the night rushed past, bringing them closer to home, whatever the game, he hoped it would last a lifetime.

* * *

MORE FROM KELLY OLIVER

The first in another historical cozy mystery series from Kelly Oliver, *Mystery in Manhattan*, is available to order now here:

https://mybook.to/MysteryinManhattan

AUTHOR'S NOTE

(WARNING: SPOILERS!)

Some of the characters and events in this novel are based on real life. The central plot revolves around a discovery I made when I was doing research at the Wade Center at Wheaton College where the Dorothy L. Sayers's archives are held. The Wade Center also has many papers from the Detection Club, which started in the late 1920s with informal dinners hosted by Anthony Berkeley and became an official club in 1930 with Gilbert Chesterton as the first president and Dorothy Sayers as the first secretary. Agatha Christie was also a founding member of the club.

At the Wade Center, I read many of Dorothy Sayers's personal letters, along with letters she wrote on behalf of the Detection Club. Through her letters, I learned that she had a secret that she took with her to her grave. In 1924, at the age of thirty, Dorothy gave birth to a son, John Anthony. Unwed and alone, she concealed her pregnancy from the world, and especially her parents, who were devoutly religious and would have disowned her. Her father was the rector of St. Mary's Church in the fens of eastern England.

At the time, Dorothy worked as a copywriter at S. H. Benson advertising agency, from which she took medical leave for a mysterious illness. No one was the wiser. In the meantime, her cousin Ivy Shrimpton had taken in several children to foster as her own. At first, Dorothy wrote to Ivy asking if she might take in the child of a friend of hers. Eventually, as the letters progressed, Dorothy admitted to her cousin that the baby was actually her own. Ivy Shrimpton raised John Anthony as her own son. Even John Anthony didn't know Dorothy Sayers was his mother until after she died and her will was opened.

I read about rumors that Dorothy was at one point the subject of blackmail. Despite my research, however, I couldn't find details or information about her blackmailer. In my novel, I've based the blackmailer on Dorothy's first lover, John Cournos (born Ivan Grigorievich Korshu), who, to my mind, used her cruelly.

Out of college, Dorothy's first job was as a schoolteacher. While teaching, she met and fell in love with fellow author, John Cournos. And while he proclaimed his love for her, he told her that he was opposed to the institution of marriage on principle. Young Dorothy believed women should not have intimate relations with a man before marriage. But given that she loved John and he refused to marry her on principle, she accepted his terms for their relationship. A year later, he left England and essentially dumped her. Eventually, he recanted his principles and married Helen Kestner Satterthwaite (1893–1960), who was also an author and published under the pseudonyms Sybil Norton and John Hawk.

Distraught by the breakup with Cournos, Dorothy fell into the arms of another man, William "Bill" White, a fellow boarder in the house where she lived. When Dorothy became pregnant, Bill revealed that he was already married and left her to deal with the pregnancy on her own. As my revenge on Dorothy's behalf, I've made her first lover, whom I've named Ivan Grigor, the blackmailer and a murder victim. He was a cad after all, telling Dorothy he didn't believe in marriage and then turning around and marrying another woman!

The novel is also inspired by Agatha Christie's first trip on the Orient Express in 1928. After her divorce from Archie Christie was final (and he married his lover Nancy Neele), Agatha was scheduled to make her first solo trip abroad to the West Indies. But at a supper party, friends told her about a marvelous trip they'd taken to the tombs of Ur in what is now Iraq, and Agatha immediately exchanged her tickets. Five days later, she boarded the Orient Express to visit a dig at Ur at the invitation of her friends Katharine and Leonard Woolley, who were archeologists. Agatha made several other trips on the Orient Express, which, as you know, became the setting for one of her most famous novels.

Finally, my novel features a cameo appearance from a young George Orwell, born Eric Arthur Blair. Reportedly, Eric Blair did not always treat women as he should and was a bit of a womanizer. In fact, there are at least two biographies of his wife, fellow writer Eileen O'Shaughnessy, that argue he was demanding and cruel and furthermore erased her from his autobiographical writings even though she helped him with every aspect of his life and work (*Eileen: The Making of George Orwell* by Sylvia Topp and *Wifedom: Mrs Orwell's Invisible Life* by Anna Funder). Like too many progressive thinkers, his ideas toward women remained retrograde. In the novel, my protagonist, Eliza Baker, is not a fan. Take my portrayal of the great George Orwell with a big grain of misogynist salt.

The Case of the Body on the Orient Express includes other

historical figures and references, but I will leave those for you to discover on your own.

ACKNOWLEDGMENTS

My heartfelt thanks, as ever, to the amazing team at Boldwood Books. Special thanks to my editor, Rachel—your encouraging words and shrewd eye inspire me. Thanks to the Wade Center at Wheaton College for allowing me to see the Dorothy L. Sayers's archives and pointing me in the right direction for information on the Detection Club. Thanks to my brilliant writing critique group—you keep me on my toes and teach me so much. As always, I'm grateful for my supportive partner, Benigno, who cheers me on and appreciates the ups and downs of writing. I'm glad we can navigate the plot twists of life together. Finally, thanks to my furry friends—Mayhem and Mr. Flan—who keep me company, making the solitary endeavor of writing more sociable... and only occasionally walk across the keyboard at crucial moments.

ABOUT THE AUTHOR

Kelly Oliver is the award-winning, bestselling author of three mysteries series: The Jessica James Mysteries, The Pet Detective Mysteries, and the historical cozies The Fiona Figg Mysteries, set in WW1. She is also the Distinguished Professor of Philosophy at Vanderbilt University and lives in Nashville, Tennessee.

Sign up to Kelly Oliver's mailing list here for news, competitions and updates on future books.

Visit Kelly's website: www.kellyoliverbooks.com

Follow Kelly on social media:

x.com/KellyOliverBook

facebook.com/kellyoliverauthor

instagram.com/kellyoliverbooks

tiktok.com/@kellyoliverbooks

bookbub.com/authors/kelly-oliver

ALSO BY KELLY OLIVER

A Fiona Figg & Kitty Lane Mystery Series

Mystery in Manhattan

Covert in Cairo

Mayhem in the Mountains

Arsenic at Ascot

Murder in Moscow

Poison in Piccadilly

The Detection Club Mysteries Series

The Case of the Christie Conspiracy

The Case of the Body on the Orient Express

www.ingramcontent.com/pod-product-compliance
Ingram Content Group UK Ltd.
Pitfield, Milton Keynes, MK11 3LW, UK
UKHW012250290726
14090UKWH00016B/575

9 781836 175568